YOU ONLY LIVE ONCE

HARIS ORKIN

YOU ONLY LIVE ONCE

www.harisorkin.com

FIRST EDITION Trade Paperback

March 21, 2018

Imajin Books: www.imajinbooks.com

ISBN: 978-1-77223-360-5

Cover designed by Ryan Doan: http://www.ryandoan.com

Praise for YOU ONLY LIVE ONCE

"A brilliant homage to everyone's favorite super-spy, and a hilarious, action-packed, made-for-the-movies thriller about a man suavely dancing along both sides of the thin line between heroism and madness." —Matt Forbeck, *New York Times* bestselling author of *Halo: New Blood*

"Pacey and unrepentant fun, Haris Orkin's *You Only Live Once* takes the James Bond mythos, gives it a swift kick in the backside and steals its wallet." —James Swallow, *New York Times* bestselling author of *Nomad*

"Fill shaker with ice. Add equal parts Ian Fleming and Quentin Tarantino. Shake (do not stir). Garnish with Douglas Adams, and you get *You Only Live Once,* a delicious martini as dry as the dusty California desert." —Dan Jolley, *USA Today* bestselling author of the Gray Widow Trilogy

"Haris Orkins' *You Only Live Once* is a tour de force, brilliant, hilarious, and moving. Written with stunning style, it's James Bond meets *One Flew Over the Cuckoo's Nest,* with a generous dollop of *Don Quixote* thrown in. All captured in prose that scintillates and pops, the book exploding in an extraordinary climax that is wildly funny and deeply moving." —David Scott Milton, award-winning author of *Paradise Road*

"If you're looking—and who isn't?—for a sexy, slapstick, razzle-dazzle, rock'em-sock'em re-imagining of Don Quixote as James Bond emerging from deep cover in a mental hospital to save the world, Haris Orkin's hilarious yet touching *You Only Live Once* is the book for you." — Charles Harper Webb, award-winning author of *Brain Candy*

"*You Only Live Once* makes for an engrossing read offering many satisfying twists and turns. Fans of thrillers will be delighted by the various nuances Haris Orkin brings to the table as he introduces a quasi-hero who ultimately faces success despite himself. A healthy dose of humor and irony is added to create a story about a misfit in search of a mission." —D. Donovan, Senior Reviewer, *Midwest Book Review*

For Kim.
Thank you for believing in me even as I tilted away at windmills.

Acknowledgements

The world can be a very unforgiving place, so I've always loved those who can laugh and joke and find the humor in everything and anything. So first I want to thank all those who brought me laughter and showed me the power of comedy; from Miguel Cervantes to Mark Twain to Monty Python to all my many funny friends. You know who you are. I've learned something from each and every one of you.

My mom loved to read and laugh and loved physical comedy, whether it was Lucille Ball or one of her kids taking a header. She was always my biggest fan and her unflagging belief in me actually made me believe in myself.

My father, a master of comedy, who taught me everything I know; from how to write a joke to how to be a father. He is the silliest man I know and he has been my biggest inspiration.

My siblings are the best and life is much easier knowing they are always there for me.

My wife, Kim and my son, Jakob, patiently read much of what I write, including this book in all its many forms. They are my sounding boards and my proofreaders and I greatly appreciate their patience and love because at times I know I must drive them crazy.

Thanks to the mentors and professors who guided me on my path; David Scott Milton, Tom McBride, Bill Goyen, Bink Noll, and Ben Masselink.

And thanks to all the brilliant authors who were kind enough to review my book in advance.

Finally, I want to thank Cheryl Kaye Tardif and her team at Imajin Books for all they've done to make this happen.

Chapter One

The waxing moon gave off a cold white light that Flynn avoided by staying in the shadows. He heard the faint harmony of dogs howling with a distant siren as he knelt below a Tree of Heaven. It was flowering and the blossoms produced a slightly acrid scent similar to semen. The odor was so strong it nearly overpowered the cigarette smoke that alerted Flynn to the security guard not thirty feet away. The guard wore dark slacks and a black polyester jacket. A Taser hung high on his hip next to a holster with a walkie-talkie. Flynn watched as the guard yawned and stubbed out his butt. He knew the guard was nearly finished with his shift and would be at his least vigilant.

Flynn emerged from the shadows, his face cautious and watchful. As a young man, he'd been a little too pretty, but now that he was firmly in his forties, life had left its mark. Tall and lean, he wore faded black jeans and a black cotton turtleneck. In one smooth motion, he slid a black ski mask over his face. The holes were askew, however, and his aquiline nose poked through the one meant for his left eye. He adjusted it so he could see into the gloom and then crept forward, moving with stealth, senses sharp.

The guard stood in the doorway to the building as he lit another cigarette. Flynn used that distraction to move. He stayed low, crouched and silent, using the shrubs for cover. Turning a corner, he came upon two more guards and ducked back. Flynn hid behind the edge of the building, calculating what to do if they stumbled upon him. He'd have to take them out—quietly—otherwise they'd sound a general alarm, putting both Flynn and the mission at risk. Luckily, they were too tired to even look up as they trudged past.

Once their footsteps receded, Flynn climbed a trellis attached to the building, grabbed a rain gutter, and clambered onto the roof. He plucked a toy dart from his fanny pack. The pink tip of his tongue emerged from the mouth hole of the ski mask and licked the inside of the suction cup. He then attached it to the window pane and used a glass cutter to etch a perfect circle, which he carefully removed. Reaching through the hole, he unlatched the lock, eased it open, and climbed inside, dropping softly to the floor.

The room was dark and silent. He approached the door, easing it open just a crack to see a large man, dressed all in white, dozing in a folding chair at the far end of the hall. Flynn took a tentative step back. A floorboard creaked. The man in white opened his eyes just as Flynn closed the door. The guard's approaching footsteps echoed in the corridor. Flynn hopped on a counter top, pushed up a ceiling panel, and pulled himself into the crawlspace above. The panel settled just as the door opened wide, flooding the room with light.

Flynn peered through a seam and watched as the man in white approached the open window. The breeze from outside rustled what was left of his hair and blew the door shut behind him. He struggled to close the window. That's when he saw the perfect circle cut into the glass.

In the darkness above the ceiling tiles, Flynn stayed quiet and still. After what felt like an eternity, the room below went dark as the man left the room and shut the door.

Flynn pulled a tiny flashlight from his fanny pack and cautiously crawled forward over pipes and conduit, careful not to make a sound as he counted every ceiling panel he passed. At number seventeen, he stopped and waited and listened. He removed the panel and peered over the edge to see someone fifteen feet down, sound asleep on a cot. His penlight revealed the luminous face of a pretty blonde in her late twenties.

She awakened with a start, surprised by the light shining in her eyes. Flynn dropped down, landing with a thump next to her in bed, his hand over her mouth before she could scream. The terror in her eyes turned into delight when Flynn pulled off his ski mask. He removed his hand from her mouth to reveal a giddy smile.

"James…"

"Thought I'd drop in. You don't mind, do you darling?" His voice was deep and his accent British, with a touch of Scottish burr.

"What if they catch you?"

"What if they *don't?*" Flynn smiled mischievously.

The blonde smiled back at him, clearly aroused by all the intrigue. Her accent wasn't British but American, from Minnesota. He caressed her face so tenderly it seemed she might swoon.

"I can't," she whispered.

"Of course you can…"

Flynn brushed his lips against her neck and she closed her eyes and moaned. "This is wrong. Very wrong."

"Which is exactly what makes it so absolutely right."

He gently pulled back the covers and softly kissed her throat and the tops of her lightly freckled breasts. As he tried to slide the comforter down further, she put her hand on his.

"Please, no…"

"You want me to stop?"

"Yes."

"You want me to leave?"

"Yes."

Flynn pulled the comforter back up to her neck and smoothed a few strands of hair off her forehead. "Another time perhaps."

Before he could put both his feet on the floor, she grabbed his wrist and pulled him close. Flynn looked into her wide hazel eyes and kissed the corner of her mouth. The blonde sighed and shuddered.

"James…Oh, James…"

The door flew open and a cold fluorescent light blinked on, flooding the room with a clinical brightness. The blonde peered past James Flynn to see a terrifying sight. Standing in the doorway, filling the entire frame, loomed a very large nurse. She stood almost six feet tall and weighed over two hundred pounds. Her hair was pulled back in a tight red bun and she didn't look like she ever had any fun. She was furious and formidable, and the blonde was petrified. Flynn offered the large nurse a welcoming smile.

"Nurse Durkin," Flynn said, "What a pleasant surprise." She glowered and took a step forward, causing the girl behind Flynn to shrink back. Flynn, however, maintained his composure. "Would you care to drop your frock and join us?"

Flynn sat on the edge of a desk in an anteroom, smiling down at an unsmiling African-American woman in her fifties. The busty, big boned woman did her best to ignore him as she typed away on a computer keyboard.

"It's a complete fabrication, Miss Honeywell. A total exaggeration." Honeywell looked at Flynn with amused skepticism and took a bite from her Ding-Dong. "You know very well that I only have eyes for you."

Honeywell smirked. "It's not your eyes we're talking about."

Before Flynn could offer a retort, a door opened and the pretty blonde nurse whose bed he'd invaded walked out in tears. Her eyes glistened as she looked at Flynn with longing.

"James." She stepped closer, wanting so badly to touch him. "Maybe now that I'm no longer on staff, maybe I could visit you and then, when you get out, maybe we could—"

A distinguished older man put his hand on her shoulder. "Miss Grouper, please."

Her shoulders sagged under the older man's hand. "I just wanted to say good-bye to James."

"Yes, and now you have, and now it's time to go."

Tears filled her eyes as she bolted from the room. The older man sighed and looked at Honeywell, who simply shook her head.

"Good morning, N," Flynn said.

The older man nodded, "Good morning, Mr. Flynn." He beckoned him into his office. James offered Honeywell a rakish grin and followed the old man inside. N abruptly closed the door and motioned to a lumpy looking couch. Flynn took a seat as N sat behind a cluttered desk, piled high with file folders and paperwork.

Various diplomas filled the wall behind the old man's head. Dr. Robert B. Nickelson had a B.S. in Chemistry from Stanford, an M.A. in Psychology from Antioch, and a Ph.D. in Psychiatric Medicine from UCLA. He was sixty-two years old, but he looked ten years older—hair gray and thinning, face careworn. His eyes were kind.

"James, we've talked about this."

"Yes, sir."

"She's the third one this year."

"I know, sir."

"The third poor girl I've had to let go."

"I'm truly sorry, sir."

"I don't think you are, James. I think you're doing this deliberately. Do you want me to send you somewhere else? Is that what you want?"

"Of course it's what I want. I need a mission. I need a purpose. Why do you think I pull these puerile pranks?"

"James…"

"I've been trapped here at headquarters for far too long. I'm rested. I'm ready. I've never been more fit. Surely, there's still danger in the world. Master criminals. Terrorists. Rogue governments. Someone could be plotting to steal a nuclear submarine. Or rob Fort Knox. Or build a killer satellite to level New York City. I'm a double-O. I need to be out there. That's what I'm trained for. To do whatever is necessary."

Nickelson smiled sympathetically. "I understand how you feel, but for now I need you here."

"And when will I be getting an assignment?"

"When we are given one that matches your…extraordinary talents."

Flynn was clearly disappointed. "But sir—"

"In the meantime, why not focus your energies on helping others here at…headquarters. Just not the nurses."

"Are we finished?"

Nickelson looked at James with affection and barely concealed sadness. "For now."

Flynn nodded and left Nickelson's office. His mood lightened a little when he caught sight of Miss Honeywell working away on her computer.

"Miss Honeywell?"

She reluctantly raised her gaze, her voice edged with irritation. "Yes?"

"Why do you do it?"

"Do what?"

"Insist on looking so luscious?" Miss Honeywell rolled her eyes and continued typing as James sat on the edge of her desk. "We really must run away together."

"You're sitting on my Ding-Dong."

James stood up to see that he had indeed smashed her snack pastry. "Sorry, darling." He kissed her on the cheek. "Next time you'll have to sit on *my* Ding-Dong."

"You don't get your ass outta here, I'm gonna kick you in your damn Ding-Dong."

Chapter Two

The social area reverberated with laughter and conversation, more like the commons at a state college than the activity room at a state mental hospital. Some of the patients could have been mistaken for students, but others were in their thirties or late forties. A few were upwards of sixty and seventy. It was like a large, dysfunctional family gathering with weird uncles, eccentric aunts, depressed older sisters, unhinged brothers, nutty mothers, and catatonic grandfathers all co-existing in one place.

Affection, tension, awkwardness and boredom commingled as they watched Bugs Bunny cartoons on TV and played Parcheesi and Chinese checkers. Some engaged in light banter while others argued, whispered or mumbled to themselves as they milled about. The furniture was worn and ugly and institutional. There were Glen Plaid couches and brown folding chairs on linoleum floors, fluorescent lights and bare white walls dotted with bright colorful posters with happy, empowering slogans:

Life is 10% what you make it and 90% how you take it.

If it's to be, it's up to me.

Keep an Attitude of Gratitude.

James Flynn wore a faded navy-blue serge suit and sat at a card table, playing Uno. He studied the cards in his hands, his gaze intense and shrewd. His partners included a rotund nineteen-year-old black kid named Ty, a beautiful, fragile-looking twenty-two-year-old named

Dulcie, and Q, a skinny, wild-eyed seventy-seven-year-old with a scraggly white beard.

Q reached for the draw pile and Ty's eyes grew wide. "Hey! What you doin'?"

"What's it look like I'm doing?" Q asked.

"It's my motherfuckin' turn."

"You just took your turn."

"No, I didn't."

"Did too."

"Did not, you stupid shit."

"Did! Did! Did!"

Flynn interjected himself into the argument. "Now just calm down, Q."

"Old man's going senile!"

"On the contrary, Ty, I believe Q possesses one of the most brilliant minds on the planet. Q, tell Ty about some of your inventions."

Q smiled at the young black man and said, "The silicon microchip. The zipper. The corn dog."

"No way." Ty wasn't buying it.

"I created it for the Los Angeles County Fair in 1962."

"Q has developed almost all our state-of-the-art spy gear." Flynn ticked them off on his fingers. "Mini-copters, laser pens, submarine cars, personal jet packs."

Ty sighed and looked at Dulcie, who'd clearly heard it all before. James Flynn patted the old man on the hand. "Q, tell us what you've been working on lately. Anything new?"

Q raised his bushy gray eyebrows and offered them all a crafty grin. "Mind control technology." He tapped his finger against his curly mop of white hair. "Invisible electromagnetic waves that actually change the structure of the brain. Bending the will. Molding the consciousness."

Flynn smiled, impressed. "That's astonishing." He glanced at Dulcie. "Are you working on this technology too?"

Dulcie looked bored and aggravated as she stared at her cards. "Yeah, sure, whatever."

Ty suddenly shouted, "Uno!"

"N-no!" Q sputtered.

"Fuck you!" Ty yelled. "I have Uno!"

"Uno means you have one card left in your hand," Flynn tried to explain. "Uno means one."

"And you have three cards," Q said, clearly exasperated.

Ty dropped two cards onto the table. "No, I don't."

"You can't do that!" Q shouted. "You need a match!"

Ty seized the old man by the front of his shirt. "How 'bout your face and a monkey's ass!"

Flynn gently grabbed the teen by the wrist until Ty let Q go.

Suddenly, Ty jumped up, knocking over his chair. "Crazy fuckin' motherfucker!" He hiked up his baggy blue jeans and backed away, screaming, "You can run but you can't hide!" Ty bumped into an orderly before charging off down a hallway.

Q sighed and set his cards down. He rose with effort, the strain showing on his face, and shuffled out of the room. He moved with a limp, the remnants of a stroke.

Flynn looked across the table at Dulcie, who dropped her cards in disgust. "Now what do we do?"

Flynn gathered and shuffled the cards. "We could always play a two-handed game."

"I don't know…"

"Unless you'd rather do something else?" He raised a seductive eyebrow.

"Are you coming on to me?"

"Why wouldn't I? You're beautiful, spirited, intelligent—"

"Intelligent? I didn't even finish high school."

"Did they send you straight to the university?"

"Don't do that."

"What?"

"Don't fuck with me."

Dulcie's long black hair framed a delicate face. Her skin was light brown and her cheekbones were high. She had an East L.A. accent and the cold, seen-it-all eyes of a chola.

"If you work for Q, you're clearly well-educated. You can't be on the cutting edge of technology and not have a post-doctorate. In what? Physics? Engineering?"

"What did I just say?"

"Bright, beautiful, and self-effacing as well."

"Look, I have a boyfriend, okay."

"So why haven't I ever met him?"

Dulcie's hard-ass attitude crumbled as emotion flooded her face. "Because he doesn't want to see me in here. And anyways, it's none of your fucking business."

"I'm sorry if I touched a nerve."

"It's okay." She scraped back her chair and stood. "It's no big deal."

Flynn watched as Dulcie shuffled off, the bottoms of her frayed jeans skimming the linoleum. A burly orderly by the name of O'Malley sidled up beside her. He was sweaty and balding with a five o'clock shadow and close-set eyes. He smirked at her as she tried to get around him, invading her space with impunity, whispering something nasty in her ear. Dulcie gave him a dirty look and pushed past. O'Malley sniggered and winked at another beefy orderly who giggled like an idiot.

Chapter Three

Dulcie glanced around at the eight patients sitting in folding chairs. Most everyone wore sweatpants or jeans or shorts or baggy T-shirts, but not James. He was dressed in an old charcoal gray suit, a shabby white dress shirt, and a faded red and black silk tie. While the others wore slippers or flip-flops, James sported well-worn Italian loafers. The daily group therapy session was held in a small white room with bright fluorescent lights and nothing on the walls. Q was there too, along with Ty and an assortment of other lost causes. A female therapist in her early forties, with short soccer mom hair and an expensive red silk blouse, smiled at Dulcie sitting slouched in her chair, nibbling at the cuticle on her left thumb.

"Is that why they fired you?" the therapist probed. "Because you called your supervisor a bitch?"

Dulcie shrugged. "That and the fact that I was totally fucked up on crank."

The therapist tried to catch Dulcie's eye, but she wouldn't look at her. She was too busy chewing on her cuticle. "Were you still living with Mike?"

Dulcie nodded.

"Was he abusing you?"

She nodded again.

"But you didn't see an out?"

Dulcie shook her head, her eyes shiny with tears.

"So, you OD'd?"

Dulcie shrugged and sucked the blood off her bleeding thumb.

The therapist patted Dulcie on the knee. "Thank you, Dulcie."

"Hey, Dulcie," Ty said. "Fuck him. Fuck that fucker. Just fuck that motherfucker."

The therapist smiled at Ty. "Thank you, Ty." A chubby guy with dark beady eyes giggled. The therapist glanced around the circle. "Does anyone else have anything to add?" She looked at Flynn, who was trying to catch Dulcie's eye. "James? You seem very quiet today."

"Maybe because I have nothing to say."

"You have nothing you'd like to share with the group?"

"I've said it all, haven't I? And no one is listening. While we sit here blabbering away, our enemies are making plans. And what do we do? Nothing."

The chubby, beady-eyed guy enthusiastically nodded in agreement.

The therapist smiled at the man. "Bob? Is there something you'd like to say?"

"I know what they're planning. I know what they're making." Bob motioned for everyone to lean in and when they did, he whispered, "Turkey Loaf."

A slab of turkey loaf covered with gelatinous beige gravy plopped onto a plate next to a perfectly spherical scoop of mashed potatoes. An elderly cafeteria lady with a hairnet handed the bland-looking meal to James Flynn, who set it on his bright blue tray next to a tiny bowl of creamed corn and a stale dinner roll. Flynn moved down the line, grabbed a Styrofoam cup and filled it with ice and Diet Coke. After grabbing his plastic utensils, he scanned the cafeteria for a friendly face and spied Dulcie alone at a table. As he moved towards her, he saw O'Malley put his hands next to her plate and lean down right by her face, his big ugly mug invading her space.

"You know you want it."

"Fuck you," Dulcie said.

"That's right. I know you want to. I can see how you look at me. You must be horny as hell, a hot little piece of ass like you."

James stepped between them, put his tray down and sat next to Dulcie. "Mr. O'Malley, may I make a recommendation?"

"Get the fuck out of here, Flynn." O'Malley whispered.

"Perhaps you should try a different approach?"

"What did I just say?"

"A little subtlety, a little romance, less penis and more panache."

"What the fuck is wrong with you?"

"Unlike us men, who prefer getting to the point, women require a little more finesse."

O'Malley grabbed James by the tie and pulled him to his feet. With his other hand, he grabbed James by the balls. Flynn's eyes went wide with pain and surprise, his voice tight, "An interesting technique."

He grabbed O'Malley's wrist and casually turned, twisting it back, using his weight and momentum against him until O'Malley grunted and released Flynn's package. Flynn continued to twist the man's arm up and back, forcing O'Malley to gasp.

"However," Flynn added. "I would recommend starting with something more subtle."

Barker, the other beefy orderly, suddenly appeared. "We got a problem here?"

"Not at all." Flynn released O'Malley's arm, the burly jerk's face now red with fury. "I was simply instructing Mr. O'Malley here in the finer points of seduction."

O'Malley pulled out a pair of plastic handcuffs. "Grab his arms." Barker nodded and reached for Flynn who effortlessly evaded him. Both orderlies charged forward, pushing Dulcie out of the way. A small Hispanic man stepped between them, grabbing Flynn by the arm.

The man was in his early twenties and wore the lime green outfit of an orderly. He was short and stocky, verging on chunky. His kind face and warm smile belied skittish eyes. "James, what are you doing, man? Are you annoying these gentlemen again?"

"Actually, Sancho, I was about to offer Mr. O'Malley a few tips on how to talk to women without making them lose their last seven lunches."

Barker and O'Malley moved forward, but Sancho put up his hands, holding them back.

"James is just having some fun with ya, man. He knows you two don't need no tips to get lucky."

"Absolutely," Flynn agreed. "What these two need is major plastic surgery."

Barker shoved Sancho out of the way just as Dr. Nickelson walked by with a tray.

"Sir, I see you're trying the turkey loaf," Sancho said, offering Nickelson a smile. "You're a brave man."

"Indeed, I am," Nickelson said. "Good afternoon, gentlemen."

O'Malley and Barker mumbled greetings as Sancho grabbed Flynn by the sleeve and pulled him away. Dulcie quickly followed. They pushed past the cafeteria line and outside into the commons area.

"That O'Malley is a menace," James said.

"So, don't mess with him," Sancho said.

"How he made it into her Majesty's Secret Service is a bloody mystery."

"You okay brother?

"Why wouldn't I be?"

Sancho smiled, shaking his head. "No reason, man. You take care, okay?" Sancho headed back into the cafeteria, leaving James with Dulcie.

"What the hell is wrong with you?" Dulcie demanded.

"I just thought—"

"I was handling it. You didn't have to do that."

"You're welcome."

"I can take care of myself."

"Of course you can."

Angry tears filled her eyes. Flynn pulled a handkerchief from his pocket and handed it to her. She wiped her tears and noisily blew her nose. When she went to hand him his hanky, Flynn recoiled, holding up his hands. "Consider it a gift."

Dulcie laughed.

"There you go. That's better. You'll be fine. You just need to mingle with a better class of gentlemen."

"You can say that again." She looked at James with real affection. "It's too bad you're such a loon."

"Come again?"

Her smile faded into something sad. "You're almost the perfect man."

James Flynn's muscular torso was drenched in sweat as he kicked and twirled and punched the air. Wearing nothing but gray sweatpants, he performed a complex karate kata in an outdoor patio area. A pretty Filipino nurse stopped to watch, mesmerized by the elegant, powerful, menacing dance. Flynn did a front jump kick, turning, punching, spinning, leaping, slashing the air with his hand. His unseen opponent beaten brutally into submission, James returned to the ready position, eyes closed. He inhaled deeply holding the breath for a count of two and then exhaled, centering himself. His eyes slowly opened and James saw the young nurse staring at his glistening body. Color rose to her cheeks when Flynn offered her a charming smirk.

Sancho, sitting at a nearby table, watched all this as he sipped an orange soda. The flustered nurse continued on her way and Sancho rose from his chair, chuckling. "Dude, you are something else. How the hell do you do it?"

"Do what?"

"Get all those women to give it up."

"They want to give it up, Sancho. The trick is to allow them to."

"Allow them to? How?"

James wiped the sweat off his face with a towel he then draped around his neck, and put on a white cotton kimono robe. He slipped on a pair of Japanese sandals and said, "Is there anyone you're interested in right now?"

"Well, there's this girl that works at El Pollo Loco over on Vineland. In the drive-through window. Her name's Alyssa."

"You know her name. That's a start."

"She has a name tag. I haven't actually, you know, talked to her. I try to, but there's always people in line behind me and she's on the headset and she's all distracted and I just, you know...What do I say?"

"Ask her out for coffee."

Sancho sighed and smiled shyly, shaking his head. "What if she has a boyfriend or something?"

"Then she'll say no. But there's also a chance that she'll say yes."

Sancho looked a little dumbfounded.

"Sometimes you have to take a risk. After all, my friend, you only live once."

"I guess."

"Taking a chance shows that you have a certain amount of confidence. Women like men who exude confidence."

Flynn clapped Sancho on the shoulder and ambled off. He smiled at two nurses, sitting at a table, sipping coffee. The nurses blushed and smiled back, whispering and giggling as Flynn left the patio.

Chapter Four

James Flynn slept next to the shy Filipino nurse who had checked him out on the patio two weeks before. She was petite and slender with long dark hair that cascaded across the frayed white pillowcase. Morning sunlight flooded through the blinds and fell across their intertwined bodies.

The door squeaked open and the sounds from the corridor prodded Flynn awake. Yawning, he opened his eyes to see Nurse Durkin poking her head in his room. James abruptly sat up and strategically arranged himself so Durkin couldn't see the beautiful young nurse naked in his bed.

"Nurse Durkin!" Flynn exclaimed. "What a wonderful ray of sunshine."

The young nurse slowly opened her eyes. At the mere mention of Durkin's name, her face filled with terror.

Nurse Durkin regarded Flynn sourly. "Time to get up."

James glanced at the imitation Rolex on the side table by his bed. "Isn't it a tad early?"

"There's a new hospital policy starting today," Durkin said gleefully. "Everyone up at 6:00 a.m."

"Why the change?"

"Chop chop, Mr. Flynn. Up and at 'em!" She clapped her hands and continued on down the hall, leaving Flynn's door wide open.

James Flynn donned a threadbare, thrift store tuxedo that was a trifle too large for him. It was long in the sleeves and a tad baggy in the seat. Nevertheless, he wore it with aplomb as he strolled into the activity room.

Immediately, he sensed that something wasn't right. The previous day the room was alive with laughter, angry words, and off-key singing. Now, however, the room was strangely quiet. The television was on, but the sound was turned down and no one said a word.

People sat scattered around the area, staring straight ahead, separate, isolated, lost in their own heads. Durkin handed out pills in little plastic cups. Flynn watched as everyone docilely swallowed pills, washing them down with Dixie cups full of water.

Ty, the rotund, black nineteen-year-old, stared at the TV in a stupor. He sat slumped on the couch next to a slack-jawed older woman. Everyone, in fact, seemed sedated. Flynn sat beside Ty who didn't even look at him. He just stared at "The Price is Right." Drew Carey was talking to a large married couple dressed like teddy bears. Ty watched this grimly, eyes dull.

"Ty," James shook the teenager's beefy leg. "What's wrong? What's going on?"

"Nothin'," said Ty as he stared straight ahead.

"Where's Q?"

"They took him away."

"Who took him away?"

"Don't know. They took Dulcie too. And Lisa. And Julie. Frank. Julio." Ty seemed to lose the thread of what he was saying and slowly swiveled his head to look at James. His energy, his personality, everything that made him Ty was trapped inside his sedated body. Only his eyes offered a glimmer of who he used to be. They were fearful and shiny with tears.

Nurse Durkin stood behind Ty and glowered at the back of his head. The teenager turned away from Flynn to fix his gaze back on the television. Flynn tapped Ty on the thigh, but he wouldn't look back at him.

Barker, the beefy orderly, handed Nurse Durkin a little plastic cup filled with pills. Durkin loomed over Flynn and offered him the meds with a chaser of water in a Dixie cup. "Time to take your meds, Mr. Flynn."

"But I've already taken my medication."

"This is a new prescription."

Flynn rose to his feet and offered Durkin a pleasant smile. "Nurse Durkin, have I told you how lovely you look today?"

She glared at him. "Time to take your meds."

"Perhaps later we could retire to my room where I would be more than happy to help you free yourself from this obviously overburdened brassiere."

Immune to his charms, she thrust the Dixie cup in Flynn's face. Flynn stared at the pills and then raised his gaze to Durkin's dark brown eyes. "No thank you."

"Doctor's orders."

James sighed, took the little cup and spilled the pills on the floor.

James Flynn barreled into the anteroom outside N's office and stopped cold when he saw that Miss Honeywell wasn't behind her desk. Instead, the disagreeable face of a dried-up looking lady in her early sixties greeted James.

"Yes?" the lady said, clearly irritated by the intrusion.

James sat on the edge of her desk, much to the dried-up lady's consternation. "Is Honeywell in?"

"Who?"

"Miss Honeywell. This is her office."

"Honeywell?"

"N's girl Friday."

"N?"

"Yes! N! I need to see him immediately."

The door to N's office opened and out stepped a corpulent man with a bald head and an insincere smile. "You need to see *whom* immediately?" the corpulent man asked.

"Who are you?" Flynn demanded.

"I'm Dr. Grossfarber."

"Where's N? Is he ill?"

"If you're referring to Dr. Nickelson, he is no longer with us."

"No longer with us. You mean—"

"He's gone."

Flynn looked stricken. "Gone? You mean—"

"It happened yesterday afternoon. He knew it was coming. He just didn't know when."

"Why didn't he say something? I could have helped him. I could have protected him. That's why I'm here."

"And you are?"

"Flynn. James Flynn."

"Ahh, of course, Mr. Flynn. Please come in. I've been looking over your file."

Grossfarber directed Flynn into the office and planted himself behind N's old desk. James sat on the couch and eyed Grossfarber skeptically. Grossfarber had files piled everywhere. He opened one in particular and scanned the dog-eared pages. Then he looked up at Flynn and said, "HMSS brought me in."

"Her Majesty's Secret Service?"

Grossfarber smiled, but only with his mouth. His eyes were cold and calculating and without the slightest trace of humor. "Health Management System Services. I'm the new senior psychiatrist, and from now on things will be very different around here."

"Where's Miss Honeywell?"

"Gone as well."

James flinched as if he were struck. "How? Who?" He jumped to his feet. "What in bloody hell is happening?"

"*Nothing* is happening and that's why I'm here. I get results. Now, please. Sit down." James remained on his feet. "Please..." said Dr. Grossfarber gently.

James Flynn sat back down. "Your file is quite fascinating, Mr. Flynn. You're a very unusual man." James shrugged, still upset about N and Miss Honeywell. "According to this, your parents were killed in a car accident when you were ten."

"What are you talking about?"

Grossfarber continued to scan the file, reading aloud snippets and passages. "No other living relatives. Went from foster home to foster home...became an obsessive fan of espionage films of the sixties...developed an imaginary persona which later became a full-blown delusion."

"What are you saying?"

Grossfarber glanced at Flynn as if he were a rare laboratory specimen. "You were helpless and had no control over your life. So, you became the most powerful person you could imagine. Someone who could handle any situation."

Flynn suddenly stood, furious. "What did you do with Q?"

"Who?"

"Q! And his colleague! Dulcinea Delgadillo!"

"Miss Delgadillo's insurance was no longer covering her stay here, so I'm afraid she had to—"

"You think I don't know what's happening?"

"Mr. Flynn, please."

"What's your ultimate plan, Grossfarber?"

"Please, sit down."

"What are you trying to do?"

"I'm trying to change the way you think."

"And the others? Do you want to change the way they think too?"

"Of course," said Dr. Grossfarber. "That's what I'm paid to do."

"Using Q's mind control technology?"

"Mr. Flynn—"

"Do you really believe you're going to get away with this?" James took a few steps toward Grossfarber and the doctor pushed a red panic button next to his intercom. Instantly the office door opened and O'Malley and Barker came rushing in.

James moved into a fighting stance, slicing his hands through the air like Bruce Lee. "Mr. Flynn, please," said Grossfarber. "We're all here to help you."

"Help me what?"

"Get well."

O'Malley and Barker stepped closer. Flynn gracefully backed away. "Gentlemen, I must warn you, I know thirty-seven different ways to kill a man with my bare hands, five of which only require the use of my right middle finger." Flynn flipped the orderlies the bird with both hands.

O'Malley snarled and lunged. James easily evaded his grasp, grabbed O'Malley's wrist, wrenched his arm behind him, and unceremoniously slammed him into a wall.

Barker grabbed Flynn in a bear hug, his beefy arms squeezing him tight. Flynn struggled as Grossfarber readied a syringe. The doctor went to plunge it in just as Flynn spun, making Barker the unwilling recipient of the powerful tranquilizer. Barker roared with anger and pain and Grossfarber looked nonplussed. The big orderly staggered backwards, ripping the syringe out of his shoulder. He rushed at Flynn, brandishing the syringe like an ice pick, but James sidestepped him and put his foot out. Barker tripped and tumbled forward, inadvertently plunging the tranquilizer into Grossfarber's chest.

Barker teetered as the powerful narcotic raced through his blood stream. When the sedative finally reached his brain, his eyes rolled back and he collapsed, falling limply across his unconscious cohort.

Grossfarber stumbled out his office door and staggered into the anteroom, the syringe still hanging from his chest. He lurched towards Nurse Durken and his secretary. "Arga hana lomma haa." As he collapsed, Flynn slammed the office door shut, locking it tight.

Grossfarber's dried-up secretary looked at her boss floundering on the floor. As he continued to mumble incoherently, Durkin calmly picked up the phone and hit a few numbers. "Can I please have security?"

James Flynn sat at Grossfarber's computer and brought up the patient data base. He found nothing for Q. But he did discover an address for Dulcinea Delgadillo. A fist pounded on the office door as he wrote the address on a scrap of paper. He could hear Nurse Durkin shouting from the anteroom, "Mr. Flynn! Open the door! Mr. Flynn!"

Flynn glanced at the image of a security cam in the top right corner of Grossfarber's monitor. He watched as two security guards rushed into the anteroom just outside the office. Nurse Durkin pointed at the door.

Out in the anteroom, Durkin impatiently watched as one of the guards pulled out a massive key ring. He fumbled until he found the right one, and slid the key into the lock. The door flew open and the men barreled into Grossfarber's office, stun guns charged, set to fry Flynn's ass.

They found O'Malley and Barker unconscious on the floor. And James Flynn? Gone. The dumbfounded guards stood there stupidly, and then Durkin heard creaking from above. She glanced up and noticed a ceiling panel was missing.

Chapter Five

The Rose Parade route begins on Orange Grove Avenue in Pasadena and continues past a mansion once owned by the founder of NASA's Jet Propulsion Laboratory. Besides being a rocket scientist, John Whiteside (Jack) Parsons was also a devotee of the infamous English occultist Aleister Crowley. Science-fiction writer and future founder of Scientology L. Ron Hubbard was a frequent house guest and would often participate in the occult rituals and "sex magick" ceremonies Parsons would hold in his living room. The goal was to conjure the anti-messiah who would overthrow Judeo-Christian civilization and lead Earth to a new Aeon.

Mrs. Doris Frawley, the oldest patient at the City of Roses Psychiatric Institute, told Sancho she came to California from Arkansas in 1948. She was fourth runner up in the Miss Arkansas pageant and her ambition was to become a movie star. Instead, she dated both Jack Parsons and L. Ron Hubbard and in 1952 gave birth to the Anti-Christ. Every day she told Sancho how sorry she was for bringing so much evil into the world. Every. Single. Day. And Sancho was starting to believe her. He had worked at the hospital for two years now and it wasn't getting any easier. The nightshift always kicked his ass and he never seemed to be able to get enough sleep.

Sancho dragged his tired twenty-two-year-old butt across the parking lot and fantasized about climbing into his saggy sofa bed. He bought the beige micro-suede futon at a garage sale. The sheets hadn't been changed in weeks. There were unknown, unnamed crumbs everywhere, but he didn't care. He just wanted to be horizontal.

Sancho spotted his rusty, dented red '92 Mustang next to a gleaming BMW 760i. The Beemer's gotta belong to a doctor, thought Sancho. Fuckers make a fucking fortune. I gotta make some changes. Gotta buckle down. Otherwise I'm gonna be wiping the asses of nutcases for the next forty fucking years.

Sancho climbed into his beater and sighed. Fast food bags, empty soda cans, and old newspapers covered the seats and the floor. He turned the key and after a few tries, the old engine finally kicked over. The muffler roared. It obviously had a hole in it, and he knew he had to fix it, but somehow, he just never got around to it. He turned on the radio and blasted heavy metal to drown the muffler out. Then he hit the gas and got his ass out of there.

The bored guard at the front gate raised the wooden arm and waved at Sancho as he pulled through. Sancho waved back. The guard, Bill Keeler, a forty-five-year-old pear-shaped guy with a bad complexion and receding hairline was always telling Sancho about his sexual conquests. Sancho didn't know whether to believe him or not. Was it bullshit? Or was Bill just banging the old, the fat, and fugly? Not that Bill was any prize. Maybe he just had a great rap. It pissed Sancho off to think that Bill might be getting more chocho than him.

Sancho yawned as he pulled out onto the highway. He looked at the Styrofoam cup in his holder and made a decision to try some of that old, cold coffee. Anything to stay awake. He took a sip and made a face and wondered if Coffee-mate ever went bad. Can it give you food poisoning? What the hell was Coffee-mate anyway? As quickly as the question entered his mind, it flitted away. He turned up the heavy metal and took another sip. Something gritty rolled on his tongue and he wondered if it was a bug. Suddenly, he felt a hand on his shoulder. He involuntarily squeezed the coffee cup, popping the plastic top off, spilling java all over his hospital pants.

"What is that bloody music?"

Sancho jerked around. James Flynn sat in the back seat, his tuxedo all dusty and wrinkled.

"What the hell?"

James leaned over the front seat and turned off the radio. Sancho couldn't believe Flynn would have the guts to touch his radio.

"How the hell did you get in here?"

"The door was unlocked. I didn't think you'd mind." James peeled a Big Mac wrapper off the front of his tux. "But Sancho, seriously, this car is a pigsty."

"Dude, they're looking everywhere for you.

"Of course they are. They want me dead."

"Who?"

"You know who."

"Dude, I don't."

"You do."

"If I knew, why would I be asking you?"

"Only you know the answer to that one, my friend," Flynn said.

"But I don't!"

"Tell me this then, Sancho. Do you know what a mole is?"

The topic of the conversation had changed so abruptly, Sancho had trouble finding his bearings. "Isn't it that like a big freckle with a hair growing out of it?"

"I'm talking about a spy. An enemy agent who has infiltrated our organization at the highest level." Sancho sighed and pulled out a cell phone. "Who are you calling?"

"I gotta let 'em know where you—" James put Sancho in a choke hold, seizing him from behind. Sancho looked panicked and terrified, swerving as he struggled to stay in control of the car. His face turned purple and his eyes bugged from his head. Flynn ripped the cell phone from Sancho's grasp and threw it out the open window. Sancho's voice was tight, strangled. "Hey, hey, hey, let go…Let. Go!"

Still choking him, Flynn demanded, "Are you working for the other side?"

"No way, man," he said hoarsely. "I'm your friend! I'm not one of them!"

James locked eyes with him in the Mustang's rear-view mirror. "If you're lying to me I'll find out and when I do—"

Sancho's lips turned midnight blue. "Honest to God, dude, I'm on your side!"

Flynn let Sancho go. He coughed and hacked and desperately sucked down oxygen as he pulled over to the side of the road.

"Sorry, Sancho. Sometimes it's hard to know who to trust." Sancho nodded and rubbed his throat. "We have to find Q and Dulcie before they break them. They're likely interrogating them, doing God knows what to them."

"Who? Why?"

"For the mind control technology, obviously."

"Riiiiiight." Sancho nodded, going along with him as if Flynn actually made sense.

Flynn pulled out a scrap of paper. "I found an address for Dulcie in Grossfarber's database. Unfortunately, I found nothing for Q." James climbed over into the front, shoving Sancho into the passenger seat.

"Hey, hey what are you doing?"

"Do you carry a gun?"

"No, man, I don't have a gun."

"Neither do I, but luckily, I have this." James reached into a pocket and pulled out a black and silver laser pointer.

"A pen?"

"Looks can be deceiving, my friend. It's actually a high-intensity laser that can cut through virtually anything. Q loaned it to me just last week." Sancho reached for the pointer, but Flynn kept it out of his grasp. "Careful, Sancho, this miracle of technology can slice through an engine block like a chainsaw through Jell-O." Sancho looked a little dumbfounded as James tucked the laser pointer away. He shifted into drive and hit the gas, burning what was left of the rubber on Sancho's bald tires.

Bodies lined the walls and filled every chair in the staff meeting room. Yet no one made a sound. Everyone stared at Dr. Grossfarber, who dominated the head of the conference table with his presence, holding an ice pack to his forehead. An oversized bandage covered O'Malley's nose. Barker looked furious and embarrassed and just a bit nauseous. Nurse Durkin stood on Grossfarber's left, glaring like the wrath of God at all the nurses and orderlies.

"James Flynn is dangerously delusional," Grossfarber bellowed. "If he hurts or kills someone, this hospital could very well be held liable. And if that happens, I promise you..." He looked at O'Malley and Barker. "Everyone responsible will be held accountable."

Nurse Durkin held up Flynn's file. "The police have been alerted but we can't just sit by and wait. We need to know if Mr. Flynn told anyone where he intended to go. Talk to the patients. Let them know that all privileges will be withheld until Mr. Flynn is captured. If anyone has any information, they need to come forward. Immediately."

"And if they don't"—Grossfarber shook his finger—"if they know something and they keep it to themselves, there will be serious repercussions."

Barker's hands balled into fists. He looked at O'Malley and saw that his compadre seethed with fury. Their eyes met and even though the communication was unspoken, the message was clear. Flynn had to be found. And he had to pay.

Chapter Six

Tujunga, California sits north of Los Angeles in the Crescenta Valley, between the Verdugo Mountains and the foothills of the Angeles National Forest. Much of Tujunga is rundown and poverty-stricken. Immigrant families live crowded in decrepit apartment complexes all along Foothill Boulevard. Farther back in the hills there are hundreds of ranch-style homes built in the forties after the Second World War. Each hillside neighborhood is a melting pot of Mexicans, Armenians, Koreans, and lower middle-class Caucasians. They're all scrabbling for their piece of the pie, so there's a fair amount of crime and quite a bit of gang activity. And because Tujunga butts right up to the Angeles National Forest, with its scenic drives that wind around sheer cliffs and tree covered canyons, Tujunga is also home to a handful of motorcycle gangs. There are local chapters of the Harpies, the Mongol's, and Satan's Slaves. All three deal in drugs and intimidation, but only the Slaves of Satan are registered as an S corporation in the state of California.

Flynn insisted on driving and Sancho couldn't dissuade him. He tried to reason with him, he tried threatening him, he tried to trick him, but Flynn was on a mission. Not much of it made sense to Sancho, but not much of anything made sense to him anymore. Sancho could have abandoned his car and let Flynn go, but his old Mustang was just about the only thing he owned. Without it, he'd be lost. He couldn't drive to work. He couldn't drive to school. Plus, as crazy as Flynn was, Sancho had a lot of affection for him. He wouldn't want to see him get hurt and he knew how the County Sheriffs could be with people they thought were powerless. He'd been arrested more than once for driving while Hispanic and knew that if Flynn resisted they wouldn't hesitate to put him down hard. So, he decided to hang around and keep an eye on his crazy compadre. Eventually, he'd find a way to cajole him back to the hospital. He was sure of it.

Flynn made a hard left onto Samoa Lane, a rundown street in a small, beat-to-shit subdivision built in the fifties. Samoa ran parallel to Tahiti and perpendicular to Bora Bora. Sancho watched as Flynn checked out the addresses spray painted on the curbs in front of the bedraggled two and three-bedroom houses. The brown foothills of the Angeles National Forest loomed above, the vegetation dry as tinder and ready to burn at the flick of a cigarette.

Sancho tugged on Flynn's arm. "James, come on, man, this is crazy. Where we going? We're gonna run out of gas." Flynn eyed a fifties era ranch-style tract house with peeling yellow paint, a black tar roof, and a scraggly front yard. "Look, man, whatever you think is happening ain't exactly what's happening. You hear what I'm saying? Am I getting through to you? Yo! James?"

James pulled the Mustang to the curb and parked it behind a late model Chevy truck. He nonchalantly glanced in the side view mirror, scanning the area for any suspicious behavior. Finally, Sancho yelled, "James! Jesus! I'm talking to you, man!"

"Shh…"

"What?"

"Hold it down, Sancho, we have to be careful. They could be watching."

"Who?"

"You know who."

"No, I don't know who, dude!" But Flynn wasn't listening. He was already out of the car. "James! Where the hell you going?" Sancho climbed out to follow him and Flynn darted behind a large shrub.

He yelled back to Sancho. "Don't follow in a straight line. Run in a zig zag. You'll be much harder to hit."

An elderly woman walking her terrier stopped next to the shrub so her little black dog could lift his leg. She took a half a step back when she saw James peering out at her from behind the bush. He put his finger to his lips. Her dog growled and James lunged out from the shrub and darted across the yard, running in a serpentine fashion, ducking behind trees and bushes as he made his way up the street.

Sancho offered the startled lady an apology and sheepishly followed after Flynn, not hiding behind anything, feeling like a fool.

A kid on a skateboard stopped and watched as James ducked behind a row of low bushes. Sancho sighed, walked over, and peered over the bushes at him.

"Down! Get down!" James commanded. "Do you want them to see you?"

Sancho reluctantly squatted down as James crawled as fast as he could across the front yard of 1543 Samoa Lane and disappeared around the side of the house. Sancho sighed, stood, and saw the boy staring at him. Sancho felt like an ass. He also felt like he should have taken that warehouse job at Costco instead of the orderly job at the hospital. I could have driven a forklift, he thought. I could have moved boxes and stocked shelves. I could have gotten huge discounts on tube socks and tires and giant boxes of Frosted Flakes. Instead I had to be a humanitarian and help motherfucking nutcases.

Flynn climbed a crumbling cinderblock wall and noticed the next-door neighbor, an elderly Korean man, watering his tea roses. The man stared at Flynn and his dusty tuxedo. Flynn offered him a smile and a quick nod before adeptly avoiding the rusty barbed wire atop the wall and dropping down into the backyard below. James Flynn crouched in the weeds, listening, looking, and carefully scanning the ratty backyard. A truck engine rested next to broken lawn chairs, a plastic trashcan, and a rusty lawnmowerFlynn slowly rose to his feet and approached a back door in need of paint. He couldn't help but notice it had the largest doggie door he'd ever seen. As the thought crossed his mind, he heard the rumbling, rhythmical sound of thundering footsteps. A massive Rottweiler exploded through the doggie door, growling, barking, snarling; its eyes crazy with bloodlust, its teeth bared and flecked with foam.

Flynn didn't move a muscle. He held his ground and locked eyes with the savage canine. They both stood stock still and glared at each other. Flynn didn't show an iota of fear. In fact, he exhibited so much self-assurance and power the dog quickly lost confidence in its viciousness. The angry growl grew less intense. Soon the dog wasn't making any sound at all. The murderous fury in its eyes transmogrified into confusion and then uncertainty and finally anxiety.

"That's right, my friend," said Flynn. "I'm the alpha dog here." The dog backed away, lowering his massive head. "Sit!" barked James and the dog sat his ass down pronto. "Down!" The dog hit the dirt and rolled over on his back, offering Flynn his neck. James rubbed his belly. "Good boy. That's a good boy!" Flynn stepped over him, ducked his head, and crawled through the giant doggie door.

Sancho stood in the front yard and stared at the house, wondering what the hell Flynn was doing in there. Gathering his nerve, he moved across the yard, and snuck around the side where he found an elderly Korean man holding a hose, watering some roses.

"Hey," Sancho said. "Did you see a guy in a tuxedo come through here?"

The old man pointed to the cinderblock wall topped with barbed wire. "He go over there."

"Great," Sancho mumbled. He grabbed the top of the wall and pulled himself up, his feet scrabbling against the cinderblock. He grunted and strained and finally clambered up. Looking down into the yard, he saw no sign of Flynn. He stood unsteadily and lifted one leg up over the wire. His pants caught on a barb. Sancho tried to pull it free and immediately lost his balance. A ripping sound preceded him hitting the ground with a painful thump. The warm breeze caressed the skin on his left butt cheek. Dazed, he clambered to his feet. Pain radiated through his shoulder and neck as he glanced down at his torn, coffee-stained trousers.

"I call police," the Korean man said from the other side of the wall.

Sancho shouted to him. "The police? Why?"

"They coming now."

"Oh, great!" Sancho said sarcastically. "Good! Perfect! Thank you!"

Sancho hurried for the house, searching for Flynn. "Hey! James! Come on, man! We gotta jam!" As he looked through a dirty window, a low growl made the hairs on his arms stand up. Turning, he found himself face to face with a snarling, one hundred and twenty-pound Rottweiler. Terrified, Sancho stumbled back, tripping over the rusted lawnmower, hitting the ground hard. The Rottweiler bared his huge teeth and—

"Down!" ordered Flynn. The Rottweiler immediately dropped to its belly. Flynn stood on the back stoop, a smirk on his face and an Oakland Raider duffel bag in his hand. "I see you've met my little friend." James approached the cowering dog and the Rottweiler tried to get even lower, whimpering pathetically. Sancho was astonished. "Remember, Sancho, hiding inside every big dog is a little dog."

Faint sirens filled the air and the dog howled along with them in unison. Sancho realized that James Flynn was already running, leaping, gracefully vaulting over the fence. Sancho hurried after, catching himself on the barbed wire once more as he clambered over, this time ripping his shirt.

The elderly Korean man, still watering his roses, smiled at Sancho as he limped forward into the front yard. "James! Wait for me, man!" The sirens were louder now and Sancho was in a panic. "James!"

The Mustang screamed up next to him, squealing to a stop. Flynn was behind the wheel, a playful smile on his face. "Are you ready?"

"Ready to what?

"Jam."

A police car came screeching around a corner as Sancho dove in the Mustang's open rear window. Flynn hit the gas and the Ford roared forward, right for the front of the police car. The surprised cop swerved, just missing the front bumper of the muscle car. Sancho managed to get his partly bare ass inside the backseat an instant before the two cars sideswiped each other. Sancho winced as metal scraped metal. The old lady walking her terrier watched as the Mustang skidded around the corner, smoke rising off the burning rubber.

Flynn appeared perfectly calm as he kept the pedal to the metal, propelling the roaring Mustang up the once peaceful suburban street.

"That's it," Sancho yelled. "That's enough! You pull over, man! You pull the hell over!"

Flynn glanced into the rear-view mirror and said, "I don't think so."

Sancho looked back. The cops were right on their bumper. "Holy shit! They're gonna fuckin' put us away!"

"They aren't the police," Flynn said. "They were obviously watching the house. In fact, I'm pretty sure they were expecting us."

Sancho noticed that Flynn now held a Smith and Wesson .44 Magnum revolver. He flicked the cylinder open to make sure it was loaded and then flicked his wrist again, snapping it shut.

"Where the fuck did you get that?"

"From whoever kidnapped Dulcie. He left it in her living room."

Sancho reached for the gun just as Flynn cut a hard left. The Mustang fishtailed, flinging Sancho sideways, his head hitting the door. Dazed, pissed, Sancho sat back up just as Flynn cut a hard right, flinging Sancho into the other rear passenger door. "Ow! Jesus!"

"You may want to put on your seat belt."

Furious, Sancho grabbed for the gun and tried to wrench it out of Flynn's hand. "Gimme that goddamn..." The gun boomed. A bullet blew right by Sancho's surprised face, punching through the rear window of his Mustang, shattering the windshield of the police car in pursuit.

The cop driving was blinded by a million shatter lines. He slammed down his brake and the patrol car squealed to a stop, skidding sideways. The driver's partner looked petrified.

Sancho stared in stunned silence at the crippled police car receding in the distance. He looked at the smoking gun in his hand. "Madre," he said, dropping it on the seat.

"Next time you want to borrow the gun," said Flynn. "Try asking for it." Sancho closed his eyes and let his head fall back.

Flynn made a left onto La Tuna Canyon Road and took the narrow, semi-rural route west towards the San Fernando Valley. They passed horse ranches and sprawling homes built into the hillside. It was as if they left Los Angeles behind and were now roaring down a country road in Arkansas.

After ten minutes, they reached the industrial area known as Sun Valley, full of junk yards, gravel pits, and manufacturing plants. It was an abrupt change of locale from residential to commercial. They passed cinderblock walls covered with graffiti, chain link fences topped with barbed wire, and auto graveyards piled high with rusty car bodies. Five minutes later they cruised through North Hollywood, heading south on Laurel Canyon Boulevard.

Flynn glanced at Sancho in the rear-view mirror. "I found a few clues as to what may have happened to Dulcie. Have you looked inside the duffel bag?"

"I don't want to."

"Sure you do."

Sancho leaned over the front seat and unzipped the battered Oakland Raider's bag to find it packed with cash. Bundles of C-notes wrapped in rubber bands. "Jesus Christ," Sancho murmured.

"There was a message on the answering machine for someone named Mike."

"Man, this isn't our business."

"Inviting him to a pub called Tiny's for some sort of rendezvous."

They heard sirens again and Sancho looked back to see another police car on their ass. "Son of a bitch! They musta put an APB out! Jesus Christ!"

"Don't worry." Flynn put the pedal to the metal. "I'll lose them."

Chapter Seven

The shrill wail of the police siren made Sancho's head vibrate like a tuning fork. "Just pull over, man! Just pull the fuck over!"

Flynn watched the pursuing police car in his rear-view mirror. It tried to pull around him, but Flynn put the Mustang in its path. The cruiser had to swerve and drop back.

Flynn made a hard right, bumping up over the curb, nearly taking out a mailbox before roaring off down a perpendicular street. He hit a dip and the car bottomed out, shooting sparks. Flynn floored it and made another hard right. He swerved around cars and SUV's and pickups, barely avoiding collision after collision—his face surprisingly calm. Sancho, however, was sure he was about to die. The police sirens could be heard howling in the distance when Flynn inexplicably began to slow down.

Sancho sighed. "Thank God."

Flynn cut from the left lane into the right, slowing down even more before abruptly squealing into the drive-thru line of an El Pollo Loco. A pickup truck pulled in line behind them and a moment later two patrol cars came roaring around the corner, sirens screaming, lights flashing, speeding right by the El Pollo Loco and on down the block, where they swerved through an intersection and continued on into the distance.

James Flynn smiled at a mystified Sancho. "Hungry?"

"Not really." Sancho was sweaty and pale and a little queasy.

"Have some lunch. On me." Flynn grabbed one of the bundles of c-notes and pulled a single bill out from under the rubber band.

"Man, have you heard a single word I've said?"

"Actually, Sancho, I haven't missed a syllable."

"I'm not hungry, okay! I feel sick, all right! You want to take my car, take it! Fuck it! You can have it! I'm done with you! I am through!" Sancho opened the car door.

"I only came here because of you," Flynn said.

"I told you! I'm not hungry!!"

"Yes, but this is the El Pollo Loco on Vineland."

"So?"

"Where the lovely young lady you've been pining for is employed."

Sancho looked flabbergasted as Flynn pulled up to the drive-thru menu. A female voice floated over the speaker, "Can I help you?"

Flynn addressed the microphone in the menu board. "Indeed, you can. I'm looking for Alyssa."

"That's me," the perky voice replied.

"Excellent. I'd like to order a Chicken Caesar burrito and a Dr. Pepper for myself and for my friend…" Flynn looked at a furious Sancho, who energetically shook his head no. "A Classic Chicken Burrito and a Coca Cola. Can I also get a Chicken Quesadilla?"

"Of course. That'll be nine fifty-two at the window."

"Thank you, Alyssa, you've been very helpful." Flynn pulled forward and they waited behind a Ford Explorer.

Sancho boiled over with anger and embarrassment. "I'm getting out of here, man."

"Yes, of course. If you want to chicken out, that's your prerogative. But Sancho, isn't this the opportunity you've been waiting for? The woman of your dreams is less than fifteen feet away. All you have to do is pose a question."

"I don't think so."

"If you try and you fail, you'll feel like a fool for a day or two, but if you don't try at all, you'll feel like a fool forever. You'll always regret that you didn't have the courage to ask a simple question. And from now until the day you die, you will always wonder what could have been."

The Explorer pulled away and Flynn cruised up to the window. Alyssa was slender and petite with huge brown eyes and a sunny smile. She was so breathtakingly beautiful that Sancho couldn't bear to look at her. Instead, he stared straight ahead, his face slowly turning red. Flynn offered Alyssa a warm smile as she said, "That'll be nine fifty-two, please."

Flynn offered her the C-note. "Why don't you keep the change?"

She looked at it with surprise. "I can't do that, sir. We can't accept anything larger than a twenty. I'm sorry."

Flynn turned to Sancho. "Do you have any cash?" Sancho sighed and pulled out his wallet, fishing out a ten. Flynn whispered, "Here's your chance."

Sancho looked mortified. He glanced at Alyssa for an instant before staring straight ahead again.

"Sir?" Alyssa repeated. "It's nine fifty-two."

Flynn handed her the ten and as she made change, he whispered, "Sancho..."

"Shut up."

"Look at her."

"No!"

"She's beautiful."

"Shut the fuck up," Sancho whispered.

Alyssa handed Flynn the change, two drinks and a plastic bag full of food, which Flynn passed over to Sancho. "You can do this."

"Let's just get the fuck out of here," Sancho pleaded.

"I don't think so."

"Dude..."

"No."

"There's people behind us, man."

"Can I get you anything else," Alyssa asked. Flynn didn't answer her, he just stared at Sancho. "Sir?"

Sancho looked at Flynn pleadingly, but Flynn continued to stare at him. "You can do this," Flynn whispered.

Sancho nervously glanced up at Alyssa. She smiled at him. There was an awkward, pregnant pause. The truck behind them beeped. James turned and gave the driver a look that shut him right the hell up.

"Can I get you anything else?" Alyssa asked again.

"Actually, my friend Sancho here would like to ask you something."

"Hi," Sancho mumbled. He opened his mouth to continue his rap, but nothing else came out.

"Hi," Alyssa said gently.

"I was just wondering," Sancho finally stammered, "If—if—if...you know...I was thinking that maybe...sometime...if you have time...you might want to...possibly...maybe...you know...go out...or...something...sometime."

Alyssa grinned, "I've seen you before, right?"

Sancho nodded, smiling shyly. "Yeah."

"You're a regular."

"Yeah."

Flynn whispered to Sancho, "How about this Friday?"

"You free Friday?"

"I work on Friday," she said. Sancho kept that smile plastered desperately to his face. His eyes, however, couldn't hide his disappointment. But then she said, "How about Saturday?"

"Saturday's good."

Alyssa wrote her number on a takeout menu and handed it to Flynn who handed it to Sancho with a grin. "Call me."

"Definitely." Sancho beamed like an idiot.

Flynn smiled at Alyssa and hit the gas, pulling away. Sancho stared in amazement at the phone number in his hand. "Son of a bitch," Sancho whispered.

"Indeed."

Sancho grinned and pumped his fist into the air, punching the ceiling of the car. "Did you see that?"

"I saw." Flynn made a right.

"She didn't hesitate or nothing."

"She was captivated by your confidence."

"What do you think I should do? Take her to a movie?"

"Take her somewhere you can have a conversation. You need to get to know each other. It's all part of the dance." Flynn pulled over to the curb behind a UPS truck, reached into the El Pollo Loco bag, unwrapped his Chicken Caesar Burrito, and took a big bite.

"You don't think she was trying to get rid of me?"

"If she wasn't interested, she would have said so," Flynn said with a mouthful.

Sancho pulled out his burrito and started to eat. They munched in silence for a few minutes. Sancho looked at Flynn, sipping on his Dr. Pepper. "So, are you ready to go back to the hospital?"

"Hospital?"

"Headquarters. Whatever."

"Sancho, I'm not sure you understand the gravity of our situation."

"Dude, I'm not sure *you* do…"

"N and Miss Honeywell are missing, possibly dead. Q has been kidnapped. Dulcie is in grave danger." Flynn crumpled up his burrito wrapper and took another sip of Dr. Pepper before pulling back into traffic.

"James, listen, man, I know that's how it seems, but—"

"A brutal enemy has infiltrated her Majesty's Secret Service. We're the only ones left. The world's last, best hope."

"James—"

"I called directory assistance and they gave me the number for Tiny's"

"What?"

"I was also able to obtain an address and a cross street. It's at the corner of Lankershim and Tiara."

"What the hell are you talking about?"

"The message on Dulcie's answering machine."

Flynn pulled into the parking lot of a grimy, mini-mall with a carniceria, a coin laundry, a Spanish-language video store and, on the far end, Tiny's Tap, a decrepit hole-in-the-wall bar. Twelve gleaming Harley's sat parked out front.

"Shit, ese," said Sancho. "You're not thinking about going in there?"

"Why wouldn't I?" Flynn said as he reached into the back seat for the .44 Magnum.

"What do you need that for, man?"

"They may be holding Dulcie prisoner, and if so they won't exactly be happy to see me, will they?" James climbed out of Sancho's Mustang and tucked the huge revolver inside his pants. It created a rather pronounced bulge under his dusty Tuxedo jacket.

"If you think I'm going in there with you, you're fuckin' nuts."

"I'm not asking you to."

"Well, you're fuckin' nuts anyway! You're gonna get yourself killed!"

Flynn ignored Sancho's warning and headed for the beat-up front door of Tiny's Tap. Sancho automatically reached for his cell phone before remembering that Flynn had thrown it out the window. He scanned the parking lot and saw a payphone at the edge of the 7-11's parking lot. He climbed from the Mustang and hurried over. The handset was off the holder and the phone was sticky with the residue of a Big Gulp. Sancho gingerly picked it up and quickly determined there was no dial tone. Then he saw that the handset wasn't even connected. The frayed wires dangled free.

"Fuck!" He unstuck it from his ear and slammed it down.

Chapter Eight

James Flynn couldn't see a thing when he first entered Tiny's Tap. The dim lighting and dark, dirty walls forced him to squint. As his eyes adjusted, he saw a few tables, a long well-worn bar and, in the rear of the room, a threadbare pool table. It was a gritty, biker bar frozen in time, ripe with thirty years worth of spilled beer, piss, Lysol, cigarette smoke, and vomit. Rough-looking assholes in greasy denim and black leather crowded the bar with their big arms, hairy beer guts, scraggly beards, long hair, bandanas, and faded tattoos. Most wore sleeveless jean jackets with a grinning devil's head patch on the back. The grinning demon smoked a fat cigar and above his head were the words, "Satan's Slaves."

James Flynn was probably the first person ever to walk into Tiny's Tap wearing a tuxedo. He seemed surprisingly at ease as he ambled in, smiling charmingly at the all biker babes, many of whom appeared to be quite taken with him.

While Flynn was busy making new friends and enemies, Sancho was having a shit fit. He pushed through the doors of the 7-11 and put his face in the face of the perplexed East Indian man working the register. "I am with someone who's insane," Sancho announced. "And I need to use your phone."

"Insane?"

"Yes!"

"I see no person."

"He's not with me!"

"Didn't you just say he was with you?"

"He's dangerous! He needs help!"

"Who?"

"The person I'm with!"

"But you are not with anyone."

"Just give me your goddamn phone!" Sancho reached over the counter. The clerk tried to hold him back.

"No, no, no…I think no."

"Don't you understand! He's out of his fucking mind!"

"Get out of here. Go!"

"He has a gun!"

"You?"

"Him!"

"Who?"

"Asshole! Just give me the fucking phone!"

"All right," said the Indian man. He reached under the counter and came up with a 9mm Glock. He aimed the automatic at Sancho's forehead. All the blood drained from his face.

"Everyone has a fucking gun," Sancho mumbled.

"Will you be going now?" the Indian man asked.

"Yes." Sancho slowly backed away. "Just put the goddamn gun down."

"I don't think so," the Indian man said.

A hard-looking bleached blonde with a huge freckled chest offered James a come-hither smile. She smoked a cigarette and wore a black halter top that displayed her cleavage like two huge scoops of cookies and cream ice cream. Her face might have been attractive a few thousand beers ago.

"Hey, baby." The blonde's voice was deep and raspy. "You seem a little lost. You looking for Starbucks?"

A couple of her biker babe friends laughed. They all looked like they'd been around the same sad block a few too many times. Too many bong hits, cigarettes, and disappointments etched permanent lines into their thirty and forty-something faces.

A skinny redhead with bloodshot eyes said, "You wanna order a double decaf nonfat latte?"

Her comment elicited more laughter as James, smiling with good humor, edged past the biker chicks and bellied up to the bar. "Actually, I was hoping for a martini."

The bartender, a fat, bald biker-type with a ZZ Top beard, glared at him. "You want a fuckin' what?"

"A vodka martini." Flynn explained, "Ketel One preferably. Four parts vodka, one part Lillet extra dry vermouth. A twist of lemon peel. Shaken, not stirred."

"What kind of vermouth?" The beefy bartender suddenly seemed a tad intimidated.

"L-i-l-l-e-t. Pronounced Lill-ay. It's French. From the Bordeaux region."

The bartender stared at Flynn, flummoxed. "I think I got some Martini and Rossi."

"Then I suppose we will have to make do, won't we?"

The bartender nodded, clearly cowed, and started mixing Flynn's martini.

Outside in the Mustang, Sancho sat behind the wheel, staring at the battered front door of Tiny's Tap. He glanced at the open duffel bag packed with cash and then noticed the car keys dangling from the ignition.

"Fuck," he said aloud.

Sancho grabbed the keys and started the car. The old Mustang roared to life. He shifted it into reverse and turned, peering out the rear window. He glanced back at Tiny's Tap. He knew he should go. Knew he should get the hell out of there. Flynn was probably already dead.

"Fuck me," he said as he looked at himself in the rear-view mirror.

Dulcie sat on a stool, looking glum, swigging from a half-empty bottle of Bud Light. The lacy, red halter top and tight black jeans only served to accentuate her skinny frame. Bored, she glowered at the pool players as the ancient jukebox blared Creedence Clearwater's "Bad Moon Rising." The raucous laughter of the biker babes brought her gaze over to the bar where she caught the incongruous sight of James Flynn offering her a grin.

Dulcie's mouth dropped open in stunned disbelief. She couldn't quite connect what she was seeing with reality. Was that actually Flynn? How the hell did he get out of the hospital? How did he find Tiny's and how did he know Dulcie would be there? Countless unanswered questions collided inside her mind. She was so busy trying to make sense of Flynn's presence, she forgot she was holding a bottle of beer. It slipped from her grasp and crashed to the floor, catching the attention of her boyfriend.

Mike Croker was tall and lean and his long muscular arms were covered with tats. An eagle's head emblazoned with the phrase, "Live Free or Die" decorated his left arm and an adorable cherub wielding a sawed-off shotgun adorned his right. To better show off his tats, he wore a tight, white wife-beater along with baggy Levies, black motorcycle boots, and a look of contempt.

"What the fuck, Dulcie? You drunk?"

All the blood drained from Dulcie's face. She put on a smile, but it wasn't very convincing. "I don't feel too good."

"You look like shit," Mike said. "You gonna spew?"

"I think I need a Coke."

"Fuckin' coke whore," Mike mumbled. His friends laughed as he went back to lining up his shot, squinting through his own cigarette smoke.

Flynn looked Croker over. He noticed twin lightning bolts tattooed on the back of his neck. Flynn recognized them as the symbol of the Schutzstaffel, Heinrich Himmler's SS. It was the favorite symbol of neo-Nazis and white supremacists, including the prison gang known as the Aryan Brotherhood.

Croker missed the shot and Flynn could hear his angry "Motherfucker!" over the music blasting on the jukebox. His two opponents smirked. One was a massive bald guy with a long, skinny, braided goatee. He said something to Mike that Flynn couldn't hear. The other player, a wiry guy with a face like a weasel, grabbed his stick, and walked around the table. Dulcie tapped Mike's shoulder and squeezed past him. "You want another beer?" she asked.

"Get me a pack of Camels."

Dulcie nodded and headed for the bar. She sidled up next to James and he offered her his most charming smile.

"Don't look at me," Dulcie whispered.

The bartender handed Flynn his martini and Dulcie put a five on the bar. "Dom, can I have a pack of Camels, please?"

The bartender grabbed the five and watched, fascinated, as Flynn took a careful sip of his martini. "Is that okay?" the bartender asked.

"This has been stirred," Flynn replied.

"So?"

"Stirring bruises the vermouth. I wanted it shaken and strained into a martini glass. This is a highball and not a very clean one."

"You kidding me?"

"Do I look like I'm kidding?"

Flynn handed the bartender the martini. Chastened, the big guy poured the drink in the sink and started over.

Dulcie peered sideways at Flynn and whispered, "What the hell are you doing here?"

"I'm here for you."

"Jesus Christ. Are you kidding me? How did you even find me?"

"I'm very good at what I do."

"Listen, you gotta get out of here."

"Not without you. We have to find Q."

"James, please."

Flynn noticed a nasty bruise by Dulcie's left eye, barely hidden by some heavy makeup. He reached out to touch it and she turned her face away. "Who did this to you?"

"If my boyfriend sees me talking to you—"

"Boyfriend?"

"Yeah. Mike."

"Is he the one with the SS tattoo?"

"He's the one right here." Mike stood directly in front of Flynn, holding a cue-stick. "Who the hell are you?"

"That's really of no consequence."

"What the fuck is that supposed to mean? Dulcie, who the hell is this guy?"

"How the hell am I supposed to know," she said nervously.

"You're the one who's having a goddamn conversation with him."

The bartender returned with Flynn's martini and watched as Flynn ignored Mike to take a sip. James gave the bartender a stern look and then smirked. "Much better. Thank you."

The bartender beamed.

Mike slapped the glass out of Flynn's hand and it crashed to the floor. The bartender looked more appalled then Flynn. "Hey, asswipe," Mike snarled. "I'm talking to you."

"Yes," Flynn said. "And so far, it's been a rather dreary conversation."

Mike swung the cue stick and James grabbed it with both hands, twisted and turned and flipped Mike right over his back. Eyes wide with surprise, the biker twirled through the air and landed on a table. It collapsed under his weight and Mike hit the floor with his face.

Mike's biker buddies looked astounded. They slowly moved forward, surrounding Flynn on all sides. Dulcie was terrified, but James calmly took her by the hand and addressed the bikers with complete confidence. "The young lady and I will be leaving now."

The bikers all looked at each other. Mike's massive bald bud, the guy with the braided goatee, blocked Flynn's path. "Who the fuck do you think you are?"

"The name is James. James—"

"Fucker!" Mike grunted. He grabbed the edge of the bar and pulled himself to his feet. A cut on his forehead dripped blood into his eyes and down his face. "You're fucking dead!" Mike slid a huge Marine combat knife out of a sheath on his belt.

Instantly, Flynn had the .44 in his hand. No one saw him pull it. It was just there as if it materialized out of thin air.

All the bikers took a half a step back, except for Mike who glared at the pistol in Flynn's fist. "What the fuck? I got a gun just like that."

"Yes, but you don't have it with you, do you? You also don't have a license to kill. I do and I promise you, I will use it without compunction."

"Without what?"

One of the bikers swung a pool clue at Flynn's head. He smoothly ducked and avoided the blade of Mike's combat knife by diving and doing a perfect shoulder roll. He came up shooting.

Click.

He pulled the trigger again.

Click. Click. Click. Click.

The bikers all grinned.

James Flynn flew out the front door and bounced down the three cement steps that led to the dusty gravel parking lot. He was followed by Mike and six other bikers who all continued to kick the crap out of him.

Flynn tasted the hot coppery tang of his own blood as he tried to focus through the pain exploding in his brain. Blood streamed from his nose into his mouth and all over his tuxedo shirt. The cold gravel cut into his hands and knees as Mike slammed his boot into Flynn's ribs, knocking the air out of his lungs. He tried to get himself upright, but the agony paralyzed him and his arms kept collapsing. His face smashed into the gravel and the smell of blood and dirt filled his nostrils.

All the yelling and laughing, cursing and grunting faded away as Flynn retreated inside himself. He folded into a fetal position as boots slammed him from all sides. The sideways world started to blur as he searched the parking lot for Sancho's Mustang.

But it was gone and so was Sancho.

Flynn felt a pang of disappointment that was even sharper than the motorcycle boots bruising his ribs. He was sure his loyal sidekick would be there.

The squeal of tires interrupted his sad and painful reverie. Flynn looked towards the sound to see Sancho's Mustang tearing across the parking lot, kicking up gravel. The hope turned to apprehension as he realized the car was careening right for him. The bikers panicked and scattered—the car missed Flynn by inches, crashing into the gleaming Harley's. The bikes went down like dominos, one after another, chrome twisting, glass shattering.

Flynn used every ounce of strength to push himself up on his hands and then his knees and then his feet. He limped for the Mustang, wincing as electrical jolts of pain shot through his ribs and lower back. His head felt like a giant balloon, numb and swollen.

The Mustang skidded to a stop, kicking up dust. Sancho waved him on. He tried to move faster, but he didn't have any control over his limbs. Sancho watched with alarm as Mike and six of his vicious compadres closed in. They were almost upon him, their beer bellies shaking as they hurried to catch Flynn.

"Come on man!" Sancho screamed and Flynn, just like Sancho did earlier that day, dove through the Mustang's rear passenger window.

Flynn's lower half hung out as Sancho hit the gas. The tires spun, kicking up a rooster tail of gravel and dust that flew into the eyes of Mike and the other Slaves of Satan.

The Mustang sped out of the parking lot, into the street, nearly colliding with a garbage truck. Sancho cut a hard right, fishtailing, squealing, rocketing south down Lankershim. He glanced in the rearview mirror to see the angry mob of bikers growing smaller and smaller. He looked at Flynn and winced. Blood and dirt covered his face and torn tuxedo. Flynn licked his split lip and tasted blood. His right eye was swollen and already turning purple.

"They beat the crap out of you, dude. Look at you. Jesus…"

James glared at Sancho. "Can I ask you a question?"

"Whatever, man."

"Did you take the bullets out of the gun?"

Suddenly, Sancho felt extremely sheepish. "Maybe," was all he would admit to. Flynn glared at him and Sancho tried to explain. "I didn't want anybody getting hurt."

Mike and the other bikers were hacked, bent, and bummed as they stared at their crushed and mangled Harleys. The door to Tiny's creaked open and Mike glanced over to see Dulcie step into the light, clearly happy as hell that Flynn was gone and presumably still alive. When she noticed the look on Mike's face, however, she realized that she probably wasn't going to be so lucky.

Chapter Nine

There were no hills in North Hills. It was in the flattest part of the San Fernando Valley, next to Panorama City, which offered no panoramas, but did have one of the largest GM plants in the world before it was shut down in 1989. North Hills wasn't known as North Hills until 1992. Previously, the area next to the 405 freeway was called Sepulveda, named after one of the founding families of Los Angeles. Gang activity, drug dealing and prostitution gave Sepulveda a bad name, so local boosters decided they could improve real estate values by changing the name to something hopeful and scenic like North Hills. It didn't exactly work.

As they cruised down Sepulveda Boulevard, Sancho watched as Flynn checked out his neighborhood. Certain blocks north of Roscoe were considered gang territory; so dangerous that the police rarely patrolled the area. They just blocked the streets off so there was only one way in and one way out. Much of the area was severely damaged by the Northridge earthquake of 1994. Many of the apartment buildings damaged by the quake were abandoned by their owners. The properties were taken over by squatters and prostitutes, gang bangers and crack addicts. The buildings that weren't abandoned had dirt cheap rents. Often entire immigrant families lived in one-bedroom apartments.

Sancho called one such building home. He rented a single on the second floor of a twenty-two-unit apartment building. There was parking available below, but since the last earthquake few tenants actually ventured down there. The lights were gone and at night the homeless claimed the area as their own. Sancho was the only resident who continued to use his space. He wasn't about to leave his Mustang on the street.

Sancho felt a little defensive as Flynn took all of this in. "Rents in L.A., right? With what I make at the hospital, I can barely even afford this shithole." They parked in Sancho's spot, right by a shopping cart and a pile of trash, the only belongings of a man named Arturo. The pile of newspapers moved and Arturo peered out from his "bed." Unshaven, skinny, and hollow-eyed, he nodded to Sancho as he and Flynn climbed from the car. Sancho tossed Arturo a five and when Flynn raised an eyebrow, Sancho said, "Arturo keeps an eye on my wheels."

Arturo scrutinized Flynn's beat up face. "You don't look too good, my friend."

"Appearances can often be deceiving."

"So, what are you saying—you usually look worse than this?"

"Arturo has a sense of humor."

Sancho smirked. "Arturo loves to break balls."

Arturo grinned and showed Flynn the last few yellow teeth left in his head. Sancho headed through a doorway and up a short staircase. Flynn followed, limping, grimacing. Every step clearly painful.

The courtyard of the apartment house had an empty pool full of trash and dried out palm fronds. A little boy on a Big Wheel rode precariously close to the edge of the pool.

Sancho smiled at the kid. "Hey, Julio, be careful, dude. Don't go falling in the pool again." The kid laughed and drove his Big Wheel over Flynn's foot.

James followed Sancho up an exposed stairwell to a second-floor landing and watched as he unlocked three deadbolts to open the door. Sancho ushered James into a one room apartment decorated in early Salvation Army. The carpeting was stained and threadbare and the walls were off-white and decorated with a single movie poster.

"I still think you need to go to an emergency room." Sancho closed the door and locked all three deadbolts. "Those assholes kicked the shit out of you."

"I'll be fine. I just need bandages and some antiseptic." He licked his split lip and winced. Sancho shook his head and led Flynn into an impossibly tiny bathroom. There was just enough room for a sink, a toilet, and a small shower stall. The walls were decorated with faded floral wallpaper and the fixtures stained with rust. A scummy looking throw rug was scrunched up on the floor and the toilet seat cover was the same brownish-gray color. Sancho directed Flynn to sit on the toilet seat. He seemed hesitant at first, but finally lowered his bottom.

Sancho opened the medicine chest over the sink. He grabbed a box of Band-Aids, a bottle of iodine, and an ancient-looking can of Bactine. Sancho studied Flynn's messed up face. "Close your eyes."

"Why?"

"Just do it."

Flynn closed his eyes and started to say something just as Sancho sprayed his face with Bactine. Flynn gagged and sputtered.

"Why didn't you close your mouth?"

"Because you told me to close my eyes."

Sancho opened the iodine and daubed a cut on Flynn's chin.

"Ow!"

"I thought you were impervious to pain, ese."

He went to daub another cut and Flynn grabbed his wrist. "I think we're done."

"You let that get infected, you'll get gangrene and they'll have to cut off your whole damn head."

"I'm fine."

"You're not fine. You're all fucked up. That cut is huge. You probably need stitches."

"I'm not worried about me. I'm worried about her."

"Who?"

"Dulcie."

"There's nothing we can do for her right now."

"What if they're torturing her?"

"What are you talking about?"

"I'm talking about a brave young woman who needs our help."

"Dude..."

"As long as she keeps her mouth shut, they won't kill her. But the second she gives them what they want—"

"You should be worrying about you. Not her."

Flynn looked hard into Sancho's eyes. "You were afraid back there, weren't you?"

"Of course, I was afraid. Those bikers would have kicked my ass from here to Oxnard."

"It's nothing to be ashamed of."

"Who said I was ashamed?"

Flynn put his hand on Sancho's arm. "I feel fear. Just as you do. The only difference is...I know how to use it. Fear keeps me sharp. It makes me dangerous..."

"Dangerous I would agree with."

"Fear is your friend, Sancho. You must face it, embrace it, and use it. For if you don't, it *will* destroy you."

Two hours later, Flynn struggled to rest on Sancho's ancient sofa. His legs hung over the threadbare armrest and a bag of frozen peas thawed on his forehead. The duffel bag of cash sat on the floor.

Sancho came out of the kitchen, eating a banana and wearing a new pair of pants. "Hey, James, you want a sandwich or something?"

Flynn's eyes popped open all the way and, for a brief moment, panic set in. He had no idea where he was or who he was or who the guy with the banana was. And then Sancho took a big bite and everything came flooding back. The panic faded, but didn't entirely disappear. It rested somewhere deep inside of him, lingering like a dull ache. "I got peanut butter, some bread and another banana and that's about it," Sancho said with a mouthful.

"A peanut butter and banana sandwich?"

"You want one?"

Flynn shook his head. He removed the bag of half-frozen peas and sat upright on the couch. He noticed some textbooks on the coffee table. College Algebra. Roman Civilization. Introduction to Psychology.

Flynn motioned to the books. "Are you a university student?"

"Junior college."

"Interested in psychology?"

"Maybe. I don't know."

"You no longer want to work with Her Majesty's Secret Service?"

Sancho smiled wistfully. "I guess that's what I'm trying to figure out."

"I wouldn't give up so easily if I were you, Sancho. I truly believe that you have the potential to be a highly adept agent."

Sancho nodded. "Maybe you should stay here while I go get some help."

"There is no help. Not for men like us." Flynn tried to stand, but his head swam. He started to reel.

Sancho grabbed his arm to steady him. "Ese, listen to me. You need to get some rest, okay?"

"You were skeptical before. I could tell. But now you see what we're up against, don't you?"

Sancho smiled and nodded and helped Flynn to sit back down. "We'll take care of it, dude. I promise you. Just get some rest. I'll be right back."

"Where are you going?"

"Where am I going? To…uh…get supplies." Sancho unlocked all three deadbolts and opened the door.

"Weapons? Ammunition?"

"Everything we need, man."

"You're a good friend, Sancho."

"I'll be back before you know it, bro." Sancho closed and locked the door. Flynn could hear the three deadbolts click.

Dr. Grossfarber hurried down an empty corridor with Nurse Durkin at his side.

"Nothing from the police?" Grossfarber asked.

"No, sir. Not a word."

"If the public finds out, if the news media picks this up, the powers that be will be very unhappy—"

Sancho came running around the corner like a madman with his pants on fire. He collided with Nurse Durkin, bouncing off her prodigious chest. "Nurse Durkin! Dr. Grossfarber! I've been looking all over for you."

"Not right now, Perez!" Nurse Durkin pushed Sancho out of the way to clear a path for Grossfarber.

"It's about Flynn!"

They both stopped dead in their tracks.

Five minutes later all three were in Grossfarber's office. Grossfarber was on the phone as Sancho and Nurse Durkin looked on. "The address is…" Grossfarber looked to Sancho, raising an eyebrow.

"1455 Lull Street in North Hills," Sancho said. "Apartment 210."

"1455 Lull Street, Apartment 210. Yes…of course…thank you, Sergeant. We'll see you there."

Dr. Grossfarber hung up the phone and smiled at Sancho. Suddenly Sancho wasn't so sure he'd done the right thing.

"They're not gonna send like a SWAT team, are they?"

Grossfarber was already putting on a jacket. "Flynn's delusional. He's dangerous."

"He's not dangerous," Sancho replied. "He's just a little…whacked."

"Is that your professional diagnosis?"

"I'm just saying—"

"I know what you're saying and I know you mean well, but Flynn has already attacked five people on our staff. One of them was me."

"I know, I just—I just don't want to see him get hurt."

"None of us do," said Grossfarber.

The neighborhood's relative quiet shattered with the arrival of five patrol cars, sirens screaming, cherries flashing, followed by an ambulance, two unmarked police cars, and a black SWAT van. Sancho stared at the front of his building— wide and blocky, typical of apartment houses built in the early sixties. It was painted a fading salmon pink, which was supposed to make the place look festive and tropical.

Instead it just looked sad; like a large old lady wearing a threadbare muu muu. Other than the traffic and the occasional private jet coming in for a landing at Van Nuys Airport, the street was usually peaceful.

The police and paramilitary SWAT guys leaped out with weapons locked and loaded. The doors on an unmarked car opened and out piled two plainclothes policemen, followed by Dr. Grossfarber, Nurse Durkin, and Sancho.

A black uniformed SWAT officer strode up to Sancho without any preamble, invading his space. "Apartment number?"

Sancho took a step back. "What?"

"I need a confirmation of your apartment number!" The man's normal tone of voice appeared to be an angry shout.

"What are you guys going to—"

"Apartment number!"

"210," Grossfarber said.

The SWAT officer moved towards his men and Sancho grabbed him by the arm. "Hold on a second." The officer glowered at Sancho and Sancho promptly removed his hand. "Officer, just let me go in first and tell him what's—"

"Sir, I'm sorry, but you'll have to get back in the car!"

"But you don't need all these guys. The dude isn't dangerous. He's just—"

"Please, sir! Get in the car!"

A plainclothes cop grabbed Sancho by the arm and pulled him towards the unmarked police car. Sancho watched helplessly as the SWAT officer shouted orders, dispatching flak-jacketed men armed with assault rifles. Sancho glanced at Dr. Grossfarber and Nurse Durkin. Both looked positively gleeful.

The plainclothes cop opened the unmarked car. "Get in the vehicle, sir."

"I just don't want the poor guy to get hurt."

"If he doesn't resist, he won't."

"But what if they see his gun? They'll think—"

"He has a gun?"

"Yeah, but it's not loaded, it's—"

The plainclothes cop yelled to another cop. "Suspect has a gun!"

"No, no, no, it ain't loaded!"

The word spread from cop to cop, all the way to the commander of the SWAT team. "Suspect has a gun! Suspect is armed!"

Now it was being bellowed from a bullhorn. "Suspect is armed and dangerous!"

"It ain't fuckin' loaded!" yelled Sancho, but no one was paying any attention to him. Sancho pushed past the plainclothes cop and sprinted towards his building.

The cop chased after him, pulling his piece. "Halt!"

Sancho yelled up to the SWAT team on the second-floor landing, "Don't shoot! Don't fuckin' shoot!"

He raced up a staircase and reached the second floor just as the SWAT Team kicked down his front door. Someone threw a flash-bang grenade inside the apartment. A muffled boom resonated followed by a weird high-pitched whine. SWAT barreled inside his apartment, screaming, "LAPD! LAPD!"

Sancho was almost to his apartment when the plainclothes cop tackled him. He heard his neighbor's door creak open and caught sight of a shadowy silhouette holding a large gun. The cop saw this too and raised his pistol. Sancho tried to get up, hitting the cop's chin with his head, bumping the revolver with his elbow. The gun went off, blowing a hole in the partly opened door. The SWAT team immediately started firing their M-4 assault rifles; sure that someone was trying to take them out. They fired wildly in a panicked frenzy. Bullets shattered glass, ripped through plasterboard, shredded furniture and punched holes in closet doors.

Sancho watched, petrified, as his neighbor's door opened wider. He could finally see the face of the silhouetted figure with the gun. It was his terrified ten-year-old neighbor, Jerome, wielding a big yellow Super Soaker squirt gun. Sancho pounced, tackling Jerome as bullets sliced through the air, peppering wood and plasterboard. The kid tried to get away, but Sancho held on tight, covering him with his body. Both were scared witless as bullets whizzed by and wood splintered and dust rose. Finally, the SWAT Team leader in Sancho's apartment screamed, "Cease fire! *Cease fire!*"

Eventually they did and in the eerie silence that followed, Sancho let the boy go and slowly rose to his feet. The cop standing on the landing trembled and stared at little Jerome, whose crotch was wet with urine. Sancho carefully poked his head into his apartment to see six assault rifles aimed at his head. He froze and took in what was left of his place. The SWAT officers were shrouded in dust and smoke and wired with adrenaline.

"Where the hell is he?" demanded the SWAT team leader as he poked Sancho in the chest with his finger. "You said he was here."

"He was."

Chapter Ten

The white, fluffy guts of Sancho's beige micro-suede sofa covered the floor. His thirty-two-inch flat screen TV lay shattered in countless pieces. His book shelves were ripped apart and his battered coffee table was cracked in half. Every wall was peppered with bullet holes. His crushed and smoking HP desktop lay upside down on the floor.

Sancho sat on his devastated sofa sipping from a can of beer and staring at a framed movie poster that, amazingly, still hung on the wall. The glass was shattered and the poster torn, but the frame still clung stubbornly to the nail Sancho had pounded into the plasterboard two years ago.

Sancho first saw Shrek when he was eleven years old. It was the only movie his father ever took him to. Sancho's dad bought him popcorn and a cherry Slurpee and Sancho laughed like crazy. He thought he'd never seen anything funnier. His dad laughed as well. He laughed so hard, he had to gasp for air. That laughter had filled Sancho with such joy. It surrounded him like a warm blanket. Like one of his mother's hugs.

His dad was a truck driver who usually left before the sun came up, to go to work. He was exhausted when he came home; too tired to talk to Sancho or even deal with him. Many nights he didn't come home until very late. One night he didn't come home at all. He never came home again. His mother never mentioned him and his absence made Sancho feel empty inside.

He and his mother moved in with his mother's parents. His grandfather was a proud man; the patriarch of his family. He didn't say much, but Sancho knew that he was loved. Often, he would work for his grandfather, mowing lawns, trimming hedges and translating for him. Sancho gave most of the money he made to his mother. But one day there was a garage sale across the street from the lawn they were cutting. Sancho saw the "Shrek" poster for sale and bought it for seventy-five cents. His grandfather thought he was crazy. Sancho took it home and hung it on the wall of the bedroom he shared with his two cousins. When he moved out Sancho brought it with him. Other than his clothes, it was only thing he took. He didn't really understand why he was so attached to it. He just knew it made him smile.

Sancho finished his beer, crushed the can, and dropped it on the floor. He leaned on what was left of the sofa's armrest and pushed himself to his feet. As he crossed his tiny apartment, the broken glass crunched under his sneakers. Sancho reached up to the poster and straightened it. He took a few steps back to make sure it was even.

"My goodness," Flynn said. "Are you all right?"

Sancho turned to see Flynn standing in the doorway to his apartment. He carried Mike's duffel bag of cash in one hand and a garment bag in the other. He was sporting a dark gray suit that fit him perfectly. The door itself was off its hinges, splintered and broken on the floor. Sancho watched as Flynn walked in, coolly surveying the damage.

"They were here, weren't they?"

"No, dude, I had a party and things got a little crazy."

"How'd they find us?"

Sancho blushed and started to stutter. "H-How the hell do I know?"

"They were probably watching your apartment."

"Yeah," Sancho nodded a little too enthusiastically. "They probably were."

"They still are."

"No shit?"

"There's an unmarked police car parked out front."

Sancho's voice went up an octave. "Did they see you?"

"Of course not." Flynn looked around the ruined apartment. "I'm surprised they didn't take you into custody." Flynn raised a curious eyebrow. "Why didn't they?"

"I don't know. How do I know?"

"Maybe they think you're still on their side."

"Maybe."

"Are they correct in that assumption?"

"No."

"Was Grossfarber here?"

"Yeah, he was here with Nurse Durkin and the police and SWAT and—Is that a new suit?"

"Armani."

"Armani? Are you kidding me?"

"When did they leave?"

"About an hour ago."

"So, they think I kidnapped you?"

"Well, yeah…Isn't that what you did?"

"No, my friend, I liberated you. We've been infiltrated at the highest level and most of our agents are completely oblivious. They are working for the opposition and they don't even know it." Flynn put down the garment bag and the duffel bag and glanced through the broken window into the courtyard below. "It's to our advantage that Grossfarber thinks you're still working for him."

"But I'm not. Not anymore. He fired me."

"Why?"

"Because I called him an asshole."

Flynn looked disappointed. "Why would you do something like that?"

"Why?" Sancho was astounded. "Because that's what he is! Look what he did to my place!"

Flynn nodded. "Well, maybe it's for the best."

"For the best?"

"Yes, because now there's no turning back."

Sancho tried to keep his cool, but finally he just blew. "Man, what the hell is wrong with you? I can't afford this shit! I got rent! I got bills to pay! I got fuckin' responsibilities."

"Sancho, a man is like a teabag." Dumbfounded by Flynn's non-sequitur, he threw up his hands and walked away. Flynn continued anyway, following after him. "You never know how strong he is until you dip him in hot water."

Sancho turned and stared at Flynn. There was so much he wanted to say, but he didn't know where to begin, so he didn't even try.

"Shall we go?"

"Go?" Sancho almost laughed. "Where?"

"To find Dulcie and Q."

"No, dude, I don't think so. Sorry, but I'm done. We're finished. I can't do this. Not anymore, man."

"I'm very sorry to hear that."

"I'm sorry too. But I can't help you anymore. And that includes loaning you my wheels."

"Well, that's fine. I don't need your 'wheels.' I have arranged for my own transportation." He smiled and held up a set of car keys. Sancho looked even more bewildered than before.

Flynn led Sancho down the apartment building's rear stairwell. He eased open the door and poked his head out to see if the coast was clear. The only person present was a seven-year-old girl playing with an ancient Barbie doll. One arm was missing and so was most of its hair. The few clumps left gave the appearance of hair plugs. As Flynn and Sancho tip-toed past the little girl, she smiled and said, "Hi."

"Hi, Rachel," whispered Sancho as they continued on to a chain link fence bordering the back of the building.

Flynn threw both bags over and quickly hopped the fence. Sancho had a bit more trouble getting over the top. Rachel watched wordlessly as he ripped his pants, yet again, and landed hard in some gravel. Flynn was already on the move and Sancho hurried to catch up. Eventually, Flynn led him to a street parallel to Lull.

He heard a low beep-boop and then the sound of a car door being unlocked with a remote. Flynn was twenty feet away, opening the door of a new Aston Martin convertible.

"Jesus Christ," Sancho blurted. "What the hell is that?"

"It's an Aston Martin DB 9 Volante."

"Don't tell me you stole it?"

"Of course not. I bought it." Flynn dropped Mike's duffel bag into the trunk."

"You used the drug money? How much cash is in that bag?"

"Not as much as there used to be."

"Is that what you used to buy the suit?"

"And the watch." Flynn held up his arm and slid back his sleeve to reveal a gold Rolex.

"Jesus. They're gonna be looking for you, dude. And if you don't have every penny you stole accounted for, they're gonna fuck you up."

"They would 'fuck me up,' as you so eloquently put it, no matter what. And as far as them finding me, I intend to find them first."

"What are you saying? You're going back there?"

"It's perfectly all right if you don't want to go."

"James, come on, man. Don't do this."

"If you want to stay out of harm's way, that's your prerogative."

"Man, you don't understand."

"Of course I do. You don't want to die. Neither do I. Personally, however, I fear death far less than I do an inadequate life." Flynn held out his hand. "It's been very nice knowing you, amigo."

Sancho hesitated and then finally shook hands with him. "I'm begging you, man. Don't go back there."

"Nefarious forces are at work, my friend. Evil in all its ugliness. Innocent lives are at stake. Innocent lives that I am honor-bound to protect."

Sancho sighed. He looked at the car. He looked at Flynn. Finally, he came to a decision, "Fuck."

Flynn smirked and climbed into the Aston Martin.

Sancho wrenched open the passenger door and sat his ass on the buttery brown leather seat.

"You might want to put your belt on," said Flynn.

Sancho glowered at him as he clicked his seatbelt into place.

Flynn met his glower with a smile. "Can I ask you something?"

"What?"

"Why'd you change your mind?"

"Because I'm an idiot."

Flynn reached over and patted him on the knee. "I like you too, Sancho."

He started the Aston Martin and the twelve-cylinder engine roared to life. Flynn rested his hand on the glossy walnut gearshift and slid the car into first. His left foot released the clutch as his right foot eased down on the gas pedal. The Aston Martin rumbled like compressed thunder, taking off faster than a rocket, laying down a ten-foot-length of rubber as it sped away.

Chapter Eleven

Dulcie's hands trembled as she lit a Marlboro Light. She gratefully sucked in the smoke, filling her lungs with the warm, satisfying poison. She knew it was killing her, but she loved it. Loved to smoke. Just like she loved Mike. Even though she knew he was killing her. Her head throbbed. Her jaw ached. The pain was everywhere. Inside and out. Her left eye throbbed where Mike backhanded her. She stood in front of the mirror in the tiny bathroom and tried to conceal the bruising with make-up. Growing up in Monterey Park, she believed her future would be very different. She thought she'd be on TV. Everyone said she was very pretty, even her step-father who would creep into her bedroom late at night to show her how much he "loved" her. Her mother knew about the nocturnal vists and pretended to ignore them, and Dulcie learned to pretend, too. Her real father died in Iraq and her mother married a balding plumber, a devout Catholic who owned his own home.

Alberto molested Dulcinea for the first time when she was thirteen. This continued for four years, until she ran away. She moved in with Nacho, short for Ignacio, a member of the Mongols motorcycle gang. Dulcie became one of his harem of three runaways, and he treated her like he treated the others. Badly. However, he did feed her and shelter her and introduced her to beer and tequila and spliffs and crack. In return all she had to do was service him and all his fellow Mongols.

Two years after moving in with Nacho, Dulcie met Mike in a bar in Laughlin. He rode with Satan's Slaves and with his long blonde hair and muscular torso covered in tats, Dulcie thought he looked like a buff,

blond, slightly beat up Brad Pitt. He'd smiled at Dulcie and she returned
the smile. She knew that he was trouble. But she didn't care. She was
nineteen years old and sick and tired of being at the beck and call of a
forty-five-year-old asshole like Nacho. Mike strolled over and they
started to talk. He offered her a beer. One of the Mongols saw this
flirtation and decided to put a stop to it.

When the fighting was finished, Nacho was no more. Dulcie didn't
care. She was on the back of Mike's Harley, her hands around his
impressively muscled torso. As they rumbled away with the rest of
Satan's Slaves, she didn't look back. Not once.

She looked at the butterfly tattoo on her inner wrist. She
remembered the day she and Mike went into that tattoo parlor in
Pasadena. Could that be two years ago? They'd had some good times.
Unfortunately, most of those good times took place the first month they
were together. Mike manufactured and sold meth. He didn't touch the
stuff, but Dulcie did, though she would never admit to being a tweaker.
Tweakers were those hopeless, toothless, bone-skinny, brain-addled
addicts you saw rooting through the garbage dumpsters behind Safeway.
Dulcie only tweaked on weekends. Besides, it helped keep her weight
down. Meth made her feel strong and confident and utterly fearless. It
was the way she always wanted to feel, but unfortunately those feelings
of omnipotence only lasted as long as her high. Six months previously
Dulcie was arrested for shoplifting and her public defender made a deal
to get her into rehab. That was where she met Flynn. And that was who
she was thinking about as she dabbed more make up on her black eye.

A fist banged on the bathroom door. "Three hundred and eight-two
thousand dollars!" Mike screamed. "Do you know what Kursky's gonna
fucking do to me!"

She knew he wanted an answer to his question, but she had a
question of her own. "How do you know it was him?"

"Because Mr. Kim fucking saw him! A tall white guy in a tuxedo!"
Mike kicked open the bathroom, slamming her into the sink. Dulcie
cowered as he grabbed her by the arm and dragged her into the living
room. "Conan was right here the whole damn time!" Mike glared at his
big Rottweiler, who tried to get as low and flat to the floor as possible.
He offered his neck, demonstrating his obedience, as Mike bellowed,
"Nobody gets past Conan!"

Embarrassed and cowed, Conan slunk into the kitchen and out the
doggie door.

Mike grabbed her other arm and pulled her close. "Who the hell is
he?"

"I don't know."

"Then how the fuck did he know your name?"

"Mikey, please…"

"I don't want to hurt you, Dulcie, but I will. I will choke the life outa you!" Mike put his right hand around her throat and squeezed. "I want to know who he is and where he is and I want to know now!"

"He's right behind you," Flynn said.

Mike turned to see Flynn and Sancho standing in his open front door.

Mike's voice boomed, "Conan! Attack!"

A moment later they heard thundering footsteps, snarling and growling as Conan came galloping into the living room. He bared his teeth, his furious eyes filled with hate, but then he saw Flynn and stopped dead in his doggie tracks. The snarling instantly ended and much to Mike's chagrin, Conan lowered his ears and slunk back out the way he came in.

Mike yelled after him. "Conan! *Conan!*

"It appears you're on your own," Flynn said.

Mike pushed Dulcie down on the couch and grabbed a baseball bat propped up against the wall. "Pal, you just made the biggest mistake of your life."

"Dulcie, are you all right?"

Mike glared at her and yelled, "Do not fucking talk to him!"

"Is that how you get your jollies?" Flynn stepped closer. "Beating up on women?"

"I'd much rather beat up on you. And that's exactly what I'm gonna do if you don't give me my fucking money!"

Sancho backed for the door as Flynn moved closer. "Does that rude, bully-boy routine usually work for you? Because frankly it isn't working for me."

Mike roared and came at Flynn surprisingly fast, swinging the bat hard. Flynn sidestepped Mike's swing. The bat whizzed by his head and crashed through a window.

Flynn glanced at Sancho. "Did you see how I did that?" Mike spun and swung again and Flynn easily ducked the blow. A lamp exploded. "You take advantage of your enemy's energy." Flynn moved his head an inch or two to the left, just enough to avoid another attack. "And turn their aggression against them." Mike's face was bright red. He was nearly frothing with fury as he swung at Flynn again and again and Flynn effortlessly avoided him.

The bat dented walls, knocked down shelves and shattered anything the least bit breakable. In the struggle to take Flynn down, Mike completely destroyed his living room. The biker's breathing grew ragged and his face shone with sweat. Furious beyond words and too out of breath to talk, Mike used his last reserves of energy to swing the

Louisville Slugger with everything he had. James parried, put out a foot, and tripped him. Mike slammed face first into the wall, cracking the plasterboard. The impact knocked him cold and he lay sprawled on the floor. Motionless. Silent.

Dulcie looked at James with utter disbelief. "Jesus Christ! What the hell is wrong with you?"

"Not a thing. I'm perfectly fine. Your numpty boyfriend missed me completely." He smiled at her with easy confidence, unruffled in his Armani.

"No, I mean why are you even here!"

"Aside from protecting you?"

Tears sprang to her eyes. "Yes."

"I'm on a mission to find Q and discover who has betrayed us. Of course, if there's anything *else* you'd like me to do…"

Dulcie stared at Mike, splayed out awkwardly on the floor. "He's going to think we're working together."

"Who?"

"Mike!"

"Well, aren't we?"

"No!"

Flynn was surprised by the vociferousness of her response. "I see."

"Well, good! I'm glad you do! Because I sure the fuck don't!"

"That's because you're under the sway of Q's mind control technology."

"Listen to me." Dulcie stepped closer to him. "That money you took? It's not Mike's. It belongs to his boss."

"Grossfarber?"

"No!" Her anxiety rose with her exasperation. "Kursky! Pete Kursky! He's not someone you want to fuck with!"

"Well, darling, neither am I."

"I'm not kidding."

"I'll protect you. I told you."

"Would you just—"

"Shh." Sancho watched with amazement as Flynn lifted her chin and looked into her eyes. "Look at me. Believe me. I will never let anyone hurt you again."

James Flynn was so cocksure and the fantasy was so seductive, Dulcie desperately wanted to believe. A tear rolled down her cheek and Flynn caught it with his thumb. He kissed her gently on the forehead and on her cheek and as he moved for her trembling lips, Sancho cleared his throat.

"Sancho, why don't you go wait in the car."

"We gotta get out of here, ese. This motherfucker's waking up."

Flynn looked at Mike stirring. He nodded then glanced at Dulcie. "Sancho's right. We have a job to do. Grab your things."

Dulcie looked flushed and dumbfounded. "What things?"

"Pack a bag, but make it quick." He clapped his hands.

She hurried into another room as Mike groaned and lifted his face off the floor. He looked up at Flynn and Flynn smiled down at him. "Are you going to behave yourself?"

"I'm gonna fucking kill you."

Flynn glanced at Sancho. "I'm guessing that's a no." Flynn kicked Mike in the head and he slumped back down, out for the count once again.

Sancho struggled with two huge suitcases as he followed Flynn and Dulcie out the front door and across the overgrown lawn.

"You may have over packed," Flynn said.

"I didn't know how long I was going to be gone."

"Can you guys help me with one of these?" Sancho asked, but Flynn was lost in thought, working out his next move.

"Do you think this Kursky has Q?"

Dulcie was beyond exasperated. "No. Look, I don't think you're listening to me."

"I'm listening, but it's clear that you don't know what you're saying. After all, they're controlling your thoughts."

"Who?"

"The ones we're hunting. The ones we must stop. They want you to think what isn't true *is* true, so if you believe they don't have Q then obviously they do."

Dulcie looked hopelessly at Sancho, but he was too busy with her luggage to commiserate. He dropped both bags by the rear of the Aston Martin.

"Whose car is this?" asked Dulcie. Sancho pointed at Flynn. She set her jaw and glared at him. "Did you lease this with the money you took from Mike?"

"Don't be absurd," Flynn replied.

"Oh, thank God."

"I bought it for cash."

A pistol boomed! All three turned to see Mike stagger out his front door, shakily aiming a .44 magnum. It was the same gun Flynn had filched earlier that day. Mike pulled the trigger and the gun thundered again, the bullet punching a hole in the Aston Martin's right rear quarter panel.

"Well, that's a shame." Flynn bent down to examine the bullet hole.

"Run!" Sancho shouted.

"I'd rather take the car, if you don't mind." Flynn climbed behind the wheel as Sancho and Dulcie scrambled inside. The big gun boomed again, this time shattering the right rear passenger window. "He's not exactly a crack shot, is he?" Flynn said as he started the car and hit the gas, shifting into first, burning rubber.

The car squealed off as Mike pulled the trigger, punching a hole in the Aston Martin's trunk. He fired again and again until every dog and car alarm in the neighborhood was either barking or shrieking and there wasn't a bullet left in his revolver.

Chapter Twelve

The Angeles National Forest was a perfect place to dump a body and, over the years, many bodies were indeed dumped in Little Tujunga Canyon. Bikers, drug dealers, gang bangers, and serial killers all took advantage of this rugged, isolated area with its nearly impassible terrain. Hikers often came upon the half-eaten remains of a gullible young model or murdered home-maker. The hills were full of coyotes and bobcats, skunks and rattlesnakes. There was even the occasional mountain lion. As society encroached, the intersection between wilderness and civilization collided. The animals had no place to retreat to and, since humans weren't about to back down, conflict was inevitable.

The Aston Martin hugged the corners of Little Tujunga Canyon Road as they headed north into the wilds of the Angeles National Forest. It was an uphill climb from the northern edge of Los Angeles County and Sancho watched as the housing developments gave way to horse property and then half-assed habitations and rickety shacks. Soon there was just dry chaparral, fragrant with sagebrush and the remnants of diesel exhaust. Higher still and Sancho saw Douglas fir and pine trees dotting the hillside.

Even with the top down, the ride was fairly quiet, and the four hundred and fifty horsepower, twelve-cylinder engine propelled the Volante effortlessly. Eventually, they were five thousand feet above sea level, zooming past huge outcroppings of granite and shale and squealing around hairpin turns. Sancho, riding shotgun, felt his stomach drop when he peered past the edge of road to see that the closest ground was hundreds of feet down.

Sancho was startled by the crack of a rifle shot and he turned to see they were cruising past a shooting range. He could hear pistols and shotguns and rifles being fired with great enthusiasm by semi-toasted, middle-aged white guys. Soon the sound of the gun fire was gone, muffled by the mountains. Sancho saw a sign for Indian Springs. It was peppered with shotgun pellets. He looked at Flynn. "Where exactly are you taking us?"

"That's what I'd like to know," Dulcie said. She sat in the back seat, looking peeved.

"Palmdale," said Flynn.

"Palmdale?" Sancho raised a curious eyebrow. "What the hell's in Palmdale?"

Flynn pointed to the little black book open in his lap. "Someone we need to pay a visit to."

"Is that Mike's phone book?" Dulcie sounded freaked.

"I found it when I found his ill-gotten gains." Flynn motioned to the duffel bag on the floor between Sancho's feet. Dulcie glanced at the open bag and saw the last of the cash, stacks of hundred-dollar bills bound with rubber bands.

"So, who do we need to pay a visit to?" Sancho asked.

"Pete Kursky. 775 Arbor Drive, Palmdale." The tiny bit of color in Dulcie's face drained away at the mere mention of Kursky's name.

Holding the wheel with one hand, Flynn pushed on a pop-up dashboard panel, revealing the hidden satellite navigation system. He keyed in the address, eyes half on the road, half on the computer screen as they squealed around another tight turn.

"Dude, what are you doing?" Sancho said nervously.

"Entering in the address. The satellite navigation system will direct us straight to Mr. Kursky's front door."

"You can't do that," Dulcie said.

"Of course I can. See." Flynn pointed to the map that now appeared on the small monitor.

"Jesus Christ." Dulcie shook Sancho's shoulder. "Do something!"

"What?"

"This motherfucker's gonna get us killed."

The Aston Martin hit a tight turn too fast and the car slipped into a skid. Sancho gaped silently at the approaching abyss as the car drifted sideways. Dulcie's scream created an irritating off-key harmony with the squealing rubber. Unperturbed, Flynn regained control of the car inches from the edge. The brush with mortality left Sancho and Dulcie deathly quiet. The only sound was the wind rushing past the car.

A soft, sexy female voice broke the silence. It came from a speaker built into the navigation system. "Please turn right on Sand Canyon Road."

Flynn squinted and peered into the distance. "Does anyone see a road ahead?"

"Maybe you better slow down," Sancho said.

"Time is of the essence, my friend. Lives are at stake. Q could be near death as we speak. He's a brave soul, but anyone can be broken and when he is—"

"Look out!" Terror filled Sancho's face as he pointed up ahead. The road split to the left and the right and in the center stood a solid wall of granite. The speedometer on the Aston Martin hovered at seventy. Flynn hit the brake and cut right.

The car slid into another skid. The sharp tang of melted rubber filled Sancho's nostrils as he watched the granite wall speed closer. It smelled like fear. Like the fire and brimstone of Hell. Dulcie closed her eyes and grabbed the oh-shit strap. Flynn, however, kept his cool and the rear tires finally caught. The rear end fishtailed as Flynn regained control. Sancho saw him smirking. The son of a bitch was enjoying this.

Sancho started to say something, but his attention was diverted by the glare of two approaching headlights. Flynn was in the left lane driving towards oncoming traffic. Sancho and Dulcie were too exhausted to scream any more. They had no more adrenaline left in their adrenal glands. They couldn't flee. They couldn't fight. All they could do was wait for the end.

Flynn tried to go right, but the panicked driver of the oncoming car turned the same direction. Flynn veered left and so did the other driver. They were in a dangerous and stupid dance, heading towards the inevitable conclusion of a collision. Flynn could have gone right again, but he made a split-second decision. The kind of decision that separates men of action from road kill. He continued to veer left, right off the road and onto the narrow gravel shoulder. The Aston Martin kicked up rock and dust as they rocketed between the oncoming car and the granite rock face, barely missing both. The sound was deafening and Sancho and Dulcie stopped breathing as everything moved in slow motion. Soon the danger was past and Flynn was back on the right side of the road, unruffled and serene.

The soft, sexy female voice with the English accent said, "Go North on the Antelope Valley Freeway."

Flynn glanced at Sancho who was holding his breath. His forehead was slick with perspiration and he felt close to blowing chunks. Flynn grinned. "Nothing like a relaxing drive in the country, eh, Sancho?"

Mike Croker stood in the middle of the street, pulling the trigger on his .44 magnum. He'd hoped to hit someone or something, but was pretty sure he didn't hit anything. He wasn't exactly a marksman. He wasn't sure why. Maybe it was his lazy left eye or the fact that he never practiced, but unless he was right on top of something he rarely ever hit it. The report of the pistol echoed in his head along with an annoying ringing. At first, he thought it was coming from his own head as the rhythm of the ringing matched the throbbing pain at the back of his skull. Slowly he realized the ringing came from somewhere else. A satellite phone. Kursky was calling him.

"Son of a bitch."

He staggered into the house. Shattered glass and cracked plaster covered the floor. He saw broken lamps and overturned furniture and finally his pride and joy, his sixty-two-inch Sony HDTV. It was the only thing in the room still standing. He limped angrily over to the satellite phone's recharging station and picked up.

"Yeah?"

"Mike?" It *was* Kursky.

"Uh huh."

"What the fuck, man? I've been calling for fifteen minutes. You said you were going to be there."

"Sorry, man...I've been...dealing with something.

"Dulcie?"

"She's part of it."

"Fuck, dude. I'm not denying she's hot. But Jesus Christ, it ain't worth it. You know what I'm saying."

"Ya..."

"I would hit that in a second, I'm not saying I wouldn't, but I'd never let a bitch that crazy move in with me. That cunt doesn't give you the proper respect; you know what I'm saying?"

"I hear ya..."

"I'm not trying to bust your balls, I'm being honest with ya." Mike heard someone saying something to Kursky and Kursky said, "Hang on a second." Mike, still dizzy from his ass-kicking, sat himself down on the couch. He clutched the satellite phone to his ear and listened as Kursky cussed someone out. Soon Kursky was back on the line. "Fucking Dave. I don't know, man. You still there?"

"Uh huh."

"Okay, listen, the buy's going down at noon tomorrow. We're meeting them at the downtown warehouse. I'll meet you in the parking lot. And don't forget the fucking cash." Mike didn't respond immediately. In fact, he didn't respond at all. "Mike? You there?"

"Uh huh."

"So acknowledge me, man. Let me know that you understand what I'm fucking telling you."

"Pete, there's…um…something going on that…um…I need to talk to you about."

"What?"

"We have a little problem."

"What kind of problem?"

Mike sighed. "Remember that crazy fucker who came to Tiny's today? The English dude?"

"The guy whose ass we kicked?"

"Yeah, he…uh…broke into my place and stole the cash."

"You fucking kidding me?"

"I think Dulcie was in on it."

"Fuck."

"I know, man. I'm sorry."

"How the fuck did that happen!"

"I don't know."

"Who the fuck is he?"

"I don't know."

"What the fuck *do* you know?"

"Pete, I'll make it up to you. I promise."

"It's not me you gotta make it up to."

"You're not telling him are ya?"

"I have to. If I don't, he'll think I'm in on it."

"I'll get it back."

"How much we talkin' about?" asked Pete.

"All of it."

"You fucking asshole."

"Just give me a little time."

"No can do, dude."

"Come on, man."

"Can't help you, Mikey. You're on your own."

"Pete?" But Pete was no longer on the line. The line was dead and Mike was afraid he'd be dead soon too. He looked up to see Conan staring at him from the kitchen doorway. The big dog tilted his head quizzically and Mike whipped the phone at him. Conan yelped and ran and Mike put his face in his hands. "Fuck me…"

Chapter Thirteen

In 1887 a wagon train of Lutherans traveled to California from the snowy Midwest to start a new life. They were told they would know they were close to the ocean when they saw palm trees. They mistook the local Joshua trees for palms and put down roots one hundred miles east of the Pacific Ocean in the western Mojave Desert. Unable to grow anything in this desolate unforgiving landscape, all but one family abandoned the settlement by 1899. Over one hundred years later, Palmdale is still home to many lost souls hoping to find the American Dream in the driest desert in North America.

Pete Kursky stood in the backyard of his palatial Palmdale McMansion and watched the light fade from the sky. A huge two-level pool with a waterfall and a massive Jacuzzi was filled with four naked, slightly overweight biker chicks. The low hills of chaparral surrounding his property were purple in the setting sun. Pete heard the mournful wail of a coyote as he stared at the satellite phone in his beefy hand. That stupid asshole. Someone has to take the fall and it isn't going to be me, he thought. No fucking way.

Kursky had a shaved walnut-shaped head. He sported a long, braided goatee tied off at the end with a tiny red bead. He stood six foot four and weighed three hundred and twenty-two pounds; exactly twenty-seven pounds lighter than on his last birthday. He was on the Jenny Craig diet, so he weighed himself every morning.

He'd struggled with his weight since he was eight years old. The kids at Fillmore Elementary school in Mesa, Arizona had teased him mercilessly. By junior high he was not just fat but tall and started fighting back. By the time he was in eighth grade, he was the biggest, most vicious bully Barry Goldwater Middle School had ever seen. At fifteen he was arrested for beating a football player into a coma and spent the next three years in juvenile hall. Upon his release at age eighteen, he found a group of friends who understood where he was coming from. These friends were members of Satan's Slaves; the most feared motorcycle gang in Phoenix.

The Slaves dealt drugs, stole cars, operated massage parlors, and sold protection. Pete quickly rose through the ranks. At age twenty-nine, he was charged with the task of starting a Slaves chapter in Los Angeles. He avoided San Bernardino, since the Hell's Angels were so well entrenched there, and settled on Tujunga in the foothills just north of Los Angeles.

The Los Angeles Chapter of Satan's Slaves now had nearly two hundred members and controlled the crystal meth trade in the L.A. area. Pete was ambitious. In fact, he was so ambitious that six months previously he made contact with one of Mexico's largest drug cartels. He was angling to be their Los Angeles distributor and the money that Mike lost was money he owed to them for the product they were bringing into L.A. The cartel's contact man was a mean son of a bitch by the name of Mendoza—and that was why Pete hesitated to call.

He liked Mike. They'd been friends a long time. He first met Mike's older brother in juvenile hall and took Mike under his wing when Mike's brother was killed in a motorcycle accident. But business was business and Mike had made a fatal mistake. Kursky punched a number into the satellite phone as the last few reddish rays of sunlight disappeared from the wispy clouds that streaked across the desert sky.

A weeping man slumped tied to a chair. He sat in a pool of light surrounded by darkness. A black hood covered his head. He shook as he sobbed, whimpering in Spanish, begging for mercy. Mendoza watched him without emotion. At six one and two hundred and eighty pounds, he was shorter and lighter than Kursky, but somehow looked bigger. His thick musculature strained the seams of his black Hugo Boss suit. He sucked on a skinned knuckle as he regarded the whimpering prisoner. Mendoza spoke Spanish with a Mexico City accent. His voice was soft and matter of fact. "Give me the name of your contact and this will all be over." Mendoza's entire presence threatened violence, but his eyes made him terrifying. They were flat, black and bottomless. "I just need the name. I'll get it out of you eventually. You know I will."

The man continued to weep. Mendoza nodded to the greasy-looking lackey kneeling behind the chair. He grabbed the weeping man's left hand. The snitch screamed. Three of his fingers were badly broken, bent at odd angles. The lackey grabbed the rat's pinky and snapped it viciously. The howling grew louder and Mendoza simply watched, giving away nothing. He raised his voice, not out of anger, but to be heard over the man's screams.

"Continue to waste my time and this will never end. After your fingers, we will break your toes. We will take your eyes. Cut off your nose. Tuco is a master. He will cause you the maximum amount of pain, yet you will not die. You will be legless and armless and yet you will still be alive and we will keep you alive until you tell me what I need to know. Everyone you love will die, regardless of what you tell us...so you see, there's no reason for you to be silent. Your bravery is pointless."

A slender young man emerged from the darkness and whispered in Mendoza's ear. Mendoza nodded and the young man handed him a satellite phone.

"Mendoza," he said, listening, his face betraying nothing. When he answered, he answered in heavily accented English. "If the money isn't found then your associate will have to pay. He will die and we will take everything he owns. And, if after everything is sold, we still haven't been properly compensated, then you will have to make up the difference."

Kursky's voice echoed over the line, "I'm sure we can find the fucker. He couldn't have gotten very far."

Mendoza's tone didn't change, though there was just the slightest adjustment in the set of his jaw. "Then find him and stop bothering me with these trivialities." Mendoza clicked off the phone and handed it back to the slender man. He looked at the snitch weeping in the chair. The jet-black Glock looked tiny in Mendoza's massive paw. "Shall we start with your left foot or your right?" Mendoza was back to speaking Spanish. "It doesn't matter to me. Left foot or right? Left or right?"

"Left!"

Mendoza shot him in the right. The man screamed and then Mendoza shot him in the left. The shriek pitched louder and then became hoarse, ragged and hopeless. Mendoza looked at the slender young man with the satellite phone. "Take over for a little while. I gotta take a leak."

Chapter Fourteen

Tiburcio Vasquez was one of California's most famous Mexican bandits. He stood five foot seven and weighed one hundred and thirty pounds. He started his life of crime in 1852. Four years later Vasquez was rustling horses by the hundreds. He was a legendary womanizer and rumored to have impregnated many impressionable and passionate senoritas. Posses in five counties were put together to track him down. Vasquez hid out in a very rugged area just south of Palmdale. Vasquez Rocks—jagged fingers of sandstone ripped up out of the ground by prehistoric earthquakes was named after the scrawny bandit. Vasquez was sentenced to hang in San Francisco. His jail cell was visited by thousands of women who wanted to catch a last glimpse. He signed autographs and posed for photographs, which he sold from the window of his cell. He used the proceeds for his legal defense. Clemency, however, was denied and Vasquez died in 1875 in San Jose, where he was hung by the neck until dead.

Sancho thought about Tiburcio Vasquez as the Aston Martin flew past the geologic park named after the long dead bandito. How the hell did that little vato get all those ladies to give it up like that? He obviously had what Flynn has, whatever mysterious thing that is. Tiburcio met a very sad end and Flynn's future didn't look much better. How will this end for them? In a hail of bullets? In a prison cell? At the bottom of a canyon in a flaming Aston Martin?

The sky was almost black and a waxing moon hung low, close to the horizon. It silhouetted Vasquez Rocks against the night sky. They stood like dark sentries, ominous and prehistoric, and they filled Sancho with dread.

The speedometer hovered at ninety. The Aston Martin blew past the other cars as if they were standing still. Since it was Sunday, the Antelope Valley Freeway wasn't very busy. Monday through Friday, at this time of day, the freeway was choked with suburban commuters heading home from work in L.A.

The wind whipped Dulcie's hair everywhere as she sat in the back seat. "I'm not a secret agent," she screamed, her voice almost lost in the wind.

"I know that," Flynn said.

"You do?" Sancho asked.

"Yes, she's a brilliant research scientist who works for Q."

"I'm a waitress and cashier!" Dulcie yelled. She turned to Sancho. "Why are we even talking to this crazy motherfucker?"

"Yes, I understand that's your cover," Flynn said. "But your innate intelligence is rather obvious."

"You are not dealing with reality! Look at me! I didn't finish high school! I'm a fucking tweaker!"

"Do you really think that's a believable cover?"

"It's not a fucking cover! It's who I am!"

"I know you're not authorized to reveal your true identity. Not even to me. But just know that we're on your side and we're here to help you. Right, Sancho?"

Sancho didn't answer. He just sighed and watched as the approaching lights of Palmdale illuminated the dark desert sky.

The satellite navigation system began to beep and a red flashing dot appeared on the map. The calm, feminine, English voice of the navigation system said, "Please exit east at Avenue S."

Sancho scooted down as Flynn drove by Pete Kursky's compound and did a reconnaissance run. The house was a sprawling six thousand square foot Spanish style McMansion on five acres of desert real estate. It was covered with salmon-colored stucco and brightly lit with motion sensing security lights. There was no landscaping. No grass. No trees. Just a dozen Harleys, a few pickup trucks, and one monster four by four parked in a front yard made up entirely of cement. A tall, black, wrought iron fence topped with razor wire surrounded the property. The only entrance appeared to be an automated gate.

Sancho watched as Flynn took in every detail. He parked a quarter a mile down the rural road in front of the next closest house and raised the Aston Martin's roof. Flynn locked down the clamps and turned off the ignition, cutting off the navigation system's ever-polite voice just as she was telling them to turn the hell around.

"James, listen to me, man." Sancho looked at Flynn hard. "We gotta think this through."

"I already have."

"Dude, they'll kill you."

"They will," Dulcie said. "They'll fucking kill you!"

"If you have nothing to die for, you have nothing to live for," Flynn replied as he opened the Aston Martin and climbed from the car. He tossed Sancho the keys. "Be ready to move."

Sancho watched as Flynn quickly made his way towards Kursky's place, disappearing into the darkness of the desert night. Occasionally, they caught glimpses of his silhouette.

Dulcie slapped the back of Sancho's head. "How could you let him go?"

"How the hell was I supposed to stop him?"

"You didn't even try." Tears filled Dulcie's eyes.

"You gotta phone?" Dulcie nodded. Sancho put out his hand.

"Who you calling?"

"Just give me the phone."

"You're not calling the cops, are ya?"

"Dulcie!"

"You can't call the cops on Kursky. If he finds out we called the cops on him…"

"How's he gonna find out?"

"They have cops on the payroll. They'll see the phone number and they'll know it was me."

"Give me the fucking phone."

"We should just get the hell out of here."

"Dulcie…"

"Start the car and let's get the fuck out of here."

"I'm not—"

"There's nothing we can do for him. He's fucking dead. The cops can't save him. It's too late. Just start the fucking car!" Sancho grabbed for her purse and Dulcie fought him for it. He dumped the contents out in his lap and found the phone. She tried to grab it and he pushed her away, opened the car door and stumbled out. She climbed out after him. "Give me back my fucking phone!"

Sancho punched in 911 and spun to avoid her as she slapped and kicked him. He put it up to his ear to listen but the phone didn't ring through. It just made a forlorn beeping sound and went dead. Sancho looked at the screen. The text read: Call Failed.

Dulcie kicked him hard in the cojones. Sancho gasped and bent at the waist. She snatched the phone out of his hand, threw it on the ground and crushed it beneath her shoe. Sancho fell to his knees, his hands clutching his injured groin.

"Why'd you do that?" Sancho groaned. "What the fuck is wrong with you?"

"What the fuck is wrong with *you*?"

Sancho tried to focus. The intense agony slowly dissipated and he was finally able to breathe. Dulcie's fear and anger gave way to remorse as she watched Sancho kneeling in the dirt, cradling his injured huevos, struggling to catch his breath.

"Are you okay?" she asked him. Sancho didn't answer. Dulcie stepped closer and put her hand on his shoulder. "I'm sorry."

"Me too," whispered Sancho.

"If they hurt him…If they…" Tears turned to mud on her dirty face as she glanced up the road at Kursky's McMansion.

Agent Johnson watched the Kursky compound through a night vision monocular and caught sight of an intruder scaling the wrought iron fence. The trespasser climbed quickly, gracefully, avoiding the razor wire as he leapt over the top and landed, cat-like, on the other side of the fence. Johnson sat in the front seat of a van parked on a hill overlooking Kursky's property. He glanced at the short, Hispanic man in the rear of the van. Agent Cordero wore headphones and monitored a laptop.

"Someone jumped the fence," Johnson said.

"What?" Cordero said a little too loudly. He could hardly hear with the headphones on.

"Someone jumped the fence!"

"Better not be LAPD."

"Nah, they know this is a DEA operation."

"What?" Cordero shouted.

"They know we're here!"

"Who?"

"LAPD!"

"So, who do you think it is?"

"I don't know," Johnson said.

"What!"

Johnson reached back and pulled the headphones off his partner. "I don't know!"

Cordero hit a button and now the voices from the Kursky compound filtered over two small speakers.

"He is such a fucking jerk," Kursky said.

"He's totally selfish," another gruff voice added.

"I don't know why she doesn't just dump him," Kursky growled.

"Who they talking about?" Johnson asked.

"Who do you think?"

The DEA agent nodded and took a swig of Red Bull.

"So, who the hell jumped the fence?" Cordero asked.

"Don't know," Johnson replied. "But if he's a hitter he's in for a rude fucking surprise."

You could have put Mike Croker's entire house in Pete Kursky's living room. The pitched ceiling was thirty feet high and the beige carpeting ubiquitous. The walls were a lighter shade of beige and bereft of anything other than paint. A strangely ornate chandelier hung down from the ceiling, illuminating the huge blank expanses of nothingness. A seventy-three-inch HDTV was surrounded by a glass and ersatz chrome entertainment center complete with a stereo, a DVD player, a DVR, a PlayStation 4, and two huge speakers. Five other speakers stood on stands strategically placed around the massive black leather sectional sofa and the three, black leather La-Z-Boys. Every chair and couch cushion had a massive biker's ass planted comfortably in its recesses.

Pete Kursky and nine of his cohorts drank beer and ate pizza while watching a rerun of "Sex and the City" on the giant HDTV.

Carrie Bradshaw quietly dressed while Big slumbered. Her inner thoughts via voice-over were picked up off the surround sound speakers by the mini-microphone hidden in the tiny white plastic piece that kept the pizza box from squishing the pie.

"When it comes to relationships, maybe we're all in glass houses and shouldn't throw stones," Carrie said. "Because you can never really know. Some people are settling down, some are settling, and some people refuse to settle for anything less…than butterflies…"

A commercial for the Sit and Sleep Mattress Gallery abruptly took the place of Carrie's face and Kursky immediately muted the sound.

"He's not right for her," Kursky said.

A lean, muscular biker with greasy blonde hair took a long pull on his beer and burped. "She doesn't know what the fuck she wants. I think she's afraid of commitment," Kursky replied.

"I don't agree," a short hairy biker took a hit of a spliff. "I think that's exactly what she's looking for."

"Doesn't mean she's not afraid of it."

A fat biker with thinning gray hair pointed at the screen. "I'd fuck her."

A biker with a red ZZ top beard shook his head. "I don't know, man, I think she's kind of horsey. I mean, what's that fucking thing on her chin?"

"That Samantha's hot," the muscular biker said.

"I'd fuck her," the fat biker added.

"You'd fuck me," Kursky said.

The guys all laughed and suddenly everything went black.

Agent Johnson, watching from the van, was surprised to see the house go dark. "The lights just went out."

"You think a fuse blew?" Cordero asked.

"Or the guy who jumped the fence cut the power. What are they saying?"

"Nothing."

"Turn up the sound."

Agent Cordero turned up the sound. The silence was deafening. They listened intently and moved closer to the speakers. Cordero cranked the volume all the way up and then both jumped at sound of an earsplitting boom.

Dulcie heard the shotgun blast, looked at Sancho and then squinted up the road, into the darkness, towards Kursky's compound. "We gotta get the fuck out of here."

Sancho started running towards Kursky's.

"Where the hell are you going?" she shouted. But he didn't answer her. He disappeared into the gloom and Dulcie couldn't believe it.

"You took the car keys! You took the fucking keys! Hey, asshole! Don't just leave me here!"

In the absolute darkness of Pete Kursky's living room, bikers tripped on furniture and bumped into walls. They cursed and collided, yelled and pushed and fought to find a way out.

"Everybody shut the fuck up!" Kursky yelled and the bikers all shut the fuck up. "Was that a fucking shotgun?"

Another massive blast shook the room.

"Indeed, it was. A Benelli 12-gauge pump-action shotgun to be more precise," Flynn explained. "Which I believe belongs to you, Mr. Kursky."

Kursky turned to face the voice's owner, but since the room was utterly devoid of light, Kursky saw exactly the same thing he saw facing the other way. Darkness.

"Who the hell are you?" Kursky's voice was full of bravado.

"Someone wearing night visions goggles," Flynn said. "Which means I can see you, but you can't see me."

"You're that jerk-off from Tiny's," one of the bikers said.

"That asshole who ripped off Mikey," Kursky added.

"Indeed," Flynn answered. "And if anyone makes a move to stop me, I will not hesitate to expunge them."

There was a long pause and then someone said, "Do what to them?"

"Pull the trigger on this shotgun and obliterate them."

"You can't take us all down," Kursky pointed out. "If we rush you—"

"You will die," Flynn replied. "You know this shotgun is a semi-automatic. I can fire it as quickly as I can pull the trigger. Of course, if you don't agree with my assessment, you're welcome to try and prove me wrong."

Kursky had no come back to that and no one made a move. "What do you want?" Kursky asked, his voice tight with anger.

"Q."

"Q?"

"Q," Flynn repeated.

"What's a Q?"

"Not what. Who."

"I don't have a frickin' clue who—"

Flynn pulled the trigger and the shotgun boomed.

Outside, Sancho jumped at the sound of the blast. The security lights were out and the grounds were so dark Sancho couldn't see squat, which is why he walked face first into the side of Kursky's McMansion. His brain lit up with pain as the stucco scraped the tip of his nose.

"Coño," he whispered as he fished around in his pocket for a lighter. Sancho was a reformed smoker. He hadn't had a cigarette in months, but he still carried his lighter out of habit. It was a chrome Zippo with a pirate's skull and crossbones. His Uncle Ernesto had given Sancho the lighter on his sixteenth birthday. Ernesto had forgotten to buy Sancho a gift, so he gave him the lighter. Ernesto had no need for it anymore since he was dying of emphysema. The Zippo contributed mightily to Ernesto's demise, but today this lighter may save someone's life. Sancho lit a flame which danced in the wind and held it close to his body, cupping his left hand around it to keep the flame alive. A second later he saw the circuit breaker box. The metal door was open and squeaking in the breeze.

Back in Kursky's pitch black living room, Flynn fed more shells into the chamber and said, "That was my last warning shot, gentlemen. There won't be another."

"But we don't know any damn Q," Kursky claimed.

"Who the hell is he?" an unseen biker to Kursky's left asked.

"He's a brilliant scientist who's currently working for your boss. Under duress, of course."

"You mean Goolardo?" Kursky was clearly confused.

"Goolardo." Flynn let the melodious name roll off his tongue.

"I'm just a dealer, dude. I don't know shit," Kursky's fear beat out the bravado now.

"You don't know about the plan?" James asked.

"What plan?"

"*The* plan."

"Goolardo has a plan?"

"Are you feigning befuddlement or do you truly not know?"

"What?" Kursky wasn't feigning anything.

"Maybe I need to talk to Goolardo."

"Dude, what the fuck are you talking about?"

"Where is he?" Flynn demanded.

"Who?"

"Goolardo."

"I don't know," Kursky said.

"Somehow I think you do."

"I don't! All I have is a phone number."

"Well that's a start."

"If I give you his number and you call Goolardo, he will not be happy," Kursky said.

"Yes, but if you *don't* give me his number, *I* won't be happy. And I have a shotgun aimed at your face."

"He'll kill me."

"Which means you're dead if you do and dead if you don't," Flynn quipped. "Of course, if you don't, you're dead a lot sooner. Say by the count of three."

"Come on, man, what are you trying to—"

"One…" Flynn heard panicked scrambling, tripping, crashing. "Two…" Running, colliding, grunting, glass shattering.

A millisecond before Flynn could say three, someone flipped the main switch on the circuit breaker, turning on every light in the compound. Flynn found himself facing the seventy-three-inch HDTV. His shot gun was aimed directly at Kim Cattrall's naked booty. Kursky and all nine bikers were right behind him. Before James could turn, the fat biker cracked him across the back of the head with a fireplace poker.

Flynn went down hard.

The biker with the ZZ Top beard was outraged. "He ain't wearing no damn night vision goggles!"

Chapter Fifteen

Kursky popped the top on a light beer and sat his colossal hiney on a La-Z-Boy. He took a sip and made a face. The light beer clearly sucked, but Kursky was determined to lose some of the unsightly blubber that made up so much of his body weight. Fifteen years previously, he was in pretty decent shape. For a twenty-four-month period, in his late twenties, he actually had visible abs. Some people said he looked a lot like Dennis Quaid. Well, one person. His mother. Now, however, he looked like a chubbier version of his big brother Randy.

Kursky could still remember when teenage girls would check him out. Not anymore. Now he was just another tubby old dude.

To Pete, losing weight meant regaining his youth. That was the reason he went to Jenny Craig. That was why he was denying himself and suffering constant hunger pangs. He wanted younger women to look at him again. Not out of fear, but desire.

Delaying gratification always pissed Pete off. Combine that with his continuous hunger and Pete's short fuse was now non-existent. The slightest provocation made him absolutely crazy, which was why he so thoroughly enjoyed kicking James Flynn's ass.

Flynn lay curled on the floor in a fetal position. Kursky had started the stomping, kicking, punching and cursing and it was all so satisfying and invigorating. But now he was out of breath and needed a break and a cold beer. He loved bonding with his buds over a serious ass-whooping.

He watched from his bar stool as the eight other Slaves of Satan beat Flynn unmercifully. Picking up his satellite phone, Kursky punched in a number. Moments later he heard Mendoza's voice.

"Mendoza." His voice was flat and without affect. Mendoza spoke from the back seat of a black Mercedes limousine. He wore a Bluetooth headset and gazed out the tinted window into the darkness.

"We got him," Kursky said.

"Who?"

"The guy who ripped off Mikey."

"Do you know where the money is?"

"No."

Mendoza noticed a spot on his tie. It looked like blood. "Chingado," he whispered. Kursky listened, but that was all Mendoza said. Mendoza opened a bottle of soda water, poured a little on a handkerchief, and rubbed the bloody spot on his tie. Finally, he said, "Do you know who he works for?"

"Not yet, but—"

"Do you fucking know anything!" The spot wasn't coming out and that seriously irritated Mendoza.

"I know he knows about some plan," Kursky said, hoping to mollify Mendoza with this new bit of probably useless information.

"What plan?"

"Goolardo's plan."

Mendoza stopped rubbing the spot. His forehead wrinkled with concern. "What else did he say?"

"Nothing. Do you want me to—"

"He had to say something. Did he tell you what the plan was?"

"No, do you want to find out—"

"No! Don't talk to him! Don't touch him. Don't lay a finger on him."

Kursky looked at Flynn curled up on the floor, bleeding and bruised and not moving. The Slaves who still had energy left continued to kick his motionless body. Kursky waved to them, shaking his hand back and forth, indicating that he wanted the ass-kicking to cease. They didn't quite understand the meaning of his miming and continued to wail away. Kursky covered the phone with his hand and loudly whispered, "Stop it! *Stop it!*" The bikers looked at him with confusion. "Get the fuck away from him!"

"I'm sending someone to pick him up," Mendoza said.

"Pick him up? When?"

"Immediately. You calling from your house?"

Kursky looked at Flynn. He didn't stir. "Yeah." Mendoza didn't say good-bye. He just hung up. The line went dead and Kursky was afraid that Flynn was equally deceased. "Shit." Kursky rose from his Laz-E-Boy and approached Flynn's prostrate form. Flynn bled from his nose and his mouth and his ears. The guy was totally limp, like a piece of bloody meat. Kursky poked Flynn. No response.

He whispered into his ear. "Dude?" Then he shouted, "*Dude!*" Nothing.

"What's going on?" the biker with the ZZ Top beard asked.

Kursky ignored him and opened Flynn's left eyelid. The pupil was rolled back and all he saw was white. "Shit."

"I think the dude's dead," the fat biker blurted.

"I fucking hope not," Kursky replied. "Because if *he's* dead, we're fucking dead."

Sancho stayed low and clung to the side of Kursky's house. Bright security lights illuminated the grounds. He hid in the sparse shadows of the shrubbery and peered in a window to see the fat biker in the kitchen, filling a bucket with water. Another biker was taking a bottle of beer out of the refrigerator. Sancho heard the distant howl of a siren and then the ragged howls of coyotes. It was an eerie, unsettling sound and it raised the hair on the back of Sancho's neck.

Staying close to the wall, Sancho moved along the house and peered in another window. The room was dark. The next window was frosted—likely a bathroom. He poked his head around the corner to make sure the coast was clear and continued on, the stucco scraping his cheek as he stayed between the wall and the shrubs.

Muffled voices filtered through a large window. Peering in, he caught sight of the bikers all standing around Flynn's motionless body. The fat biker with the bucket doused Flynn with water. Flynn didn't move. He just lay there. Sancho's stomach tightened with dread. Was he dead? Did they waste him? Why were they throwing water on him? He was so distracted by the troubling thoughts rattling around his head, he neglected to hear the quiet footsteps approaching him from behind. He didn't realize he was compromised until he felt the cold barrel of a gun pressed against the back of his neck.

Dulcie whacked the steering column with a crowbar. She was trying to hot-wire the Aston Martin, but really had no idea how. She'd watched Mike hot-wire a half a dozen cars and thought she understood the basic principle, but couldn't figure out how to remove the steering column and access the necessary wires.

The car came with a rudimentary set of tools which Dulcie did not know how to use. Desperate, she took the edge of the crowbar, inserted it into the ignition, and twisted it hard. Something cracked, but she didn't know what and she didn't see any wires. Frustrated, she hammered the steering column again and again. She made so much noise she didn't notice the rapping on the window until she finally stopped whacking. She turned to see Pete Kursky's face peering at her through the glass.

He was smiling.

He didn't seem upset at all. In fact, he seemed glad to see her. He tried to open the door, but she'd locked it. He motioned for her to unlatch the lock and she shook her head. Pete stopped smiling. He disappeared from view and when he returned he had something in his hand. It was a rock, which he used to smash the driver's side window glass. Kursky reached in and roughly grabbed her by her slender arm. He pulled her through the window and the edges of the safety glass clawed at her as he dragged her from the car.

Dulcie couldn't catch her breath and barely managed to stand as Kursky held her upright with two huge hands. "Where's the money, Dulcie?"

"It's in the duffel bag! In the backseat! He spent some of it, but—" Kursky let her drop, reached in the window, and unlocked the car. He found the duffel bag, unzipped it, and looked inside.

Dulcie lay on the shoulder next to the highway. Tears ran down her dirty face. "You can sell the car—If you sell the car—"

"Come on," Kursky ordered. He pulled her to her feet and dragged her along the side of the road, the duffel bag in one hand, Dulcie in the other.

Mendoza, still ensconced in the limo, entered a number into the satellite phone. He listened and waited and watched as the shadowy shapes of the night rushed by. When he finally spoke, it was in Spanish.

"It's me. We have a situation." Mendoza listened for a moment. "Someone took our money off Kursky. But that's not the problem. The problem is he found the piece of shit who ripped him off and apparently the joto knows about the plan." Mendoza winced as the voice on the other end grew angry and loud.

When the person finally stopped berating him, Mendoza took a breath and continued, "I don't know. He didn't say. He just said he knew about the plan."

The voice on the other end was a bit calmer now, and as Mendoza listened sweat beaded on his forehead.

"That's what I'm doing. I'm picking him up. I was gonna interrogate him personally and find out—" Mendoza was cut off mid-sentence. He listened and nodded. "Are you sure?" The loud response from the person on the other end caused the blood to drain from Mendoza's face. "No, sir, I wasn't questioning you. I would never..." The voice continued to castigate him and then, "No, sir. Yes, sir. I will, sir." Mendoza clicked off the phone and sighed heavily.

He looked up to see the eyes of the limo driver watching him in the rear-view mirror. "What the fuck are you looking at?" he spat. The driver quickly faced front as Mendoza wiped the perspiration off his forehead with the palm of his hand.

Chapter Sixteen

Flynn felt like he was falling into a deep, dark, bottomless chasm. The void was endless and the emptiness filled him with an unbelievable sadness. There was no one. There was nothing. And there was no escape. He was about to give up hope and surrender to the darkness. Let it swallow him. Let it consume him until he became one with the nothingness. But then he felt a hand. A soft, warm, gentle hand. Next, he heard a voice. Dulcie's voice.

"You okay?

Flynn opened his eyes. It was so bright. He squinted into the light, but it burned. His head throbbed painfully. The agony wasn't centered in any one place in particular. It was everywhere; a deep, pulsating, unrelenting misery. Soon, however, he was able to open his eyes wide enough to see the source of the painful incandescence. It was the huge, ornate chandelier hanging from Pete Kursky's ceiling.

Dulcie gazed down at him, her fingertips on his face. She had tears in her eyes. She looked so sad.

"What's the matter?" Flynn asked.

"Look what they did to you."

"I'm fine," Flynn replied. He tried to smile, but flexing those muscles made little explosions go off in his head. Dulcie knelt by his side and held his hand. His face was covered in blood and starting to swell.

Flynn tried to sit up but an electric pain shot through his side. A broken rib? Maybe it was just bruised.

"Help me up." It was then, he saw Sancho, standing next to Dulcie, staring down at Flynn with horror and revulsion. "Do I look that bad?"

"You look like one of those dudes in Dawn of the Dead."

Flynn attempted a smile. "What doesn't kill me, makes me stronger."

"I don't buy that Nietzsche bullshit," Sancho said. "It sure the hell didn't work for him. Dude had a nervous breakdown; ended up a mumbling idiot, pissing in his pants."

"You studied philosophy?" Flynn asked.

"Enough to know it's mostly bullshit."

Flynn tried to grin again, but the size of his swollen lip made that difficult. "Can you help me up?"

Sancho and Dulcie grabbed him under his arms and managed to get him on his feet. Flynn wavered and nearly fell. Sancho and Dulcie kept him upright. Two of Satan's Slaves watched from the couch.

Kursky came barreling into the room, angrily munching on a piece of pizza. When he saw Flynn, he winced. "Jesus Christ, I told you to get him cleaned up."

"I'm trying to," Dulcie snapped.

"Get him in the bathroom and get that blood off his face. He looks like he got the shit kicked out of him."

"Wonder why?" Dulcie said caustically.

"You want to look just like him? Keep it up, bitch."

"Watch your mouth," Flynn said.

Kursky lunged at him, but then realized he couldn't lay a hand on him. Instead he took a huge bite of pizza and said with a mouthful, "Get him the fuck out of here!"

Dulcie glared at Kursky and took Flynn by the arm. "Come on, Sancho, give me a hand."

Sancho and Dulcie helped Flynn to one of Kursky's palatial bathrooms. There was a glass-enclosed shower stall, a large Jacuzzi tub and a purple throw rug that matched the fuzzy toilet seat cover. Sancho sat Flynn down on the toilet and Dulcie wet a washcloth with warm water. She cleaned the scrapes and cuts and dried blood that covered Flynn's face. He didn't wince once. He just gazed gratefully into her eyes as she tended his injuries.

"Thank you for this," Flynn said. Dulcie shrugged. "And you too, Sancho. You could have driven off and left me here, but you didn't."

"Yeah," Sancho said, his voice dripping with sarcasm. "Good thing I hung around."

"We'll get out of this, my friend. I know it looks like they have the upper hand, but it's all part of the plan."

"Are these multiple ass-kickings part of your plan? Because if they are, you might want to come up with a new one."

"If they wanted us dead, we'd be dead. But we're not dead, are we?"

"Not yet," Dulcie said.

"Someone's coming to see you," Sancho said. "I heard them talking. That's why they want you cleaned up."

"Ah, yes, excellent. Just as I thought. Kursky and Croker are simply muscle. Thugs. Soon we'll meet the man behind the curtain. The one pulling the strings."

"I can't listen to this shit anymore," Sancho mumbled. He abruptly walked out of the bathroom to find two bikers standing guard.

The fat biker had a sawed-off shotgun. "Where the fuck you going?"

"Nowhere," Sancho replied.

"He cleaned up yet?"

"She's working on it."

"So, go sit your ass down." The biker motioned to a spot on the floor. Sancho sat and waited and watched as the fat biker lit up a cigarette.

Back in the bathroom, Dulcie unbuttoned Flynn's shirt to wipe the dried blood off his chest. "They really did a number on you, didn't they?"

"This isn't all my blood," Flynn said. "Besides, I have a very high threshold for pain."

"Your ear's still bleeding," Dulcie leaned in close to examine and it and Flynn turned his head and touched his lips to hers. She took a half step back. "What the hell was that?"

"That was a kiss. And not a very good one."

"Are you kidding me?"

"No, I'm actually considered a very good kisser. At least that's what I've been told."

Dulcie smiled at that. "Dude, you are such a fucking dork."

"I must admit, I've wanted to do that for quite some time." He leaned in to kiss her again and this time she didn't back away. Flynn gave her a soft, gentle, lingering kiss.

Finally, she pulled free. "This is crazy."

"Danger awakens all the senses. It's the adrenaline. It floods through the blood, making everything sharper. Your body goes into overdrive to keep you alive. Self-preservation is a very strong instinct. A near death experience is a powerful aphrodisiac. The body wants to perpetuate itself. Pass on its DNA. It goes to our deepest animal instincts."

Flynn put his hand firmly on her ass and pulled her closer. Dulcie resisted for an infinitesimal moment before surrendering. This third kiss was deeper, longer, and more passionate than the first two. Dulcie started to kiss him back and Flynn winced, gingerly licking his fat lip.

"Sorry."

"It's not you, it's me," Flynn said. "My kissing equipment is bit wonky at the moment. Once I recover, I promise I will kiss you the way you deserve to be kissed. Properly. Well. And often."

Dulcie grinned. "Dude, that has to be the lamest line anyone has ever laid on me."

He smoothed the hair off her face and tenderly kissed her on the cheek and on the corner of the mouth and on her lips.

They felt it before they even heard it. A low rumbling that shook the air. Flynn moved away from Dulcie, suddenly all business. He looked at the bathroom ceiling and listened as the rumbling grew louder.

"Earthquake?" Dulcie asked.

"Helicopter."

Agent Johnson saw the helicopter before he heard it. The lights were high in the sky, skimming the mountains to the south. Soon he could hear the beating of the blades. The roar grew louder as the lights grew brighter.

The chopper swooped over Kursky's compound and slowly descended, dust rising, as it touched down in the middle of street.

Cordero tore off his headphones and climbed into the van's front seat, next to Johnson.

"What the hell?" Cordero grumbled.

Mendoza and two huge goons climbed from the copter, ducking below the slowing rotor. Each goon lugged a large M-249 SAW machine gun as they headed up the walkway towards the front door.

Kursky stood in the open doorway, a nervous smile cracking his ugly mug. "Mr. Mendoza!" Kursky put out his hand and Mendoza walked right past him, followed by his two massive goons.

Flynn, Dulcie, and Sancho stood against a wall in the living room, flanked by two bikers, both well-armed. Mendoza studied Flynn's bruised and battered face and turned towards Kursky. "I told you not to lay a hand on him."

"He tried to escape."

Mendoza looked at Kursky with his cold eyes and the biker felt the hair rising on the back of his neck. Mendoza held Kursky's gaze until Kursky had to look away.

"Who are these other two?" Mendoza mumbled.

"The girl's the squeeze of one our guys. The other one…I don't know."

"Did you attempt to interrogate them?"

"Not after I talked to you. No."

"Before you talked to me?"

"I might have asked them a few questions."

Mendoza nodded. "Why didn't you tell me there was more than one?"

"I didn't think it mattered."

"You didn't think. It's not something you know how to do. So why do you even try?"

Kursky's guys looked a little surprised to see someone talking to their boss like that. They were even more surprised that Kursky swallowed it.

"We'll be taking all three."

Kursky nodded.

"Taking us where?" Dulcie asked.

"Shut the fuck up!" Kursky bellowed.

Mendoza leaned closer to Kursky. "Didn't I say not to talk to them?"

Kursky nodded. He was fighting an internal battle. He was capable of eating a certain amount of shit, but only a small serving. By the look in his eyes it was clear that Kursky couldn't take another bite. It was a look that intimidated most men. Kursky took it for granted that he could scare the shit out of virtually anyone alive. But not Mendoza. The fact that Mendoza wasn't the slightest bit intimidated not only chilled Kursky to his core, it irritated him to no end.

Mendoza stepped closer to Dulcie and gazed into her face. "You have a question?"

Kursky could see that Dulcie was trying to play Mendoza the way she tried to play him; submissive and seductive with just the hint of a smile. "I was just wondering where you were taking us."

Mendoza smiled back and that only made his gaze more frightening. "I'm taking you to see someone."

"Who?"

The smile disappeared. He nodded to his goons. One took Flynn. The other grabbed Sancho. Mendoza put his massive hand on Dulcie's back and pushed her towards the door. The bikers watched silently as Mendoza marched them outside.

Kursky shouted after them. "What about the money? You want what's left? Or should we use it to make a buy? Mendoza!" Mendoza didn't answer him. Kursky shook his head and whispered, "Fat fucking spic." A couple of the bikers heard the insult and grinned. That was the Kursky they knew and feared. No one gives shit to a Slave of Satan and just walks away.

Mendoza's two goons walked back inside with their machine guns. "Go get your boss," said Kursky. "I got a question for him."

The two goons raised their weapons and pulled their triggers. The Slaves with the shotguns were mowed down first. The other bikers tried to flee, but they couldn't outrun the machine guns. Kursky was last to go as five high-velocity bullets splattered his brains all over his beige walls.

Outside, even over the sound of the helicopter, Flynn, Sancho, and Dulcie heard the machine guns cut down the Slaves of Satan. Sancho and Dulcie both looked nauseous. Flynn didn't seem the least bit surprised.

Down the street in the pizza van, Agents Johnson and Cordero heard the carnage over the little speakers in the rear of the van. The shouts and screams were nearly drowned out by the staccato thunder of machine gun fire.

"What the fuck!" Cordero shouted.

Johnson half opened the van door. "What do we do?"

"What *can* we do."

"Fuck!"

They watched as Mendoza's two goons walked back outside Kursky's palatial McMansion and closed the late biker's ornate door. Mendoza had an Uzi in his hand. He used it to motion to Flynn and the others.

The DEA agents watched as Mendoza ushered his captives onto the chopper.

Johnson picked up a pair of binoculars and tried to get a closer look. "Who the hell are these guys?" Cordero shook his head.

The blades of the helicopter began to spin, faster and faster, kicking up dust as it rose into the air and headed east into the Mojave Desert.

Johnson grabbed a handset and called in on the radio. "We have possible multiple homicides at 775 Arbor Drive in Palmdale. I'm requesting police back up and EMTs."

"Is the suspect still on the premises?" asked the female dispatcher.

"We don't know," Johnson snapped. "Just get those EMTs here!"

Cordero leaped from the van, gun in hand. Johnson climbed out and drew his weapon as well. "Come on," Cordero said and he started running towards the McMansion. Johnson followed a few steps behind him.

When they reached the front walkway, the house exploded. The shockwave blew both men off their feet. They hit the ground hard as burning bits of building rained down.

They were already miles away and the roar of the main rotor was deafening, but the sound of the blast was unmistakable. Flynn glanced back to see the fire rising into the sky. What was left of the house was engulfed in flames, a bright, blazing bonfire illuminating an otherwise dark desert floor. Sancho was speechless, but not Dulcie.

"They can't let us go now," she said. "We're witnesses." She was only seven feet away from her captors, but the chopper was so loud, only Flynn and Sancho could hear her.

"Witnesses to what?" Sancho asked, his voice frantic with fear. "What did we see? We didn't see nothing. When we left they were still alive! Right?"

Flynn smiled grimly and watched as the fire consuming Kursky's pride and joy grew smaller and smaller.

Chapter Seventeen

The New River flows north from Mexicali, directly into the Salton Sea. It is considered the most polluted river in North America. That pollution, combined with the fertilizer runoff from surrounding farms, has coated the sea in a thick layer of algae, resulting in the demise of countless fish, suffocated by the lack of oxygen. The thousands of dead tilapia create an unbelievable stench. Pelicans eat the diseased fish and die and their rotting carcasses contribute to the odious aroma of death. In the summer, when the temperature rises above one hundred and ten, the place looks, feels, and smells like hell on Earth. From seven thousand feet up, however, the Salton Sea can be a beautiful sight.

Sancho, Dulcie and Flynn watched as the sun rose in the east, reflecting red off the Salton Sea. The helicopter soared over the vast expanse of water and, if Sancho hadn't been in fear for his life, he would have enjoyed the view. He winced at the stench when it finally reached his nostrils. Dulcie held her nose. Mendoza looked depressed. Flynn, however, seemed to be having a wonderful time. There was a half-smile on his face as he watched the passing landscape and for some reason that pissed Sancho off to no end.

"Where do you think they're taking us?" shouted Dulcie. Only Flynn and Sancho could hear her.

"That's the Salton Sea, so we're probably heading to Mexico," Flynn said.

"Baja?" Sancho asked.

Flynn nodded.

Rows and rows of ten-story tall wind turbines covered the hills near the border, the propellers spinning and generating power. They looked like space-age windmills; sleek and white and spinning in perfect unison. Sancho watched as they passed over them. He glanced at Flynn. He looked haggard, older, and not nearly so happy-go-lucky. The half-grin was gone. Sancho saw uncertainty now. Anxiety. Maybe even doubt. Flynn looked tired. He hadn't slept in twenty-four hours. There was stubble on his face and his eyes were rimmed red. Dulcie had dozed off, her head on Flynn's chest, lulled to sleep by the roar of the chopper blades. Sancho closed his eyes. Adrenaline could only keep pumping for so long. He was crashing and he knew it. He longed for the oblivion of sleep and it wasn't long before he had his wish.

When Sancho opened his eyes, a jolt of panic shot through him. The helicopter was heading directly into the side of a mountain. Sancho couldn't hear himself scream over the din of the rotor reverberating off the wall of solid rock. Sancho squeezed his eyelids shut and braced for the collision. It would all be over soon. But it wasn't. It wasn't over at all. He opened one eye and then the other and saw that they'd crested the top of the mountain and were swooping down towards an amazing sight.

A Moorish castle perched on a rocky promontory overlooking the Sea of Cortez. The massive brick and stone structure had turrets and towers, spires and parapets. Sancho thought it was a strange sight to see on the coast of Baja; like something out of a medieval fairy tale.

"What the hell?" Sancho asked.

"The lair of our nemesis I imagine," Flynn mused. "Now we're finally getting somewhere."

Dulcie yawned and opened her eyes as the helicopter landed on a helipad in a courtyard in the center of the castle. A cadre of dangerous looking men with automatic weapons awaited the chopper's arrival. They looked like pirates, squinting into the dust kicked up by the chopper.

Mendoza climbed out first, followed by the pilot. The last man in the copter pushed out Flynn, Dulcie, and Sancho. The thugs surrounded them and devoured Dulcie with their hungry eyes. James offered her a smile full of bravado and held out his arm. She took it gratefully. They followed Mendoza into the castle, their footsteps echoing between the high stone walls.

Flynn watched as two tall wooden doors, carved in an intricate Moorish design, opened wide. Mendoza led the little parade into a marble-floored foyer. He looked up to high, ornate ceilings, decorated with carved wood and gold leaf. The walls were constructed of huge blocks of smooth stone. A massive wrought-iron candelabra chandelier hung down from above. The light bulbs were shaped like candles and burned with a flickering reddish flame. He glanced at two gleaming suits of conquistador armor that stood on either side of the door. Both had breastplates adorned with brass lions. One empty suit held a double-edge great sword. The other was posed with a tall halberd; a battle-axe topped with a vicious-looking spike.

Flynn sized-up the weapons, but didn't glance at them directly. Instead he pretended to admire the dazzling twenty-five-foot-tall stained-glass window; a royal crest with castles and lions, intertwined with roses. Opposite the window was a long winding staircase that led to a second floor.

At the top of the staircase stood a tall, lean man with a receding a hair-line. The hair that remained was black and thick and shot with gray. He wore a well-cut Versace suit that emphasized his wide shoulders. His eyes were dark and twinkled with humor or anger or maybe both. The man looked at Sancho and Dulcie and then rested his eyes on Flynn. He studied him carefully, and then glanced at Mendoza. "Is that him?"

Mendoza nodded.

Flynn offered the man a charming smile and said, "Mr. Goolardo, I presume."

"And you are?"

"Flynn. James Flynn."

"Welcome to my humble home, Mr. Flynn." Goolardo moved gracefully as he made his way down the spiral staircase to greet them.

"It's a Spanish castle, is it not?" Flynn queried. "Modeled on the Alcazar of Segovia?"

"Indeed," Goolardo said, delighted by Flynn's observation.

Mendoza, Dulcie, and Sancho looked at Flynn with astonishment as he went on to explain, "The Alcazar of Segovia was built by Muslims in the eighth century. It was the favorite residence of the kings of Castile and each monarch put their mark on it. Isn't this where Queen Isabella married King Ferdinand the Second?"

"Correct," Goolardo agreed, his smile growing wider.

Flynn looked at Dulcie to see she was staring at him in stunned wonderment. "The Alcazar is where Columbus asked Queen Isabella to fund his expedition to the New World."

Goolardo turned to Mendoza. "It appears that our guest is very well informed." Goolardo now looked at Flynn. "What else do you know, Mr. Flynn?" Flynn smiled cryptically and the humorous twinkle left Goolardo's eye.

"You want me to take them down to the dungeon?" asked Mendoza. "See what I can find out?"

For the first time since Sancho met the man, Mendoza showed a
flicker of enthusiasm. Dulcie blanched at the mention of the word
dungeon. Flynn laughed. "You want to put me on the rack, Mr.
Mendoza? Perhaps fit me for an iron maiden?"

"I hardly think that's necessary," Goolardo said.

"And not very hospitable," offered Flynn.

"I agree." Goolardo chuckled.

"In fact," Flynn said. "You have yet to offer us any refreshments."

Goolardo laughed again. "Well, why don't you join me then?
You've had a long journey. Do you enjoy daiquiris?" Mendoza looked
perturbed. Goolardo caught the dark look. "Mr. Mendoza, do you have a
problem with daiquiris?"

Mendoza shook his head. He looked as spooked as Dulcie and
Sancho did.

Goolardo offered the entourage a charming smile. "Let's have our
drinks in the throne room."

As Francisco Goolardo led them forward, Flynn probed him. "Is
that a Brazilian accent I detect?"

"Indeed, it is," Goolardo admitted. "I was born in Brasilia, the son
of Roma gypsies, the descendants of those driven out of Spain during the
Inquisition. Gypsies were considered heretics and sorcerers and many
were exiled to South America. My great, great, great, great grandfather
was involved in the slave trade and smuggling and the selling of vices of
all kinds. At least that was the family mythology. You see, I come from
humble origins, Mr. Flynn. My father, a grifter and a pickpocket, was
murdered when I was nine. My mother moved us to Rio, where she fell
ill. Spinal meningitis. I lost her at ten and since then have been on my
own."

"Not an easy life."

"At nineteen I was convicted of armed robbery and sent to Ilha
Grande. It was during the years of the military dictatorship and common
street thugs were often incarcerated with members of the guerrilla
movement working to overthrow the government. That's where I met my
mentor, Emilio. He became a surrogate father to me, you see. He taught
me how to read and how to think and, after six years in prison, I had the
equivalent of a university education. I learned about economics and
literature and science and politics. I learned how to turn a spoon into a
knife and how to kill a man with my bare hands."

"A renaissance man."

Goolardo smiled and led them down another corridor. "Emilio
taught me that the drug dealers in the slums were a perfect microcosm of
capitalist society. That there was a pecking order and hierarchy just like

in any other corporation. One year before I was released from prison, Emilio was beaten to death by a guard. He had become too popular among the prisoners and was fomenting dissent. That was something the warden would not tolerate. Upon my release, I tracked the guilty guard to his home, cut his throat, killed his wife, his mother, and his children."

"You were making a statement."

"I was staking a claim. Over the next few years, I used everything Emilio taught me to revolutionize the drug trade in Rio. I was a revolutionary, fighting the status quo. I allied myself with the largest of the Mexican and Columbian drug cartels and made myself a millionaire many times over. On the tenth anniversary of Emilio's death, the warden of Ilha Grande Penitentiary was found dead in his bed, decapitated. His head was nowhere to be found and never seen again."

Flynn understood then that Goolardo's Alcazar was a monument to himself. It proved to the world that he had worth. That he was someone to reckon with. Not some gypsy orphan, but a man of substance. A man of respect.

James sipped his cocktail and examined a huge detailed mural that dramatized the coronation of Queen Isabella the Catholic. Flynn, Dulcie, and Sancho were in a long dramatic room with stained glass windows depicting the Spanish kings. Precious oriental carpets covered the floor. At the head of the room sat two ornate thrones. One of them was occupied by Francisco Goolardo.

"Enjoying your daiquiri, Mr. Flynn?"

"Very refreshing."

"Most of the men I deal with don't have the knowledge or the breeding to appreciate the finer things."

Mendoza looked insulted. He stood by the stained-glass window depicting the arrival of Columbus in the New World, sipped his cocktail and sulked.

"A daiquiri isn't a proper daiquiri without Cuban rum," Flynn said as he took another sip and glanced at Goolardo. "Five-year-old Anejo reserva?"

"Very good."

Sancho looked at James with amazement. Mendoza rolled his eyes. Dulcie, however, wasn't even listening. She was chugging her drink down, desperate to numb her brain with alcohol as the anxiety of crystal meth withdrawal crawled through her veins.

"We've enjoyed a cocktail and some pleasant conversation, but I still feel as if I don't know anything about you, Mr. Flynn."

"What is it you'd like to know?"

"Who are you and how is it you know about my plan?" Goolardo asked.

Flynn smirked and sipped on his daiquiri.

"You want me to ask him?" Mendoza said.

"I was hoping we wouldn't have to resort to that sort of unpleasantness, but—"

"He's an escaped mental patient," Sancho blurted. "From City of Roses Psychiatric." He felt horrible saying that in front of Flynn, but he felt he had no choice. "He thinks he's some kind of…secret agent or something."

Mendoza looked stunned. Goolardo raised an eyebrow. "A mental patient?"

Sancho nodded. "I'm an orderly there and he escaped, like, two days ago."

Flynn stared at Sancho as if *he* were the escaped mental patient.

"How interesting," Goolardo said as he drained the last of his daiquiri. "Is this true, Mr. Flynn?"

Sancho cut in. "He doesn't know he's crazy. He thinks he's—"

"Shut your fucking mouth," Goolardo snapped. The menace in his voice was palpable. Sancho shut up as Goolardo smiled again, turning on his charm like a switch. "I was talking to Mr. Flynn."

"Nice try, Sancho," Flynn said. "But Mr. Goolardo is no idiot."

"No, I am not," Goolardo agreed. "If you're going to concoct some sort of story, I'd appreciate something a little more believable."

"Sancho's still in training," Flynn said. "He doesn't yet know that half-truths make the best lies."

"Indeed," Goolardo said as he put his hand on Flynn's shoulder. "This man penetrated my organization, uncovered a top secret covert operation, and you want me to believe he's an escaped lunatic?" Goolardo laughed. Mendoza looked irritated. Dulcie was on her third daiquiri. "He's obviously a man of substance. Accomplished. Experienced." Goolardo addressed Flynn directly now. "I'd rather not have to turn you over to a man like Mendoza, but that is exactly what I will be forced to do if you continue to refuse to confide in me. Mendoza is crude, but very effective. Eventually he will get you to talk. He always does. By then you and your friends will have met a very sad end."

"I suppose there's no reason not to tell you what I know," Flynn replied. "My guess is your plan is about mind control."

Goolardo's eyes widened with surprise. "Go on."

"And if you're going to be controlling minds, why not control the minds of men who can give you what you want."

"My sentiments exactly."

Sancho was stunned. "He's right? Are you serious?"

"How do you know about this?" Goolardo probed.

"It's my job to know," Flynn said.

"And to stop me."

"Yes."

"Well, I'm sorry, my friend, but it's too late. In less than twenty-four hours the ten richest men in the world will be in my thrall."

Flynn's eyes lit up as he connected the dots. "Angel Island." Flynn smiled, nodding. "Randall Beckner's private resort. On a clear day, you can probably see it from this Alcazar's highest tower. It's in the Sea of Cortez and every year Beckner hosts a retreat for the world's ten richest men. Tycoons meet to exchange ideas, make deals—"

"And collude to continue the oppression of the working man," Goolardo said.

"So, you're a socialist like your mentor?" Flynn raised a surprised eyebrow.

"I'm an enlightened capitalist. I believe in social responsibility and a more equitable distribution of wealth. Pure socialism doesn't work. People need incentive. They need to be rewarded. Otherwise you end up with what happened in the former Soviet Union."

"And that's why you're taking control of them?" Flynn posited. "To distribute the wealth from them to you?"

Goolardo laughed. "Give me more credit than that, Mr. Flynn."

"You're kidnapping them?" Sancho was still a little confused.

"He's doing much more than that," Flynn said "That ransom for those vatos has gotta be—"

"Nothing," Flynn continued. "Compared to what Mr. Goolardo will make when the stock market crashes on the news of their disappearance."

"Very good, Mr. Flynn. Yes, my entire fortune is poised to take advantage of the market's downturn."

"You're short selling all the stock and then once it drops, you'll buy low and when you release the tycoons…"

"The market will rise…"

"And you'll make…."

"Billions.".

"Brilliant," Flynn said.

Goolardo smiled with pride. "Thank you. It's a pleasure to finally meet someone who understands. I do believe that fate has finally handed me an adversary worthy of my talents. I'm just sorry that our dance couldn't have lasted a bit longer."

"Yeah, too bad," Mendoza mumbled as he grabbed Flynn by the arm.

"I agree," Flynn replied. "I'm sorry I won't be able to see your plan in action. It's always entertaining to watch a master at work, no matter what the endeavor."

Goolardo continued to grin. "You know, I do believe Mr. Flynn has a point. I'm thinking perhaps he and his friends should stay as our guests for at least a little while longer."

"Stay where?" Mendoza choked on his daiquiri. "Here?"

"In the guest rooms. Of course, you'll keep them under guard. But my victory will be that much sweeter if I can share it with someone who isn't an idiot."

Mendoza looked offended. "You think I don't understand your plan?"

"Mr. Mendoza, please, you're very good at what you do. But this…is a bit beyond you."

"You're kidnapping billionaires and when the stock market goes down, you'll make a lot of money. Right?"

"How?" asked Goolardo. "Can you tell me how I make money when the stock market goes down?"

Mendoza started to open his mouth and then closed it. Angry color rose to his cheeks. He glowered at Flynn before abruptly downing the rest of his drink.

"We dine at nine," said Goolardo. "Mendoza will show you to your rooms. Take a nap. Freshen up. We'll see if we can find you some clean clothes to wear. Something more appropriate for dinner."

Flynn smiled and glanced at Mendoza, who watched him the way a lion eyeballs a wildebeest just before it pounces.

Chapter Eighteen

Dulcie thought she would fall asleep as soon as her head hit the feather pillow on her Duxiana bed. It was a well-appointed room in one of the towers. A window overlooked the Sea of Cortez, but Dulcie wasn't interested in the view. She was interested in being unconscious. She had enjoyed a long bath, which had helped to relax her jangled nerves. They even supplied her with a tab of Valium. She was so tired, so exhausted from being terrified. Unfortunately, as hard as she tried, she couldn't sleep.

Her mind raced. It was partly the meth withdrawal, but partly the fact that she couldn't figure out Flynn. He was a total headcase, but he had this Goolardo wrapped around his little finger. Did Flynn really believe what he was saying? Or was it all part of some elaborate scam designed to keep them from getting killed? And what was this attraction she felt? She knew he wasn't all there, but still…there was something about him. He seemed so sure of himself. So confident.

Mike had pretended to be confident, but that was mainly to cover up his deep insecurity and self-loathing. She knew Mike was beaten daily by his dad and that frightened little boy still remained inside of him. He created a tough guy front to protect himself, but inside he was weak. He attacked Dulcie because he knew she wouldn't fight back. He was a coward and a liar. But so was she, so maybe he was exactly what she deserved. Flynn, on the other hand, seemed like the real thing, even though, deep down, she knew he couldn't be. Maybe the only people with complete confidence are the crazy ones.

Sancho was in another room in the same tower, across the hall. Five hulking killers with AK-47's guarded the inner foyer just outside his door. Sancho knew this because he'd tried the door earlier and was surprised to find it unlocked. Upon opening it, however, he found five AK-47's pointed at his face. He closed the door without a word and they bolted it shut behind him. He too had bathed, though he opted for the shower.

The stall had been huge and decorated with colorful tile in an Aztec theme. There were three nozzles. The pressure was intense and the water was perfect and a large window offered a dramatic view of the sea. Once he was in there, he didn't want to leave. The hot water pounding his back felt so good. From here, it would all be downhill.

He knew they were going to be killed. The only question was when. Flynn couldn't keep this crazy charade going forever. Eventually they would figure out that Sancho was telling the truth and that Flynn was a total loon. And now that Goolardo had laid out his plan, he couldn't let them live. Before Goolardo had spilled the beans, there was an infinitesimal chance of survival, but now there was none. No way was he going to let them walk. Fucking Flynn. He should have let Kursky and his crew kill him in Palmdale. What was he thinking? He should have listened to Dulcie. Now they both were going to die and it was all his fault.

Flynn's room, right next door to Sancho's, had a window which overlooked the palace courtyard. Sixty feet down he could see the helicopter. It was surrounded by guards lounging about laughing, smoking, automatic weapons dangling from their shoulders. If he tied his sheets together to use them as a rope, there was a good chance they'd see him rappelling down. If the bullets didn't kill him, the fall surely would.

He leaned out over the edge of the window and felt a rush of vertigo. Adrenaline surged through his blood. Fear was fuel for Flynn. It charged him up and filled him with purpose. There was a ledge right below the windowsill and it apparently ran around the circumference of the tower. If he could edge his way around the ledge and reach another window, perhaps he could find Dulcie and arrange for some sort of escape. The fools had left him his laser pen, believing it was harmless. He could use it to cut through his door and take down the guards, but lasers are dangerously powerful and difficult to control. In the heat of battle, he might accidentally slice through another door and cut Dulcie in half. No, there was only one option. He would make his way out the window and around the ledge, find Dulcie, and free her before anyone knew he was gone.

Mendoza never let anyone know what he was feeling. That was his power. That was how he kept control. Like an expert poker player, he never gave anything away. He had toughened his body and toughened his mind to a point where he was untouchable. These emotional calluses started growing soon after his parents were murdered by a right-wing death squad. They grew even thicker when he found his first wife in his brother's arms and had to kill them both. This was why he had no friends and no family. This was why he had no one but himself.

He was completely self-contained; impervious to pain. He was beholden to no one and loyal to only one, Goolardo, but over the course of time his loyalty had become something else entirely. Somehow, emotion had seized control of his cold, calloused heart. Mendoza felt anger. He felt jealousy. He was jealous that Goolardo was so interested in this Flynn, confiding in him, joking with him, and telling him things he had never told Mendoza.

Goolardo insulted me to my face, Mendoza thought. He called me an idiot. Not in so many words, but the intention was clear. Mendoza was nothing but muscle in Goolardo's eyes. A gun. A thug. A pendejo. He knew he wasn't in Goolardo's league, but he thought he had the man's trust. The man's respect. What if Goolardo never killed Flynn? What if he offered the puto a job? What if he bought him off like he bought *everyone* off and made him his righthand man? Where would that leave Mendoza?

Mendoza called a private detective in Los Angeles, someone he had worked with before. The man's name was Soto and he was an ex-LAPD detective who'd lost his job after the Rampart scandal. He narrowly avoided jail by testifying against his fellow officers. Now, he worked for criminal defense attorneys, helping to find evidence to protect the very drug dealers he had once tried to put away. Soto lived in Burbank. Married for over twenty years, he had seven children with an eighth on the way. So, Mendoza knew he could use the money.

Soto answered his cell phone. He was on a stake-out in Glendale, across the street from the Vagabond Inn, looking to find dirt on a local judge. The judge was cheating on his wife with another man and Soto was documenting the whole sordid affair. The man screwing the judge was a gay hustler in Soto's employ.

"Soto," he said. There was no caller ID, but then most of his clients blocked their numbers.

"It's Mendoza. I got a job for you."

"I'm kinda tied up right now."

"This needs to be done right away."

"I'd like to help, but I got a lot on my plate."

"I don't care what the fuck you got. This is an emergency."

"Come on, man…"

"If you make me ask you one more time, I'm going to kill your wife and all seven of your snot-nosed niños."

Soto sighed. "Fine. What? What is it?"

"I want you check out some asshole named James Flynn. I want you to see if they have any record of him at City of Roses Psychiatric. If they do, I want his file. Everything you can find. Can you do this for me?"

"How soon do you need it done?"

"If it takes longer than four hours, it ain't gonna fucking matter."

"I'll see what I can do."

But Mendoza had already hung up.

The ledge was slippery with bird guano. Flynn kept his right cheek flat against the warm stone as he edged his way along. He could hear the guards talking sixty feet down. They were directly below so, luckily, the ledge blocked their view of him. It was only a foot wide so Flynn couldn't avoid any missteps. The hand holds were few and far between, but he kept creeping along and soon the voices of the guards grew faint. His hand found the edge of a window. Flynn glanced in and there was Sancho, sitting on the bed.

Sancho was very surprised to see Flynn smiling at him. He tried to help Flynn in, but Flynn resisted.

"I have to find Dulcie."

"Dude, you're crazy."

"Just stay put."

"Where the hell am I gonna go?"

But Flynn was gone, edging his way past Sancho's window and around the tower. His fingertips were raw by the time he reached the window of Dulcie's quarters.

Dulcie was resting in bed, wearing an open robe, when she heard a loud, "Pssssst." She followed the sound to the window. Flynn grinned at her with bravado. The wind gusted and pushed him sideways. His cocky smile was replaced with a look of surprise as he stepped on a large pile of bird droppings. His left foot slid off the ledge. Flynn scrabbled against the stone. He caught the edge of the ledge just in time. Dulcie was up and running to the window. She grabbed Flynn's wrist as his fingers slipped, and pulled with everything she had. He grunted and got his leg up and then the rest of him tumbled through the open window head first.

"What the hell is wrong with you?" Dulcie was electric with fear and adrenaline.

"Nothing a stiff drink wouldn't fix." He stood and smirked and dusted himself off.

"What are you doing here?"

"Rescuing you, of course."

"We're like ten stories up."

"More like four."

"I don't care! I'm not—"

"We have no choice, Dulcie. Goolardo's toying with us and eventually he's going to kill us."

Her eyes grew shiny. "So why don't you just let me fucking die."

"Is that what you want?"

"Yes."

"Why?"

"Because I'm fucking over it, okay. I just wanna close my eyes and never fucking open them again."

"You want to let them win?"

"They already did!"

"I don't believe that."

"I don't care what you fucking believe! Just leave me alone." Tears ran down her face. "Can you do that? Can you just leave me the fuck alone?"

"I don't think I can."

Dulcie sobbed in earnest now. Her shoulders shook and Flynn put his arms around her. She tried to push him away, but he was as firm as he was gentle and she finally couldn't fight him anymore. He held her tight and she rested her chin on his shoulder and cried. He cradled her like that until she was exhausted and empty and didn't have a single tear left.

He whispered to her softly. She so desperately wanted to believe him. "Let's rest now," he said. "Get some sleep. When the sun is down, we'll make our move."

He laid her down in bed and climbed in beside her. She put her head on his chest and could hear his heartbeat. It was strong. Constant. Confident. Too bad he was such a fucking psycho. Within seconds, she was asleep.

Chapter Nineteen

Mendoza was now hurt, angry, *and* humiliated. Goolardo had requested Mendoza's presence in the throne room. He thought the big man wanted to confide in him, bond with him, apologize for insulting him. He thought Goolardo would reveal his true plans for Flynn. That he was playing Flynn, using him, trying to get information out of him. But instead Goolardo praised the irritating son of a bitch.

He kept going on and on about how impressive he was. How educated. How high-class. How unflappable. It was hard for Mendoza not to blow, but he kept his fury in check and tried to look inscrutable. And then Goolardo handed Mendoza three different designer suits: Huge Boss, Armani, and Dolce & Gabbana. He wanted Mendoza to take them to Flynn to see if they fit him. He also had dresses for Dulcie; dresses that belonged to the big man's girlfriend. Fucking designer dresses. Goolardo wanted them to dress for dinner.

He stood there with his arms out, feeling like a pendejo as Goolardo piled clothes on him. Then he asked Mendoza to find some clothes for Sancho. Will the abuse never end, he wondered? Is he testing me? Mocking me?

Mendoza stood outside Flynn's room, holding the suits. The guards were eyeballing him. Were they smiling? They'd better not be.

"Open the door," Mendoza ordered. One guard unlocked the deadbolt and another guard opened the door.

Mendoza threw the suits on the floor. "Goolardo wants you to put one of these on." He waited for Flynn's clever retort. The bastard always had some snotty limey comeback. "Did you hear what I said!" Mendoza poked his head in the room and didn't see Flynn anywhere. He drew his weapon and motioned with his head to get the guards to follow him. He glanced behind the door. He looked in the closet. Under the bed. What the hell? Then he spotted the open window. Mendoza hurried to the opening and looked down. He couldn't have jumped. It was a sixty foot drop straight to the courtyard. The guards would have seen him and raised an alarm.

And then he noticed the ledge.

He leaned out a little further and felt a rush of vertigo. He wasn't fond of heights, but he steeled himself and poked his head out a little further to see that the ledge continued around the tower.

"Chingado!" He rushed from Flynn's tower room and hurried across the hall and threw open the door to Dulcie's room. The guards were right behind him with their AK-47's.

Dulcie was in bed alone. Asleep. She awoke with a start, surprised to find a furious Mendoza staring down at her. He pointed his pistol at her face. "Where is he?"

"Who?"

He pulled the trigger and the gun boomed. The bullet missed her face by inches. Dulcie screamed and Flynn poked his head out from under the bed. "If you hurt that girl…"

"What? You'll be angry with me?"

Flynn rolled out from under the bed and checked on Dulcie. She was terrified, but uninjured. Then he leveled his gaze at Mendoza. "I'm disappointed in you, amigo. You didn't seem to be the sort of sadist who got his jollies frightening defenseless women."

"What sort of sadist do I seem to be?"

"The kind who enjoys torturing men like me."

"Well, yes, I must admit, *that* I would enjoy. Wiping that smirk off your face would give me great pleasure. So, you know what? I think I won't shoot you. Not right now. Right now, you should get dressed, so you can have dinner with Goolardo. It's important that you keep your strength up, muchacho. That way later, when I do torture you, it will last a very, *very* long time."

The Armani suit was the closest to fitting Flynn correctly. Goolardo was broader through the chest and shoulders, so the jacket was a little big and the arms a tad long. Flynn was also taller, so the trousers didn't quite reach his shoes, but somehow Flynn carried it off with panache. He wasn't the least bit self-conscious, unlike Dulcie, who wore a sexy, red, silk dress designed by Donna Karan. It was knee length, but low cut. She wore red pumps with pointy toes and high stiletto heels. She wasn't used to walking in heels so high, so she looked unsteady and embarrassed. Her eyes were full of apprehension, but Flynn wasn't sure if she was afraid of Mendoza or of simply falling on her face.

Sancho looked equally uncomfortable. He wore Goolardo's Hugo Boss suit and, being much shorter, it looked like he was wearing his daddy's clothes. The sleeves dangled down past his hands and the pants hung low off his butt, bagging up around his ankles.

The three followed Mendoza and four guards down a long corridor. Flynn dropped back a bit to check out the situation and get an eyeful of Dulcie from behind. He noticed that Sancho was doing the very same thing. So were all four guards. The only one who wasn't checking out her booty was Mendoza. Dulcie could feel the scrutiny and looked back, irritated with all the attention. "What the hell are you looking at?"

"A thing of beauty," Flynn said. Sancho grinned. So did the guards, but not Mendoza. He looked irritated.

Hearst Castle in San Simeon was Goolardo's inspiration. It rose above the Pacific coast, resting high atop "La Cuesta Encantada." The Enchanted Hill. Goolardo called his creation "Alcazar del Goolardo." And the promontory upon which it rested was known as, "Protuberancia del Misterio."

Dulcie tried not to grin when Goolardo told her this. He said it so proudly, with such a flourish, rolling his R's, widening his eyes. "Protuberance of Mystery" was what it meant in English and, for a moment, she wondered if Goolardo was putting them on. When he didn't chuckle, or offer them a grin, she knew he was deadly serious. Sometimes, when she was terrified, she became dangerously giddy. It was a nervous reaction and it used to make Mike furious. He would beat her savagely, yelling at her to stop laughing at him, but she wasn't laughing at *him*. Not exactly.

She felt the laughter bubbling up and she fought to keep it down. Flynn saw the smile fighting for control of her face. She was going to lose it and he knew it, so he grabbed her and started tickling her. Her laughter burst free and she let it out gratefully, relieved.

Goolardo was a bit taken aback by Flynn's spontaneous tickling attack, but continued on with his tour, down a hallway lined with Mexican art, and into a vast dining room which rivaled the grand hall at San Simeon. The walls were paneled in oak and decorated with tapestries. Dulcie saw sculptures of gargoyles and suits of conquistador armor and in the center of the room, a ridiculously long antique table.

Flynn whispered to her. "I believe Mr. Goolardo is overcompensating for something."

"You saying he has a tiny package?"

"A protuberance of mystery."

She laughed and Flynn smirked and Goolardo glowered at them both. "What are you two giggling about?"

"Nothing you would find amusing," Flynn said. "But I must say, I *am* impressed by the size of your table." Dulcie almost lost it again. She bit her tongue as Flynn continued. "Everything here is quite grand. Was that an original Rivera back there in the corridor?"

"Indeed, it was."

"And an original Jose Orozco and a David Alfaro Siqueiro?"

"You know Mexican art?"

"I know a little bit about a lot of things."

Mendoza rolled his eyes.

"I must say, Mr. Flynn, you never cease to impress me. Have a seat. Everyone. Dinner is about to be served. I hope you enjoy langosta."

"Mexican Lobster?"

"Rock Lobster, yes. It's not as sweet as Maine lobster, but it can be quite tasty and it's indigenous to our local waters. Have you ever been to Puerto Nuevo? It's very quaint. A tiny village on the west coast of Baja made up entirely of cantinas that serve fresh lobster, tortillas, rice, and beans." Goolardo smiled at Mendoza just as the big man was planting his ass in a chair. "Mr. Mendoza, I'm sorry, but I hadn't planned on having you join us."

Mendoza looked stunned as Goolardo, who, still smiling, motioned for him to rise. Embarrassed color rose to his cheeks as he scraped back his chair and stood.

"Perhaps next time," Goolardo said.

Mendoza left the room, barely containing his anger. He wanted to hurt something. He wanted to find a living thing and cause it pain. His first choice, of course, would have been Flynn. He imagined putting his massive hands around the man's neck and squeezing the life out of him. He almost punched a Diego Rivera painting, but held himself in check. He wanted Goolardo to know he was angry, but he didn't want to owe the big man three and a half million dollars.

Mendoza found a quiet spot outside, on a second-floor landing, behind a parapet. Pulling out his satellite phone, he punched in a number and gritted his teeth as it rang. Finally, he heard a voice on the other end.

"Soto," the private detective said.

"It's Mendoza."

"I know."

"What else do you know? Did you do what I ask?"

"I did. And you won't fucking believe what I found out."

"What do you have?"

"I greased a few palms. It didn't take long. Though it wasn't cheap and you're gonna have to reimburse me for—"

"*What do you have?*"

"His medical file. A police report. The motherfucking mother lode, my friend. I'm scanning the documents as we speak. You have an e-mail address? I'll send it as a PDF."

Chapter Twenty

"This Champagne"—Flynn swirled the pale amber liquid—"it's Krug, isn't it? Clos du Mesnil '95."

"If one can afford the best…" Goolardo said. He left the sentence unfinished.

Sancho's plate was full of empty lobster claws and clam shells. He ate with gusto. This was probably my last meal, he thought. I might as well enjoy it.

Goolardo gave Dulcie a long look. He was a man used to taking what he wanted. "That dress suits you, my dear." Dulcie avoided his eyes, but Goolardo was persistent. "I have a lady friend who visits now and then. A fashion model. Rather well known. That dress is hers and she looks very good in it, but I think you look even better. Maybe you would like to sit next to me?"

In an attempt to change the subject, Flynn pointed out a shrunken head on display under glass. "So, what happened to *that* poor unfortunate gentlemen?" The head was gray and shriveled and about the size of a baseball. The hair was white and stringy and the eyes and mouth were sewn shut.

"I told you the story of the warden of Ilha Grande Penitentiary and his missing head? He rubbed me the wrong way, and well…the result was not good for him…as you can see."

"Did you shrink the head yourself?"

"I enlisted the aid of a local Amazon tribe. The Jivara. They believe, as I do, in the total annihilation of one's enemies. The head is a trophy. A tsantsa."

Sancho stared at the little wrinkled head with horror. "That's a real head?"

"The process is fascinating and very involved. The face is peeled off, turned inside out, and scraped. Believing that such a violent death unleashes a soul bent on revenge, the lips and eyelids are sewn shut to trap the spirit. The skull and brain are then removed and what's left of the head is simmered in a pot. The skin tightens, the head shrinks, and sand is poured inside the neck." Sancho looked like he was about to spew. "The head is then shaken like a maraca until the flesh is like leather. The hair is trimmed, for it continues to grow for a short while even after the head is separated from the body. And there you have it." Goolardo motioned to the itsy-bitsy head. Sancho put down his fork and pushed away his plate. "Shrinking a head is not something you want to leave to amateurs," Goolardo explained. "I'm a firm believer in hiring only the best for whatever job needs to be done. Which is why, Mr. Flynn, I would like to offer you a position in my organization."

"I'm flattered."

An astonished Sancho looked across the table at Dulcie. Neither one could believe what they were hearing.

"Your talents are being wasted. How much do you make working for your government? I'm sure it's a pittance."

"I have modest needs."

"I doubt that, Mr. Flynn. A man whose palate is educated enough to appreciate and identify a Clos du Mesnil '95?"

"What would you have me do for you?"

"Whatever is necessary."

"Implement your plan?"

"I could certainly use someone with your intelligence and sophistication."

"So, who came up with this operation? Was it Dr. Grossfarber?"

"Who?"

"You deny he's part of your organization?"

"Who?"

"Grossfarber."

Sancho and Dulcie continued to stare at each other, afraid to look at anyone else, afraid if they did they would lose it. Goolardo just seemed perplexed. "I'm sorry, but I don't know anyone by that name."

"Plausible Deniability. I understand."

"Understand what?"

"I understand many things. For instance, this plan you have concocted? It's quite mad."

"Mad?" Goolardo's smile started to fade.

"You are clearly insane if you think you can penetrate the security surrounding Angel Island. It can't be done."

"Are you calling me crazy?"

"If the shoe fits."

"What if I said it *could* be done?"

"Impossible."

"Then perhaps I should explain to you exactly how I intend to do it."

"This should be entertaining," said Flynn. He smiled at Dulcie.

Goolardo's face darkened with fury. He was trying to stay calm, but Sancho could tell he wasn't used to being challenged or mocked. He scraped back his chair and stood from the table. "My plan is already in motion. At this very moment, I have a man…"

Mendoza barged into the dining room, breaking Goolardo's concentration. He had a file folder packed with papers and his eyes were full of fire. "I have new information!"

"This can't wait until later?" Goolardo was spitting nails. "*I'm trying to enjoy my fucking dinner!*"

Mendoza thrust the file folder in front of Goolardo and Goolardo tore it from Mendoza's hand and threw it on the floor. "What the fuck is wrong with you? I said *later!*" "It's from my contact in Los Angeles! Information on Flynn." Mendoza reached down and picked up the file folder. Goolardo invaded Mendoza's space. They were eyeball to eyeball, but Mendoza wasn't about to back down. He opened the file and held it out for Goolardo to see. Goolardo glanced down at a picture of Flynn. It was a photocopy of the front page of the Pasadena Star-News. The headline read, "Escaped Mental Patient still on the loose."

The fury on Goolardo's face morphed into confusion as he read the two-paragraph story. He looked at James with disbelief as Mendoza flipped to Flynn's psychiatric file. Inside Goolardo found photographs. Documents. Histories.

"This can't be," Goolardo whispered.

Sancho rose and peered over Goolardo's shoulder. When he saw the file, he literally went white. Dulcie caught his eye and knew that it had to be bad. Flynn seemed almost disinterested. Not the least bit concerned.

Goolardo pulled out a family photo of a handsome couple and an adorable seven-year-old-boy. He held it up for James to see and Flynn, for the first time since he escaped from the hospital, seemed apprehensive.

"This is you?" Goolardo crossed closer to Flynn and Flynn tried to look away, but Goolardo thrust the picture in his face. Sancho watched as sadness and pain welled up in Flynn's eyes. "Your mother and father and you?"

James closes his eyes, raised both his hands and backed away. He seemed rigid and afraid; like a child with autism. Goolardo leafed through the file and read select passages aloud. "Born in Van Nuys, California…Orphaned at age ten…passed from foster home to foster home…grossly obese…a chronic bed wetter."

Sancho and Dulcie watched sadly as Flynn crumpled in on himself. He seemed to be shrinking right in front of their eyes.

Goolardo pulled out a photo of a fat, pimple-faced twelve-year-old. He had a black eye and he looked as if he was about to cry. He set the picture on the table and continued to read. "…developed a delusion so severe…institutionalized at the age of…" Goolardo looked up from the file to see that Flynn sat slumped in his chair, staring at some imaginary nothing ten feet in front of him.

Flynn sat deep in thought, thinking about a recurring nightmare he often had. Everything was dim and vibrating and there was always music playing. A country western song. It was upbeat and lively and it filled him with such happiness. He was riding in the backseat of a car. A man drove. A woman was asleep in the passenger seat. She was curled up on her side and Flynn could see her face in profile.

"The girls all get prettier at closing time," the singer sang. "They all begin to look like movie stars."

In the dream, Flynn would look at his hands and see they were the size of a child's. His legs were small too, dangling over the edge of the seat. He wore Keds and a seat belt and a t-shirt with the L.A. Dodgers logo.

"The girls all get prettier at closing time," sang the singer. "When the change starts taking place, it puts a glow on every face, of the falling angels of the back-street bars."

Images from the nightmare flashed through his mind: the glowing radio dial. the speedometer pegged at seventy; the little words below it which read *Cruise Control*; the man driving looked at Flynn in his rear-view mirror. His eyes were kind. So full of love. He nodded at Flynn and smiled and for some reason that made Flynn ineffably sad.

"The girls all get prettier at closing time," sang the man with the Texas twang. "They all begin to look like movie stars."

In his dream, the head of the driver would start to dip. And snap back up. And drift back down. He'd shake himself awake. And stare at the oncoming highway. Flynn would look out the passenger side window to see only darkness rushing by. The man driving and the sleeping woman seemed so familiar. Who were they? Why was he with them? Where were they going?

"The girls all get prettier at closing time, when the change starts taking place..."

The driver's chin would finally sink to his chest and the car would start to drift. Then it would begin to bounce up and down, throwing Flynn around. This would always awaken the man and he would frantically grab the steering wheel. By then bright headlights were blazing through the windshield. At that point the woman would scream.

"When the change starts taking place," the singer happily sang. "It puts a glow on every face."

The sound that ended the song was always explosively loud. What made it seem even louder was the absolute silence that followed. And darkness. Total darkness.

Flynn would feel so lonely and empty and hopeless. This bottomless hopelessness came from deep inside his soul and it hurt like nothing had ever hurt before. When the pain became unbearable, so unbearable that Flynn just wanted to die, he would awaken from this nightmare and all would be fine. The sun would be shining, and he would be who he was. Masterful. In control. Powerful. A hero.

But for some reason, this time, Flynn wasn't waking up. The nightmare wouldn't stop. The darkness continued to surround him and the unbearable hopelessness and loneliness would not let him go. If this pain didn't end soon, he knew he would die. His body would give up the ghost. Nothing was worth this much suffering.

Sancho was stunned by Flynn's transformation. Every ounce of confidence was gone. His face didn't even look the same. The spark was missing; the dash, the daring, the bravado. It was as if someone had let all the air out of him.

"I told you who he was," Sancho said, quiet and sad.

"But how did he know about my plan?"

"He didn't," Dulcie said.

"He *did*!" bellowed Goolardo.

"Dude," Sancho said. "All he knows is what you told him."

Goolardo saw Mendoza's satisfied smile. Rage burned in his blood like fire and he blindsided the big thug with a backhand that sent him reeling. Mendoza was stunned. His nose bled. The boss man now had a gun in his hand. A gun aimed at Mendoza's face. "Are you laughing at me?" Mendoza's smile was long gone. He quickly shook his head no.

Goolardo's mind raced in fifteen different directions as he frantically searched his memory. Did Flynn really know nothing? He seemed to know something. What did I tell him? He knew there was a plan. How did he know that? Goolardo looked down at the file folder open on the table. At the pictures of Flynn. At Flynn himself. He now looked far more like the fat, pimple-faced pre-teen than the man of action he seemed to be but moments before.

"Look," Sancho said. "It was a mistake. An honest mistake. It's kind of funny, if you think about it." He offered up a tiny smile, but there were no takers. "He doesn't know anything. Not a damn thing. And neither do we."

"You know something now," Mendoza said.

"Who are we going to talk to? Who would even believe us?"

Dulcie's eyes filled with tears. She knew what was going to happen. She knew there was no talking their way out of it, and when Sancho saw the look on her face, he knew that there wasn't anything he could say that would save them.

Goolardo holstered his pistol and sat back down at the table. He sipped a little champagne then said, "Kill them."

"Come on," Sancho pleaded. "We're nothing. We're nobody. We can't hurt you. There's no reason to—"

"*Kill them all!*"

Chapter Twenty-One

The tall wrought iron gates of Goolardo's Alcazar opened and a convertible Humvee trundled out. The driver had wide shoulders and no-neck and a bald head the size of a basketball. It was stubbly and lumpy and his ears were an angry red. The killer riding shotgun was even uglier, thought Dulcie. His greasy black hair was tied back in a ponytail and his beard looked ratty and thick. A vicious scar puckered the left side of his face.

Dulcie tried to move, but her hands were bound tightly behind her with rough twine. Sancho sat on her left, hands tied, squinting into the dust and wind. He looked angry. He looked bitter. He looked like a ten-year-old trying not to cry. Flynn sat on Dulcie's right. He, too, was tied up, not that it mattered. He was a sad, sorry, shrunken husk of his former self.

Mendoza occupied the seat right behind them. If Dulcie turned, she could see him out of the corner of her eye. He looked serene and relaxed. A Mac-10 machine gun was cradled in his lap.

The killer with the ponytail turned around and smiled at Dulcie. Quite a few of his teeth were gold and the puckered scar twisted his smile off-kilter. His grin lit a fire inside of her. "What the fuck you looking at?"

The killer laughed and shouted to the driver. "Es una puta muy guapa!"

The driver grinned and nodded. "Diene un chichis muy grande!"

They both cracked up. Dulcie wanted to kill them both. Cut their throats. Bash their heads in with a baseball bat. But she couldn't do anything. She couldn't even move. The anger turned into tears.

Sancho saw the tears on Dulcie's face and it pissed him off. "Hey! Come on!" he shouted at the thugs. "Have some fucking respect!"

The killer with the scar turned and smiled, savagely back-handing him. He wore a huge gold ring and it split Sancho's lip. Blood spurted out and ran down his chin. Sancho didn't react with fear, but with fury. He licked his fat lip and smiled at the killer with bloody teeth. "Why don't you untie me and try that?"

"What's the matter, little man?" asked the thug. "You don't like being bitch slapped?" The driver laughed at that and shook his big ugly head. "You wanna bitch slap me back? Is that it?" He drew a huge combat knife from a sheath, and turned around, kneeling on his seat. He held the tip of the blade to Sancho's throat. The Humvee hit a rut and the tip punctured his skin. Sancho leaned back to get away from the blade, but there was nowhere to go.

"Leave him alone!" Dulcie shouted. The thug struck her in the face with the hilt of his knife, breaking the skin on her cheek. He then put the knife point inches from Sancho's left eye. The blade ominously jumped around as the Humvee bounced down the dirt road.

"You'll have your chance to be a hero, chilito, as soon as we get to where we're going to dump your body. The only reason you're not dead yet is because I don't want to carry your fat ass around." They hit another rut and the blade cut Sancho right below the eye. The thug smirked, turned back around and faced front. He slipped the knife back into its sheath and mumbled, "Joto."

The driver laughed and in that split second, Sancho didn't care whether he lived or died. He stood up and arched back, slamming his head into the nose of Mendoza. He then lifted his legs up and scissored them together, banging the driver's head into the thug's. The killer was stunned, but the driver was unconscious. The Humvee swerved off the dirt road and down an embankment. Dulcie screamed when she saw the cliff they careened towards, overlooking the Sea of Cortez.

Mendoza was dazed. Blood spurted from his nose. His Mac-10 clattered on the floor. Mendoza leaned out of his seat and finally got his hands on it just as the Hummer bounced in and out of a deep gully. Mendoza bounced as well. Right out of the vehicle. He landed on his head and skidded in the dust, skittering and somersaulting as the Hummer sped away.

The killer in the passenger seat grabbed the steering wheel as Sancho squeezed him around the neck in the scissor hold. They struggled and the Hummer bounced and flew and lurched closer to the cliff. Dulce struggled to free her hands, but they were tied too tight. She looked to Flynn, but he was no help, just a blank-faced bobble head with the mental capacity of a potato.

They were going so fast, yet everything seemed to move in slow motion. The killer struggled to steer them away from the cliff with one hand, while the other hand was busy trying to free himself from Sancho's legs. Sancho tightened his grip, choking the thug out as he desperately fumbled for his Glock. The pendejo tried to stand, lifting Sancho half in the air and blindly aimed the gun. The Hummer hit another rut and the killer flipped off the side of the vehicle, almost dragging Sancho along with him. The driver bounced awake just in time to see the precipice. Without a word, he leapt off the side of the vehicle. Seconds later the Humvee roared right off the edge of the cliff.

Dulcie caught Sancho's eye and together they screamed to high heaven. It was a panicky, high-pitched wail of existential terror.

"*Silence!*" Dulcie abruptly shut up to stare at Flynn, who was now back in charge and sharp as a tack. "Keep your heads about you, for God's sake!" Dulcie and Sancho tried to maintain, but their eyes belied their panic. "When I say jump, jump. *Jump!*"

And they did.

Chapter Twenty-Two

The woman in Flynn's nightmare wouldn't stop screaming. Soon the scream split into a grating harmony; two distinct screams blended into a discordant chorus. The lower pitched scream began to fade and soon only the higher pitched one remained.

Dulcie.

The sound penetrated the darkness that surrounded him like the weak beam of a penlight. Dulcie was in danger. That much was clear. He followed the light and it led straight up. A tiny circle of brightness hovered high above. The light tugged on him, lifting him, pulling him like a rope, faster and faster until the world came flooding back in a riot of sound and color and physical sensation.

All at once, he knew where he was; the backseat of a speeding Hummer, flying off the side of a cliff.

Mendoza tasted dirt. It crunched between his teeth as he lay face down on the ground. Every square inch of him hurt. He pushed himself to a sitting position and spit out the grit that coated his tongue. He gagged and almost vomited. His gun was gone, his shirt was torn, and he was bleeding from more places than he could count. Grunting, he pulled himself to his feet and saw the killer, sitting in the dirt a few dozen yards away. The driver stood at the edge of the cliff, looking down at something far below.

Mendoza staggered forward. A sharp pain shot up his leg and into his lower back. He saw the Mac-10 and picked it up as he continued on his way, past the dazed thug, and all the way to the cliff.

Mendoza looked over the edge. The surf crashed into jagged rocks two hundred feet down. He felt a flutter of vertigo and stepped back. There was no sign of the Humvee. No sign of James, Sancho, or Dulcie.

The driver had a huge, bloody scrape on the side of his face. He glanced at Mendoza. "What do we tell Goolardo?"

"All he needs to know is that they're dead."

"No one could survive such a fall."

"They're gone. That's all that matters."

"What if he asks about the Hummer?"

"He won't. But if he does, I'll tell him I decided to make it look like an accident." Mendoza continued to stare into the violent surf. He licked his split lip and touched a finger to his broken nose. As he looked at the blood on his hands, his eyes burned with rancor. "I'm just sorry I didn't have the opportunity to make his death more unpleasant." Mendoza grimaced, turned, and limped back in the direction of the Alcazar. The thug and the driver followed, wincing with every step.

The Sea of Cortez roiled and bucked as it crashed into the rocks at the base of the cliff. The sea had carved a cove into the bottom of the palisade, creating a haven protected from the violence of the most powerful waves. The water would rise and fall as the ocean rushed into the inlet. Flynn's face burst to the surface as the water descended. He gasped and coughed and sucked in a huge lungful of air. He kicked his legs hard, treading water, leaning back to keep his face above the sea.

A moment later Sancho popped to the surface, choking and hacking and sinking back down. Flynn's arms were still tied behind him. Letting himself sink below the surface, he raised his legs up and pushed them through his tied-together wrists. Then, Flynn swam back to the surface, grabbed another lungful of air, and dove back down, undulating like a dolphin. He seized Sancho by his shirt and dragged him above water. He kicked his legs hard to keep them both afloat as he scanned the sea for Dulcie.

A huge wave exploded into the rocks, raising the water level, pushing them from the protected area. Flynn was exhausted and in pain, but he wasn't about to let go of Sancho. He fought the rip current and kicked and pulled until he caught a wave which they rode all the way to a rocky little beach.

Flynn didn't want to move. Nothing had ever felt as comfortable as that hardscrabble beach. He didn't mind the rocks poking into his bruised ribs or the gritty sand against his face. He just blissfully breathed in that negative ion-rich oxygen; sweet with the smell of rotting fish. Sancho vomited on the sand, expelling seawater and seafood and whatever else was inside of him. Flynn untied Sancho's hands and Sancho returned the favor. They were cold, they were wet, but they were alive—and that's when Flynn thought of Dulcie. Where was she?

He struggled to his knees and then to his feet. He searched the water, but there was no sign of her. And then he saw a shoe farther down the beach, partly buried in the sand. He headed towards it and as he drew closer he saw it was a red pump with a pointy toe and a high stiletto heel. Sancho watched as he picked up the tiny shoe. She had such small feet. Flynn glanced back at the sea. He looked so melancholy. Sancho felt as bad for him as he did for Dulcie. What a short, miserable life she had. She never had a chance. And now she was gone.

Flynn headed back up the beach with the little shoe and showed it to Sancho. "I told her I would protect her. I told her nothing would happen to her."

"Well, maybe you shouldn't make promises you can't keep." Sancho's comment took Flynn by surprise. When Sancho saw the hurt in his eyes, he mumbled, "I'm just saying."

"You're right." Flynn said. "It was arrogant of me. I should have told her the truth."

"Dude—"

"I just didn't want her to afraid anymore. I just wanted her to feel—"

"Dude!" Sancho pointed out to sea. Flynn followed his finger to a flash of red bobbing amidst the white caps.

Flynn dropped the shoe and ran for the water. He dove in head first and swam hard and fast, full of hope and crazy energy. He hit the riptide and felt it pull him forward. A wave lifted him and he saw her. She was floundering, gasping, her face slipping beneath the water. The current kept pulling her away. Flynn used its power to propel himself forward and, finally, he grabbed a handful of dress. As James swam for shore, Sancho waded into the water, the waves nearly knocking him down. Sancho grabbed onto Dulcie's cold arm and together they dragged her to the rocky beach where Flynn gave her mouth to mouth. She coughed up water and vomited and finally started breathing.

"Dulcinea? Are you all right?"

"I'm fine." Dulcie spit and wiped her mouth. "For someone who just fell off a *fucking cliff*!"

Flynn gently untied her wrists and ankles and she glared at him the entire time. Her eye make-up was smeared and ran down her face. Her dripping hair was plastered to her head and her Donna Karan cocktail dress was soaked and decorated with dirt and seaweed. But it didn't matter. She was alive.

Sancho sat beside them, exhausted, dazed and wet. "I can't believe this is really happening. There's really a mastermind. There's actually a plan."

"Well, of course there is," Flynn replied. "What do you think we've been doing all this time?"

Flynn finished untying Dulcie and she rubbed her wrists. They were red and raw where the twine had cut into her skin. She watched as Flynn stood and scanned the cliffs above them. He looked strong and determined, and he offered Dulcie a confident smile, which just pissed her off even more.

"You're loving this, aren't you?"

"Danger, mystery, a ruthless enemy. What more could one possibly want?"

"A hot shower and some dry underwear."

Sancho tried to stand and teetered off balance. Flynn grabbed his arm and steadied him. "Are you all right, my friend?"

"I'll live." Sancho pushed his wet hair out of his eyes. "What about you, homes. You okay?"

"Never better."

"'Cause you like totally shut down back there, man. He brought up that stuff about your family and…" He hesitated, afraid such talk would take Flynn back to that painful place.

"I had to make Goolardo think I wasn't a threat."

"So that was all an act?" Dulcie seemed skeptical.

"Absolutely."

"But that file was real, right?" Dulcie asked. "All those pictures. Wasn't that you? Weren't those your parents?"

Flynn's self-assured smile faded and Sancho grabbed him by the arm. "That's just a cover story," Sancho said. "That's just some, you know…made up…umm…"

"Carefully constructed fabrication," Flynn continued.

"Exactly," Sancho said.

Dulcie raised a skeptical eyebrow. "A cover story?"

Sancho ignored her. "So, ese, we're not exactly home free and clear. How the hell are we gonna get back to L.A.?"

"We're not. Not yet."

"What?"

"We have a job to do and until it's done—"

"Job?" Dulcie couldn't believe it. "What the fuck are you talking about?"

"Angel Island." Flynn knocked the sand out of his shoes. "We have to warn Mr. Beckner and stop Goolardo."

"Stop Goolardo? Are you kidding me?"

"You're frightened. That's to be expected. You're not a field operative. You're—"

"Shut up!" Dulcie shouted. She turned Sancho. "Would you please talk to him."

"What do you want me to say?"

"Tell him the truth!"

"The truth is"—Flynn smoothed her damp hair off her forehead—"the fate of the world is in our hands."

She grabbed Flynn by the soggy lapels of his suit. "Listen to me, you psycho. I'm done with this, okay? I am *through*! We're lucky we're alive. You wanna go off and get yourself killed, have fun. Not me. I'm going home."

"How?"

"I don't fucking know." She looked at Sancho. "Are you coming or what?"

Sancho shook his head.

"You're going with *him*?" She pointed at Flynn.

"We can't just walk away," Sancho said.

"You're crazy as he is!"

Sancho met Flynn's gaze. "If you have nothing to die for…".

"You have nothing to live for," Flynn finished. Dulcie threw up her hands. She couldn't believe that Sancho was now as committed to this insane enterprise as Flynn.

"Fine," she said, her anger now tempered with melancholy. "Get yourself fucking killed." Tears filled her eyes.

"We better start moving." Flynn scanned the horizon. "They may already have that helicopter out looking for us. And if they find us…" He left the thought unfinished. Sancho and Dulcie looked up at the sky, suddenly fearful.

Dulcie's shoes were in the sand. Flynn picked them up and cracked off the stiletto heels. "Jesus Christ!" Dulcie said, her voice rising. "Those are Manolo Blahniks! They're like five hundred dollars a pair."

"And totally inappropriate for our purposes." Flynn threw them at her feet. "When we flew in, I noticed a small fishing village a few miles north of here." He started walking up the beach, his wet shoes squeaking with every step. Sancho followed and Dulcie angrily put on her mangled Manolo Blahniks and brought up the rear, cursing to herself quietly as she struggled not to fall behind.

Chapter Twenty-Three

The most beautiful time of day in the tiny fishing village of Puertecitos was at sunset, when the town was shrouded by the shadows of the surrounding mountains. The islands and hills across the bay would glow with a soft blue-violet light. The ramshackle houses and rusted trailers looked less run-down at twilight. The dirt roads were darker, which made it harder to see the trash and discarded auto parts. The turquoise waters of the sea dimmed to midnight blue as the sun disappeared. The islands faded away. Even the sounds grew gentler. In the daytime, you could hear mothers yelling at their crying children, howling dogs, and fishermen laughing and arguing as they cleaned their morning's catch. You could hear sea lions bark, sea gulls squawk, and blue-footed boobies whistle and squeak as they did their strange mating dance. At night, the only sounds were the waves lapping against the fishing boats and the occasionally eerie shriek of cats fighting over fish guts.

Flynn, Sancho, and Dulcie reached Peurtecitos a little after midnight. They were exhausted, having walked somewhere between five and seven miles. All Dulcie wanted to do was lie down. She couldn't take another step, but Flynn insisted they press on.

A door squeaked open and a middle-aged man stumbled outside to take a leak in the bushes in front of his shack. Many residents of San Felipe didn't enjoy the luxury of in-door plumbing. He was surprised to see Flynn, Sancho, and Dulcie walking down the narrow dirt road, dressed in elegant designer fashions. They looked like aliens from another world in their torn and dirty, wrinkled and seaweed encrusted dinner wear. Flynn nodded to the man and the man nodded back as they strolled past him.

"Do you think there's like a motel or something here?" Dulcie asked.

"I doubt it," Flynn said.

"They got phones though, right?"

"Maybe."

Flynn eyed the dilapidated docks where the fishing boats rested in their slips. There was an area with wooden tables where the fishermen cleaned their daily catch. A Pemex station with one fuel pump appeared to be boarded up. Dulcie held her nose and tried not to gag from the aroma of the quaint little pueblo. They had smelled Puertecitos a half a mile before they arrived. The stench grew stronger the closer they came, and now that they were there, the odor was almost overwhelming. It wasn't just the dead fish. It was dead fish mingled with the sickeningly sweet smell of raw sewage.

"Jesus Christ," Dulcie said with her nostrils pinched shut. "What the hell is that smell? How do people live like this?"

"They get used to it," Flynn replied.

"You never notice your own stink," Sancho pointed out.

"Maybe *you* don't," Dulcie said.

Flynn approached the docks and Sancho followed. Dulcie tagged along only because she didn't know where else to go. "We may have to borrow one of these runabouts," Flynn said.

Dulcie was not happy. "Do you even know how to drive one of these things?"

The boat Flynn selected was a forlorn-looking wooden craft with aluminum fittings. The blue paint peeled and the metal was spotted with rust, but it looked sturdy. There was a large hold for the fish, a couple of berths, and a main cabin paneled with plywood. Flynn opened a metal compartment that revealed an old engine dirty and sticky with oil.

Sancho watched Flynn try to start it up. It was clear that when it came to boats, Flynn didn't his know his ass from a poop deck. Flynn pulled levers and turned cranks, pushed buttons, and flipped switches— and the engine didn't do anything but lay there and look up at him with pretty much the same expression Dulcie gave him. Sancho's cousin had a boat and he had some experience working on it. So, unlike Flynn, he wasn't a complete nitwit when it came to things nautical. Sancho pulled out a knob, which he assumed was the choke, primed the engine, and pushed the ignition. The engine roared to life. The quiet, peaceful little pueblo suddenly wasn't so quiet.

"Jesus Christ!" Dulcie yelled. Her voice was barely audible. "You're gonna wake up the whole town!"

"What?" Flynn couldn't hear her.

"What did you say?" Sancho asked.

"The engine!"

"Who?" Flynn said.

"What does she want?" Sancho shouted.

Dulcie threw up her hands. "I'm out of here!" she screamed. But neither one could hear what she said. She stormed off the boat and jumped back to the dock.

"Where the hell is she going?" Flynn wanted to know. Sancho shook his head. He didn't hear what Flynn said.

Dulcie walked towards the little village square, still holding her nose, angrily mumbling to herself. "How the hell do I always end up with assholes? I'm like an asshat magnet. What the fuck did I ever do to deserve—" Dulcie abruptly stopped mumbling when she saw a half-dozen villagers running towards her. Six irate guys wielded crowbars, baseball bats, and machetes. She turned on her heel and ran the other way. Lights flickered on and doors crashed open. The village awoke. Dulcie raced away from shouts and running footsteps as the angry fishermen closed in on her.

"Hey!" she screamed to Flynn and Sancho as she hurried for the boat. "*Hey!*"

Sancho saw her first. He tugged on Flynn's sleeve, but James was busy looking at a nautical chart. He tugged harder and Flynn turned to him, irritated.

Sancho pointed.

Dulcie ran like her skirt was on fire. The furious villagers were right behind her, shouting at her in Spanish.

"Time to go!" Sancho shouted.

Flynn shut the top on the motor, slightly muffling the sound. He untied the boat from the dock as Sancho ran to the wheel and revved the engine. The hull banged into the dock, nearly knocking Flynn into the drink. Sancho quickly put the engine in reverse. Dulcie shimmied along the dock now, the pissed-off residents of Puertecitos almost upon her.

The boat backed away from the slip, leaving the dock, leaving Dulcie.

"Wait!" she screamed.

Flynn leaned off the front end, one hand on a fitting as his other hand reached out for Dulcie. She glanced back to see the enraged faces of the fisherman and their various improvised weapons.

"Jump!" Flynn shouted.

The gap between the front of the boat and the dock steadily increased, but Dulcie had nowhere else to go. She ran as hard as she could, which wasn't much faster than she was already running, and jumped off the end of the dock, diving hard for Flynn's hand. She missed his grasp by about a foot and hit the water with a painful belly flop. It was so loud that some of the pursuing fisherman actually winced. Dulcie immediately went under and Sancho tossed Flynn a bright orange life preserver attached to a length of rope. Flynn searched the dark surface of the water and finally saw Dulcie pop back up, coughing and screaming. He threw the life preserver like a Frisbee and it bounced off her head.

"Grab!" Flynn shouted.

She flailed for the preserver, finally caught a piece of it and pulled herself out of the water, choking and gasping and calling Flynn every curse word she knew in English and Spanish. A few of the older fisherman were shocked to hear a woman use such rough language, but most of them were too busy shouting at Flynn and Sancho to notice or care.

"Mi barco!" shouted a squat little man waving a baseball bat. "Traer detrás mi barco!"

"Don't worry!!" Flynn shouted back. "We'll be very careful with it! Tomaremos el buen cuidada do el! No preocuparte!" They slammed backwards into another docked boat and the collision nearly threw Flynn into the drink with Dulcie. The squat Mexican was jumping up and down now. His wife was right beside him with two small kids and all three were yelling at the top of their lungs. Even their ratty little dog barked at them.

Sancho put the engine into drive and turned the craft towards the open sea. Dulcie dangled off the front, barely hanging on to the life preserver. Flynn pulled her in closer, grabbed her by the top of her dress, and hauled her on board. She was wet and cold, shivering and spitting mad. "Pendejo! Why the fuck didn't you wait for me!"

"I didn't know you were coming," Flynn explained. She punched him right in the mouth. Flynn staggered back a bit and smiled at her with surprise. "That's a pretty good right cross." She swung at him again, but this time he caught the punch, holding her fist in his hand. She swung at him with her other hand and he caught that one too. "Are you through?" Dulcie slammed her knee into his groin and Flynn grunted, the condescending smile disappearing from his face.

Chapter Twenty-Four

Goolardo was preoccupied—Mendoza was just fine with that. His boss stood on a balcony outside his master suite, overlooking the dark sea, talking with someone on a satellite phone about something that had something to do with "the plan." Goolardo held up his hand to indicate that Mendoza should keep his mouth shut.

"So, we'll be ready in time." Goolardo's query was less a question and more of an order. "We need to move quickly. We can't afford to—" He frowned and his eyes flashed with anger. "That was nothing. *Nothing!* He was a nobody and he knew nothing!" Goolardo's anger barely stayed in check. "It is nothing to worry about. I just needed to be sure and now I am and now it's time to put it behind us and move forward. Okay? Adios!" Goolardo clicked off the phone and glared at Mendoza. "What the fuck happened to you?"

"There was an escape attempt."

"From who? The psycho, the puta, or the pendejo?"

"What does it matter? They're dead."

"What about the bodies?"

"No one will ever find them."

Goolardo nodded. "No one must ever know about this."

"I understand."

"You understand nothing. But that's all right. I don't pay you to understand. I pay you to do what needs to be done."

Mendoza opened his mouth to say something smart and thought better of it.

Sancho couldn't tell up from down. There was no moon and no stars. The sky was overcast and a thick fog blanketed everything. The lights on the boat penetrated only a few feet forward. It was like they floated in nothingness. The tiny vessel listed to one side as it puttered forward in the mist. The boat was taking in water from the collision back in the harbor.

Sancho watched as Flynn poured over a navigational chart like he actually knew what he was doing. Dulcie looked on, hugging herself to stay warm.

"So, what direction are we heading now?" Flynn asked.

Sancho consulted the globe compass. "According to this…south by south east." Flynn nodded and squinted at the chart. Sancho tapped the globe and the marine compass changed its reading. Now it appeared they were heading south by south west. He started to tell Flynn, but then let it go. What was the point? They were lost and they were almost out of gas and slowly sinking. Any direction they headed would take them to the same place; the bottom of the Sea of Cortez.

"Change our heading ten degrees south," Flynn instructed. "According this chart, Angel Island is about fifty miles out."

Sancho nodded and turned the wheel, but there was no way to tell which way they were going. The mist was so thick, it felt like they weren't moving at all. The only indication was the sound of the engine and the wind in their faces.

"You were skeptical before, weren't you?" Flynn steadied himself as the boat rocked. "You didn't quite believe me. But now you see what we're up against."

Sancho didn't know what to say. He glanced at Dulcie to see she was glaring at him. He looked back at Flynn.

"Look, dude, I'm all for saving the world and whatever, but first we gotta save ourselves. This boat's like sinking and we're almost out of gas and who knows where we're going."

"We're heading for Angel Island," Flynn said.

"Would you stop listening to him?" Dulcie was losing it.

"Listening to who?" Flynn asked. "Sancho?"

"You!"

"Me?" Flynn was truly perplexed.

"Jesus Christ!" She was talking to Sancho now. "Turn this goddamn boat around and take us back to that stinky ass town before he gets us all killed!"

"Just follow my lead and you'll be fine," Flynn said.

"Fine!"

"Wasn't I right about the plan?"

"No!" screamed Dulcie. "You weren't!" She was on her feet now, off-balance as the boat bounced about. "You didn't know about his plan until Goolardo told you! It's a fucking coincidence!"

"There is no such thing as coincidence. And you make your own luck. I may not have known the specifics, but that's why you do an investigation."

The boat lurched over a white cap and Dulcie almost flipped overboard. Flynn grabbed her by the arm and pulled her close. She was frantic and afraid as she shouted into his ear. "James! Jesus! Just listen to me. We have to go back! If we don't go back, we're gonna drown."

"Dulcinea—"

"No, please. Just…take us back to Puertecitos. We'll call the police. We'll call the FBI. We'll tell everybody everything. You'll still be a hero and we'll still be alive."

"I'm sorry," Flynn said. "But the police could easily be in Goolardo's employ."

"What?"

"I can't leave this to someone else. I have a responsibility."

"Please…" Tears filled her eyes.

"I've been in much more dangerous situations than this one and each time, I came out unscathed. Do you know why?" Dulcie didn't offer an answer. She was too upset. "Because I never gave up. I never gave in. As bad as things can sometimes seem, there's always—"

Just then the boat engine went dead. The gas gauge needle settled on empty. Sancho tried to restart it, but it was futile. It was official. They were screwed. Dulcie sobbed and James tenderly rubbed her back.

"One time, I was strapped to a stainless-steel table with an industrial-strength laser inching towards my scrotum. I could have given in. I could have told them everything. But I didn't. I said to the villain, do you expect me to talk? No, he said. I expect you to die." Flynn smiled. "Another time, brutal thugs threw me into a salt water swimming pool filled with hungry sharks. I was cut and there was blood in the water. I could have given up, but instead I kicked and fought and punched those sharks right in their ugly snouts. And do you know why?"

"Because you're fucking crazy."

"Maybe I am. I don't know. I do know this though. The only way to fail for certain is to surrender. As long as my heart is beating, as long as there is a breath left in my body, I know we have a chance."

Dulcie looked at Sancho, "I'm gonna fucking kill him."

"We're going to find Angel Island." Flynn tapped the map. "We're going to foil Goolardo's plan, and we're going to do it all by Friday."

The specificity of the date took Dulcie by surprise. "Why by Friday?"

"Tell her, Sancho."

"Tell her what?"

"He has a date on Saturday."

Suddenly Sancho remembered. "Oh, yeah, Alyssa." Sancho nodded, half-smiling.

"The beautiful Alyssa. The princess of El Pollo Loco," said Flynn. "You can't disappoint her now, can you? Now that you've raised her expectations?"

Dulcie extricated herself from Flynn and crossed to the other side of the boat. Defeated and demoralized, she sat on the deck and immediately realized her butt was under water. She scrambled back to her feet, adrenaline surging into her blood. "Oh, my God! We *are* sinking!"

"So, start bailing," Flynn said. "We have to stay afloat. We don't have much farther to go."

"How do you know? You don't even know where the hell we are!"

Sancho pointed at something in the distance. "What's that?"

Flynn followed his finger and smiled. "Lights. Land."

"Angel Island?"

"What else could it be?"

Dulcie saw the lights as well. "Oh, thank God!"

The lights grew larger quickly, but the engine was dead and they were out of gas. Sancho wondered how they could be traveling towards Angel Island with such velocity. The current couldn't be moving them that fast. And then he realized that they weren't moving at all. Only the lights were.

A thundering roar filled the air and Sancho looked up to see even more lights. A helicopter hovered above, blasting them with a hurricane-like wind. Sancho stumbled back, nearly blown overboard, but Flynn held him by his belt. The approaching lights belonged to three speedboats manned by men in black uniforms, armed with assault rifles. They aimed their weapons and bright red laser dots danced on Flynn, Sancho, and Dulcinea.

Flynn held his hands over his head. "That date with Alyssa…You may need to reschedule."

Three cigarette boats cut across the dark, choppy water. Each boat had twin eight hundred horsepower engines that generated speeds of up to sixty knots. Every boat held a different prisoner. Flynn found himself handcuffed and on the deck with an Israeli-made Galil assault rifle trained on his face. Besides the pilot, there were three other commandos keeping watch. With the sun peeking over the horizon, Flynn could make out the chopper hovering above. It was a Super Cobra attack helicopter with a 20 mm Gatling gun and heat-seeking Hellfire missiles.

The sun climbed even higher and the fog began to burn away, revealing Angel Island on the horizon. It was a bright coppery brown, topped with a deep verdant green. Light sandy beaches ringed its edges. Soon Flynn could make out buildings and structures and a small harbor. Buildings were in the Southern California style; stucco with red tile roofs. As they approached the harbor, the helicopter buzzed overhead and off to a helipad a short distance away.

A reception party waited for them on the docks. In the center stood a tall man in a dark suit, flanked by a dozen commandos in flak jackets. The tall man wore mirrored sunglasses. He wasn't smiling and didn't look happy to see them. Flynn and the others were led up a short ramp to where the man in the dark suit waited. He was taller than Flynn and had wide-shoulders. His voice was flat and Southern with the clipped cadence of a military man.

"Welcome to Angel Island. My name is Mr. Harper."

Chapter Twenty-Five

William Walker, an American doctor, lawyer, journalist, and mercenary, organized a private military expedition to Baja, California in 1853. His plan was to conquer the Baja peninsula and steal it away from Mexico. He commanded a force of forty-five men and managed to capture La Paz. He appointed himself President of the Republic of Lower California and held onto power for three months before being chased out of the country by the Mexican army. In his mind, he was conqueror, destined to create a new American Empire. Some saw him as a bold champion of Manifest Destiny. To others he was simply delusional.

Randall Beckner didn't need an army to take Angel Island. Just money. Even so, he never bought into the notion that "whoever dies with the most toys wins."

There were only so many toys a man could play with. He was more concerned with his legacy. His father had made a small fortune in real estate. Beckner took that small fortune and turned it into 16.2 billion dollars. He was lionized and respected, criticized and vilified and he knew that all that attention, good and bad, was simply the price of doing business. As long as he could push along his agenda, he didn't care what the press said about him. He believed in the free market and free trade, in the global economy and cheap labor. He believed that a rising tide raises all boats. Of course, if some of the boats were leaky and couldn't stay afloat, that was just too bad. That was just the natural order of things. Natural selection. Survival of the fittest. After a ninety-minute massage, a snifter of Remy Martin, and a half an Ambien, Randall Beckner teetered on the edge of sleep. The sudden thunderous roar of the helicopter pumped him with adrenalin and woke his ass right up. He stared at the ceiling. "Son of a bitch," he muttered. He considered getting up, but it was 3:00 a.m. and he needed his rest. The conference started again in six hours and he needed to be fresh. Alert. On top of his game.

He created the annual Angel Island Conference to extend his influence and cement his power—modeled it on Herbert Allen's Annual Sun Valley retreat for communication moguls and the titans of Wall Street. Ten of the richest men in the world would gather and confer and discuss the future. They'd exchange ideas and make deals, go deep sea fishing and play poker. They would give talks and have round table discussions, frolic in the surf, and get hot oil rubdowns.

Beckner believed, like most billionaires, that the reason that billionaires were billionaires was because they were smarter than mere millionaires. The fate of the world wasn't in the hands of governments or presidents or kings. It was in the hands of multinational corporations run by men like Beckner. He believed that putting all that brain power together for a week, once a year, would help not only them, but contribute to the well-being of the entire world economy.

He pulled off his CPAP mask, climbed out of bed and looked out the window to see what all the ruckus was about. There were boats and lights and security men and that damn helicopter landing on the helipad.

He brought billionaires to Angel Island to impress them. And all this commotion at 3:00 a.m. was not exactly impressive.

What *was* impressive was the centerpiece of Angel Island; his ten thousand square foot manor house built on the crest of the highest hill. Surrounding the manor house were lush landscaped grounds dotted with ten opulent guest villas, each with its own private terrace, native Mexican art, and luxurious furnishings. There were three infinity pools and four large Jacuzzi's adorned with colorful hand-crafted ceramic tiles. There were conference rooms, huge dining patios, tiki huts with rope hammocks, a driving range, and a private airport.

Beckner watched as security led three people off one of the cigarette boats. It was too far to see who they were, but he assumed they were local fisherman. They often strayed too close to the island. Guards marched them towards the security compound on the other side of the estate. It accommodated a company of one hundred commandoes. Most of the men were ex-military, now working as private contractors. Many were veterans of Iraq and Afghanistan. The structure also contained an interrogation room that doubled as a large holding cell. Beckner climbed back into bed, took the other half of the Ambien, reattached his CPAP mask, closed his eyes, and hoped for the best.

Dulcie, Flynn, and Sancho sat side by side at a long table in the interrogation room. They were damp and dirty and tired as hell. Their clothes were torn, they had bruises and scabs, and Dulcie, for one, was in desperate need of a hair brush. All three had their wrists bound in front of them with Flexi-cuff plastic handcuffs. Mr. Harper sat on the opposite side of the table. He looked relaxed as he watched Sancho and Dulcie drink water from Dixie cups. Armed commandoes stood in each corner of the room.

Flynn was agitated. "You're wasting precious time! Mr. Beckner and his guests are in great danger!"

"You claim that men are coming here to kidnap them."

"Yes! Why do we keep going over this?"

"And you're with who?"

"I told you! Her Majesty's Secret Service!"

Harper saw Dulcie roll her eyes. "What about you Miss? Are you with Her Majesty's Secret Service?"

"Yes!" Flynn said, but Dulcie shook her head no. "Dulcie, it's okay! We don't have to maintain our cover! They need to know the truth."

"And what is the truth?" Harper asked.

"I told you! What in God's name is wrong with you?"

"You wanna calm down, sir?"

Flynn started to rise and one of the commandoes forced him back down.

"He's telling you the truth!" Sancho said.

"He's a secret agent with her Majesty's Secret Service?"

"Well, no, but—"

"He has a license to kill?"

"Well, no, but the part about the kidnapping, that's totally—"

"Are *you* a member of Her Majesty's Secret Service?"

"No, dude, just listen to me—"

"You have no identification. Nothing. Just a cockamamie story about some drug dealer. For all I know you could be al-Qaeda. Or Isis. Or Hezbollah…"

"al-Qaeda?" Sancho almost laughed. "Look at me, man! I'm from East L.A.!"

"Quite a few terrorist types are coming across the border, passing themselves off as Mexicans," Harper replied.

"We have no weapons," Flynn pointed out. "If we were terrorists, wouldn't we have weapons or explosives or—"

"Maybe. Or maybe you're trying to play us. Make us think you're on our side, so we let our guard down and you can use our weapons against us."

"Are you out of your bloody mind?" Flynn asked.

Harper focused on Dulcie, who hadn't yet said a word. "Sweetheart, I know you want to tell me the truth."

"We have been!" Flynn shouted. "Why won't you listen to me!" He jumped to his feet and the armed guard pushed him back down, but this time not so gently.

Harper stood, put both hands on the table, and got in Flynn's face. "Why won't I listen to you? Because you're not making any sense! The security on this island is tighter than a nun's pussy, pardon my French, ma'am. Angel Island is impregnable. We got radar, we got gun boats, Apache helicopters, anti-aircraft guns. A mouse can't fart within ten miles of here without me knowing. It just ain't possible."

"You can't defeat Goolardo with conventional weaponry. He's using highly-advanced top-secret technology."

"What kind of technology?"

"It's top secret."

"So, you can't tell me."

"No."

"How 'bout a hint?" Harper smirked at one of the guards.

"Do you think this is a joke?"

"No, Mr. Flynn, I do not. How about I contact Her Majesty's Secret Service and see if they know who you are?"

"They will disavow any knowledge of me. It's standard procedure. I'm a double O."

"So, you can't prove who you are and nobody else can either. We are gonna be attacked by some Mexican drug dealer using cutting-edge top-secret technology that you can't tell us about. Does that pretty much sum it up?"

Flynn bolted to his feet, angry, frustrated. "He's not Mexican."

Harper looked at one of the guards and he grabbed Flynn from behind. A sap somehow appeared in Harper's hand. He brought it down hard on Flynn's collarbone. Flynn grunted and the guard shoved Flynn back into his chair. Harper was about to hit him again, when Sancho stood up to stop him. The guard slammed the butt of his rifle into the back of Sancho's head. Sancho fell to floor. Dulcie was horrified.

"I have boys here who worked in Iraq," Harper said, his voice surprisingly calm. Contractors. Interrogators. They aren't as gentle or understanding as I am. They've worked with terrorists and know what it takes to make 'em talk. So, you either stop fucking around with me, pardon my French, ma'am, or you three are gonna find yourselves in a world of hurt."

"All right," Sancho said. He was still on the floor. "We didn't tell you everything, 'cause some of it might make you think that some of us are…you know…a little crazy or something." Harper nodded to a guard and he pulled Sancho to his feet and planted him back in his chair.

"Go on."

"Sancho, the man doesn't have a high enough security clearance," Flynn whispered. "You can't just tell him—"

"You shut up," Harper said. "Or I'm gonna shut you up! You understand me, boy?"

"I work in a mental hospital in L.A. I'm an orderly. Flynn was one of the patients." Harper glanced at Flynn. Flynn wouldn't meet his gaze. Sancho's explanation came out in a rush. He talked as fast as he could to fit it all in before Harper could cut him off. "He escaped and carjacked me and we found Dulcie, who was also a mental patient. And her boyfriend kicked Flynn's ass and he stole a bunch of cash, and then later we kicked *his* ass."

"Who's ass?"

"The boyfriend's ass. But the money wasn't his. It belonged to some vato named Kursky and Flynn thought he had Q."

"Who?"

"Another patient. But he didn't and he caught us and then his boss thought Flynn knew about his plan."

"Who's boss?"

"Kursky's boss. Goolardo."

"Flynn knew about his plan?"

"No, he thought he did."

"But he didn't?"

"No, it turns out he did. But not the plan he thought he had. He had a different one."

"Who? Kursky?"

"No, Goolardo. So, he tried to kill us and we got away and stole a fishing boat because Flynn wanted to warn you."

"About what?"

"The plan!"

Harper stared at Sancho. He looked at Dulcie. He scratched his chin.

"I'm gonna take a piss, grab some coffee and have a cigarette." Harper backed for the door. "Then I'm gonna get the boys I was telling you about. Those interrogators who know how to make terrorists talk. They're gonna get you to stop fucking with me. Pardon my French, ma'am."

Harper nodded to a guard. He opened the door and Harper and the four guards left, locking the door shut behind them.

Flynn looked at Sancho. "Good try, but I don't think he bought it. That whole mental hospital cover just may be a little too hard to swallow."

"What did he mean about bringing in boys who know how to make terrorists talk?" Sancho asked.

"They're going torture us."

"T-torture us?" Dulcie's voice grew tight with fear.

"No matter what they do to us, we can't reveal the existence of Q's mind control technology," Flynn whispered. "We don't know who we can trust and who we can't. It's likely, in fact, that this room is wired for sound."

Dulcie looked like she was about to cry. "Jesus fucking Christ! This is so…fucked up."

"Why would they torture us?" Sancho was beside himself. "We can't tell them anything!"

"My point exactly," Flynn said.

"Fuuuuuuck." Sancho sat down on a chair. With his wrists Flexi-cuffed together, Dulcie watched as Flynn had to contort himself to reach into his inner jacket pocket. He retrieved his silver laser pointer. "Luckily, they neglected to confiscate this. They must have thought it was harmless."

"What is it?" Dulcie asked.

"A laser pointer," Sancho said listlessly.

"Shhh," Flynn whispered. "It looks innocent, but, in fact, houses an ultra-high-intensity laser. It's one of Q's most ingenious creations. A CO_2-based terawatt laser that breaks new ground in axial flow resonator design." Flynn turned it on aimed the red beam at the metal door. He slowly moved it across the brushed aluminum surface, tracing a square big enough for him to step through.

Dulcie sighed and looked at Sancho, who wasn't even paying attention to what Flynn was doing. "I don't understand it," Flynn whispered.

"You and me both," Dulcie said.

"It doesn't seem to be penetrating the metal. This door must be constructed out of some super-anodized titanium steel alloy."

Dulcie's eyes filled with tears as Flynn stubbornly continued to shine his laser pointer on the door.

Chapter Twenty-Six

Randall Beckner crossed his colossal terrace and admired the magnificent terrazzo floor that reflected the natural environment of the sea, the sun, and the sand. Imbedded in the floor were native shells, slivers of sea glass, semi-precious stones gathered from the beach, and hand-painted ceramic tiles. The terrace extended off the east side of the manor house and overlooked the small harbor and the Sea of Cortez. There were fruit trees and flower beds and a five-foot-tall burbling fountain made of granite and copper. The bright early morning sun was partially shaded by the long white pergola that covered half of the veranda. Below it was a long, glass-topped table made of teak surrounded by chairs filled with the butts of billionaires. The table was laden with platters of indigenous fruit, pitchers of freshly squeezed orange juice, bottles of Veuve Clicquot, and silver carafes steaming with dark, Mexican coffee. Small Mexican servants wearing white, flitted about unobtrusively, serving the billionaires their preferred breakfast foods.

Eighty-three-year-old media mogul, Quinton Blackstone, looked with horror upon Richard Cook's full English breakfast. "What the hell is that?"

"Poached eggs, baked beans, smoked kippers, black pudding, and a bit of bubble and squeak," Cook said as he cut into a kipper with relish.

"Those runny eggs and beans are bad enough," seventy-nine-year-old Warren Davis said. "But those little kipper fish are fricken' scary-looking. And what the hell's black pudding?"

"It's coagulated pig blood," Rupert Breen chuckled. "Mixed with fat, suet, barley, and oatmeal. It's an English delicacy."

"Also known as an oxymoron," joked fifty-one-year-old Prince Adnan Bin Hasan.

"Well at least the English don't eat that nasty Vegemite," Cook said. "That's strictly an Australian delicacy."

Sergei Belenki, at thirty-five, the youngest member of the group, munched on a breakfast burrito and asked, "What *is* vegemite exactly?"

"A brownish, salty paste made from brewer's yeast and mashed marsupials," Cook replied.

Warren Davis laughed and tucked into his blueberry pancakes.

"It's no worse than that nasty Marmite," Lakshmi Mandar added. The fifty-eight-year-old info-tech king, currently residing in London, unfolded his napkin

"I think we need to stop teasing Sir Richard about his breakfast," Davis said. "He needs to keep his strength up if he's going make another attempt to circumnavigate the globe by hot air balloon."

Most of the billionaires laughed, including Cook.

"Yes," Breen said. "Don't let us put you off your bubble and squeak. A man with your death-defying hobbies needs all the energy he can get."

"So does a man married to a hot wife fifty years his junior," Cook cracked.

"Guilty as charged." Breen smiled with satisfaction. "My dear Natalie has perfected the art of making an old man happy. Not an easy task."

"I would agree with that," Quinton Blackstone mumbled.

Warren Davis chuckled. Sergei Belenki checked his Blackberry.

Eighty-something Ingvar Knudson, the Swedish born real estate tycoon, didn't crack a smile. He did, however, crack the top on a single boiled egg. Like Warren Davis, and seventy-nine-year-old Hong Kong Billionaire, Li Chu Young, Ingvar was a man who lived modestly. He drove a fifteen-year-old Volvo and only traveled economy class. Davis lived in the same house in Kansas City that he bought in 1958 for thirty-two thousand dollars. Li Chu Young favored cheap shoes and plastic watches. He was the tenth richest man in the world since the death of Canadian Kenneth Thomson, the baron of Fleet Street.

Software mogul Bill Munson poked at his eggs. "These seem a little runny." He tapped Li Chu Young on the shoulder. "Do these seem a little runny to you?" The Hong Kong business man shrugged as Munson handed the plate to one of the Mexican servants. "I think these are a little runny."

Randall Beckner smiled at his assembled guests. He wore perfectly pressed chinos and a blue, silk, Guayabera shirt. He was tall and slim and slightly balding. As the President of Beckner International, he was the fifth richest man in the U.S., and the seventh wealthiest in the world. He approached the head of the table and one of the Mexican servants pulled out his chair. But he didn't sit; he just stood there, smiling down the length of the table.

"Good morning, gentlemen. Welcome to day three at Hacienda Del Beckner. I trust you all slept well?" Three billionaires nodded, three smiled, one frowned, and three didn't pay any attention at all. "We have a lunch meeting at 1:00 p.m. with the head of the Federal Reserve. Before then, may I suggest some snorkeling or tennis or, for those less athletically inclined…" Beckner clapped his hands and half a dozen stunningly beautiful Asian women walked out onto the terrace in single file. "Direct from Phuket, six of Thailand's most accomplished masseuses, expert in Shiatsu, Swedish, and exotic Tantric techniques."

Sergei Belenki grinned. Bookish and bespectacled Bill Munson looked like a startled deer, staring into six very bright headlights. "Are we talking happy endings here?" Quinton Blackstone queried.

"Gentleman, you are the authors of your own destiny, so the ending is entirely up to you," Beckner said. "Our hacienda spa also offers an astonishing Fig and Cassis Body scrub, a detoxifying hot tub, chakra balancing, and the very latest in aromatherapy."

"For those who believe in that sort of bullcrap," Warren Davis said.

"Exactly," Beckner replied. "But then one man's bullcrap is another man's belief system." Beckner was about to sit down to breakfast when he noticed Harper standing by the entrance to the terrace. "Excuse me, gentleman. I have something to attend to. I promise you, I'll be right back."

As the billionaires buttered their various types of toast, Beckner crossed over to where Harper stood.

"Sorry to disturb you, sir," Harper said. "But about last night…"

"More lost fishermen from San Felipe?"

"No, sir. Actually, the trespassers claim to be U.S. citizens."

"Lost?"

"I don't think so, sir."

"So, what are they doing here?"

"That's what I intend to find out, sir. I just wanted to keep you in the loop."

"Can you do something else for me, Harper? Can you figure out a way to do your job without making such a goddamn production out of it? That helicopter woke up not only me, but most of my guests."

"Sorry, sir."

"That kind of commotion makes my guests nervous. Which is exactly the opposite of what I'm striving for here. If they're not relaxed and open, they can't be creative, innovative and inspired. Do you understand what I'm saying?"

"Yes, sir. I'm very sorry, sir. It won't happen again."

"I think we're done here."

"Yes, sir." Harper started to salute, caught himself, and nodded curtly before turning on his heel and heading off. Beckner returned to his guests and his breakfast. When he saw that the masseuses were still standing there, smiling awkwardly, he clapped twice and motioned for them to go. As they filed away, Rupert Breen caught the eye of the tallest of the tiny beauties. He waved at her with a baby banana while Bill Munson carefully sniffed a piece of pineapple.

Flynn heard someone approach the holding cell door. He quickly turned off his laser pointer and slid it into his back pocket as the door clanked open and Harper walked inside. He was followed by four hulking commandos and a squat muscular man in camouflage pants and a tight black t-shirt. The muscular man carried a nasty looking stun baton. It was black and thick and eighteen inches long. The short muscular man flicked a switch on its base and six electric arcs danced around, crackling with a flickering blue light that filled Dulcie with terror.

"Mr. Dugan is carrying an Omega Star Warrior Baton," Harper said. "It delivers a charge of one hundred and fifty thousand volts. Now, I'll give you one more opportunity to come clean, Mr. Flynn. The only question you need to ask yourself is how much pain do I want to suffer? Personally, I don't like this kind of thing. I prefer less brutal methods of interrogation. But Mr. Beckner is not a patient man."

"I've been worked over by the best, Mr. Harper. I've been stripped naked and tied to a bottomless chair and beaten about the scrotum for hours. I didn't talk then and I won't talk now. I'm here to help to you. If you can't see that then I don't know what to tell you."

Becker looked at the man in the camouflage pants. "All right, Mr. Dugan, let's get it done."

A commando took each of Flynn's arms and forced him into a chair. A third soldier produced a roll of duct tape and wound it around Flynn, fastening him tight.

"Let him go!" Dulcie screamed. She stepped forward to stop them and Dugan blocked her with the stun baton. The arcing electricity crackled less than an inch from her frightened face.

"Sit *down!*" Harper ordered. Dulcie immediately sat on the floor, cowed and docile. Sancho watched sadly from his chair. There was nothing he could do either, and he knew it.

"Mr. Harper," Flynn's voice was firm and not the least bit afraid. "When you finally realize that all I've been trying to do here today is help you, you will feel quite foolish."

Flynn's scream reverberated off the walls, high-pitched and raw. After five
seemingly endless seconds, Dugan pulled back the baton and Flynn's head slumped forward, his body shaking and twitching involuntarily.

"You're killing him!" Dulcie screamed.

"No, lassie, I'm simply encouraging him," Mr. Dugan countered. He had an Irish accent and that, combined with his tiny size, created the impression of a sadistic leprechaun. "The electricity is overwhelming Mr. Flynn's natural nerve impulses, causing his muscles to contract at an insane rate of speed. This instantly converts his blood sugar to lactic acid, causing intense pain and muscle cramping. He's disoriented and more passive as you can see, but he's in no danger, unless of course he has a heart problem."

"Mr. Dugan," Flynn's voice was hoarse from screaming. "I detect a Northern Irish accent. Ulster is it?"

"Indeed," Dugan said.

He pushed the stun baton directly into Flynn's groin and Flynn wailed even louder this time; a ragged, hair-raising shriek of animal agony. Dulcie screamed along with Flynn, tears streaming down her face. Flynn literally pissed himself as he continued to twitch and spasm. Spit dribbled from his open mouth and he looked like someone you'd find strapped to a table in a mental hospital after a lobotomy.

Dulcie looked at Sancho to see him fighting tears. "Fucking cowards," Sancho said.

"You're next, Mr. Perez," Harper replied. "But this is Mr. Flynn's turn. Unless, of course, he's had enough of this and is now ready to tell us the truth."

Flynn struggled to control his twitching and lifted his head to glance at Harper. He smiled at Dugan.

"You want the truth?" Flynn said. "It's simply this…" His voice was very hoarse now and difficult to hear, so Harper and Dugan had to lean in closer. "They're always after me Lucky Charms."

Dugan lost it and slapped the baton against the side of Flynn's head. Electricity ripped through his skull and every tendon stood out on Flynn's neck. His shriek was so shockingly loud, no one heard the door open. Not until Flynn stopped screaming, could they finally hear the young commando standing in the doorway.

"Sir, I'm sorry to disturb you…"

Harper seemed irritated by the interruption. "Spit it out, Jackson. What is it?"

"Some sort of vessel has surfaced in the harbor."

"What do you mean surfaced?"

"It looks like some kind of mini-sub."

Flynn glanced past Dugan and caught Sancho's eye. "So, it's begun."

"What the hell are you talking about?" Harper growled. "*What* has begun?"

"Goolardo. He's here."

Harper glanced at Dugan. "We'll pick this up later." He turned to Jackson. "You stand guard right outside this door. No one goes in or out." He left the room without another word. Dugan followed along with young Jackson and the other commandos. The metal door slammed shut. Sancho heard the deadbolt click.

Dulcie immediately went to Flynn and lifted his chin. Even though he was still mildly twitching, he offered her a rakish smile. "Do you think could unfasten me?"

Dulcie found the end of the gaffer tape and started to unwind him from the top. Sancho worked on his legs. After a minute or so, Flynn was free. He tried to stand and staggered off balance, dizzy, weak. Sancho helped him back into the chair.

"Just chill, muchacho."

"But Goolardo's here. He has to be stopped."

"How's he gonna get past Harper and his private army? The dude doesn't stand a chance."

"Don't be so certain. Harper has the men and arms and equipment, but Goolardo's exceedingly clever." Flynn retrieved his laser pointer from his jacket pocket.

Sancho sighed and caught Dulcie's eye. "It's all right," Dulcie whispered. "It'll keep him occupied."

Flynn flicked it on and aimed the red beam at the frame around the door. "If it doesn't work on the door itself, perhaps it'll cut through the surrounding structure," Flynn said. Slowly, methodically, he moved the red dot of light on the wall around the door.

Dulcie heard something that sounded like a siren. It was very faint, but continuous. "Do you hear that—"

Sancho nodded.

"That's an alarm," Flynn said.

Chapter Twenty-Seven

Beckner and the other billionaires were just finishing breakfast when the alarm sounded. The pneumatic horn fractured the air, painfully vibrating eardrums everywhere. Rupert Breen leaped to his feet with his hands over his ears. "What the hell is that?"

Beckner, shouted over the siren, "That is the sound of someone who is about to be fired."

"Is there some sort of security breach?" Lee Chu Young asked.

"Probably just another local fisherman who drifted off course," Beckner said. "I'm sure it's nothing to worry about."

"Your men don't seem to think so." Breen was standing near the edge of the veranda, looking down upon the harbor. The other billionaires joined him and were not reassured by the sight that greeted them.

A black mini-submarine slowly cruised towards the docks. Over a hundred commandos armed with sniper rifles, assault weapons, and Stinger missiles were poised and in position to take the craft out.

"What the hell is happening here, Beckner?" The CEO of Blackstone Communications was clearly irritated.

Beckner shook his head. He had no answer.

In the corridor outside the holding cell, the young commando guarding the prisoners, heard someone pounding on the door from the inside.

"What's going on in there?" he shouted.

The pounding stopped. A moment later it started up again. He was told to guard the holding cell even though he knew all hell was breaking loose in the harbor. He wanted to be where the action was. He wanted to shoot a Stinger missile and blow shit up. But instead he was stuck inside here, guarding who knows who. The constant pounding was beginning to concern him. What the hell were they doing in there? Were they trying to break through the wall?

"Hey! What's that racket?" The pounding stopped. Silence. Thirty seconds later, it started up again. He grabbed the keys off the hook on the wall and unlocked the deadbolt. The pounding halted again, but he didn't care. He drew his 9mm, released the safety, and kicked the door open.

The door banged into Dulcie who bumped into Flynn who instinctively hid the laser pointer behind his back. Sancho stood stock still.

"What do you have there?" the young guard demanded.

"Nothing," Flynn said.

"It's gotta be something."

"It's nothing."

"Let me see it."

"There's nothing to see."

The guard stepped past Sancho and Dulcie and aimed his pistol at Flynn's face. "I'll strip you naked and do an anal search if you don't show me what the hell you're hiding."

"It's just a laser pointer," Sancho said.

"Show me."

Flynn reached into his pocket and came out with the laser pointer. Turning it on, he shined the beam in the guard's eyes. The young commando angrily grabbed it as Flynn hooked his foot behind his leg and brought him down. The guard fired. A slug tore into the wall, inches from Sancho's head. The sound was deafening. Dulcie stood stunned as Flynn kicked the pistol right out of the young man's hand. The weapon skittered across the floor and Sancho scooped it up. The astonished commando immediately raised his arms. Flynn took the gun from his compadre and aimed it at the young man's nose.

"What the hell are you doing?" Dulcie said.

"Escaping," Flynn replied. "Hands on the wall. *Now!*" The young commando sighed and turned and put his hands against the wall. Flynn kicked his feet apart to throw him off balance. "Dulcie! Cuff him!"

"What?"

"The plastic handcuffs on his belt. Bind his wrists behind him." Dulcie reluctantly cuffed him. "Now do his legs."

When the commando was trussed and still standing with his feet fastened together, Flynn peered out the open door into the hallway.

"You're on an island in the middle of nowhere," the young commando said. He was smiling, trying to be cocky, but it wasn't really working. "You got no place to go and nowhere to hide."

"He's right," Dulcie said.

"They got an army out there."

"What if they do?" Flynn said.

"They'll kill you," Dulcie answered.

"They'll try to," Flynn replied.

Flynn noticed the laser pointer on the floor. The beam was on and shining on Flynn's foot. "I'm going to have to talk to Q about that laser device. It is seriously underpowered." He set the pistol down and used the folding knife on the young commando's belt to cut the plastic handcuffs off Sancho and Dulcie. Sancho returned the favor.

"Come on, man, don't go out there alone," Sancho pleaded.

"I wasn't planning to," said Flynn as he picked up the pistol. "I assumed you were coming with me."

"Me?"

Flynn handed Sancho the young commando's knife. "Dulcie, you stay put."

Before she could answer him, Flynn was gone. Sancho peered into the hallway. "Fuck me," he said as he followed after Flynn.

"Hey!" Dulcie shouted.

"Get me out of these!" The young commando looked desperate and embarrassed.

"Yeah, right," Dulcie replied. She took off after Flynn and slammed the door.

Harper stood on the dock, flanked by twelve stone-faced commandos. He watched with curiosity as the mini-sub approached. A hatch opened with a hiss and Harper watched as a man emerged wearing black combat fatigues, shiny black boots, and a jaunty black beret. He was followed by two large thugs and an even bigger thug, who had to struggle to squeeze his massive body through the hatch. All were dressed in the same black fatigues as their boss.

"Thank you for the rousing welcome, gentlemen," the man in the beret said.

Harper stepped forward. "And you are?"

"Francisco Goolardo and this is my associate, Mr. Mendoza. We're here to pick up Mr. Beckner and his guests."

"And what if they don't want to go with you?"

"I'm afraid they have no choice." Goolardo saw the billionaires watching from the terrace and offered them a friendly wave. "But I can assure you, they will be very comfortable. This isn't just any luxury submersible. This is the Nautilus 1000."

"You do realize that you're surrounded by over a hundred armed men."

Goolardo chuckled. "I do indeed."

"That's funny to you?"

"What's funny is the fact that you're all dead men walking and you don't even know it."

"Excuse me?"

"Funny more to me than you, obviously."

"Pardon me, if I appear to be dense, sir. But you gentlemen don't seem to be armed."

"Nevertheless, if you don't comply with my demands, you all will be dead in two hours' time."

Harper almost smiled, but something about the look on Goolardo's face told him this was no joke. "Why *two* hours? Why not just take us out now?"

"I can tell by your question that you don't believe me. I'm being too vague, aren't I? Sorry. It's just that I love the drama. The rising tension. The suspense. But time is at a premium, so perhaps we should get down to brass tacks."

Goolardo stepped closer and Harper raised the barrel of his gun. Goolardo pushed it away with his finger and said, "There is a sous chef who works in your kitchen. An assistant. His name is Armando, and last month I kidnapped his entire family; his parents, his grandparents, his wife, and his five children. He was told that they would all die if he didn't do something for me." Harper's eyes flickered with apprehension. "Good. I see I have your attention now." Goolardo paused, relishing the fact that Harper now hung on his every word. "Last night Armando poisoned your entire water supply per my instructions. The toxin is quite virulent. It can be ingested or absorbed through the skin. So, whether you drank some water, washed your face, or simply brushed your teeth, you have introduced this toxin into your system."

The stone-faced commandos were suddenly not so stone-faced.

"Poison?" Harper asked.

"It's an extremely rare bio-toxin. Unbelievably deadly. In two hours' time, everyone on this island will be dead." The faces of the commandos were now deathly white. "At first you'll suffer flu-like symptoms. Nausea. Dizziness. Diarrhea. Soon after that you'll lose control of your limbs, then your mind, then you will bleed out of every orifice you have. I understand that at the end, it's quite grotesque."

"If what you say is true, then why the hell wouldn't I just shoot you?"

"Because I have access to an antidote and I'll supply you and everyone on this Island with it. But only if you do exactly as I say."

Harper didn't know what to believe. He searched Goolardo's eyes, looking for some hint, something that would tell him what to do.

"Of course," Goolardo said. "Your other option is blow my head off and rush everyone to the mainland. You may not have time to make it to the States, but I'm sure you could reach the finest hospital in Baja. The doctors will do their tests and when they finally determine why it is you're dying…it will be too late. At least they'll be able to make your last minutes a little more comfortable."

Harper was starting to sweat. Fine beads broke out on his forehead. It was only seconds, but it felt like hours before he finally he said, "And what if I don't believe you?"

"Then you and everyone on Angel Island will die a painful and hideous death."

Sancho struggled to keep up with Flynn as he charged straight up a steep hill directly behind the security compound. Dulcie struggled even more. It was a dry island, so there was very little vegetation for them to hide behind. They slipped on the loose dirt and grabbed whatever scruffy native plants they could get their hands on as they scrambled up the hill. There were no commandos or guards patrolling the area, for they were focused on the confrontation in the harbor.

Flynn headed for the back door of the Manor House and Sancho called to him, sucking wind something bad, "Dude, where you going? We gotta find some place to lay low until this bullshit blows over."

"I have to talk to Mr. Beckner."

"Are you kidding me?"

"He's in danger. They all are."

"I'm sure Harper has it under control…"

The backdoor was unlocked and Flynn walked in like he owned the place, disappearing inside. Sancho sighed and followed after and found himself in the Manor House kitchen. The cooks and dishwashers looked very surprised to see him.

"You see a white guy in a suit?" Sancho asked in Spanish. "He's about this tall." Sancho lifted his hand to show how tall Flynn was, not realizing he still had the knife. Petrified, they all pointed towards a door. Sancho hurried after Flynn and Dulcie hurried after Sancho.

They climbed the stairs to the second floor and headed down an ornate corridor. A terrified maid burst out of a room and bumped into

Sancho. She shrieked and ran even faster when she saw the knife in his hand, her little legs pumping as she brushed by Dulcie.

Sancho peered in the door she burst from to find a master suite. He also found Flynn opening a large set of French doors. They were polished mahogany and led to a balcony above the terrace where the billionaires were breakfasting. The titans of industry were all watching the confrontation in the harbor. Sancho and Dulcie joined Flynn on the balcony. They were much too far away to hear what Harper was saying to Goolardo. They could, however, make out Mendoza. Over a hundred commandos surrounded the area and every weapon was aimed at Goolardo and his miniscule crew.

"Look, ese! They got 'em! Dude's going down. Big time."

Goolardo's smile faded into something ugly and mean. He held Harper's steely gaze. "Tell your men to put down their weapons."

Harper's stare didn't waver. He didn't like surrender, but what if this battle was already over? What if he was dying? What if his men were already dead? "I don't think I can," he said.

"Do you feel nauseous? A slight dizziness? The symptoms will soon be quite apparent, Mr. Harper. Don't wait until it's too late."

Harper looked at his men. Each one was brave and resolute. Every one of them would die for him without question. He turned around farther to see the billionaires on the terrace. Personally, he didn't give a rat's ass about any of them. He hated rich bastards like that, but he was hired to protect them. That was the mission and he was ex-Delta Force, and Delta Force always completes the mission.

Sancho watched as Harper shouted an order loud enough for him to hear. "Put down your weapons!" Harper's men hesitated. They seemed confused. Harper shouted the order again. This time louder, with an edge of anger. "*Put down your weapons!*"

Harper's men complied. Over one hundred weapons were laid on the ground; assault rifles, machine guns, pistols, and Stinger missiles.

"What the hell are they doing?" Sancho was stunned.

"They are in Goolardo's psychic grip," Flynn said.

"Oh, my God," Dulcie hissed. "He's right, it's…"

"Mind control," Sancho said with amazement. He looked at Flynn with wonderment. James had the guard's Glock in his hand and it was pointed towards the sky. "Dude, what are you—"

Boom!! The pistol shot echoed in the relative silence. Goolardo, Mendoza, Harper, his men, and the billionaires, all turned to see James Flynn standing on the balcony high above them.

"Mr. Harper!" Flynn shouted. "Your mind is under the control of Francisco Goolardo!"

Everyone was surprised to see Flynn on that balcony. But no one was more surprised than Goolardo. He glowered at Mendoza, who looked mortified. "I thought you said he was dead."

"You must fight to free your mind!" Flynn shouted. "Mr. Harper! You can do it! Don't let them win!"

Flynn aimed the Glock at Goolardo and squeezed the trigger. The pistol jumped and Goolardo could hear the bullet whiz over his head.

He crouched and glared at Harper, his voice a sinister hiss. "If he kills me, he kills you!"

"Arm yourselves!!" shouted Harper.

Harper picked up his rifle and his men followed suit and Flynn grinned. "Yes! That's it! Fight!"

But then Harper and his men turned around and aimed their weapons at Flynn. "Shoot that stupid son of a bitch!" Harper shouted.

"Fuck," was all Sancho was able to say before everyone started firing.

Flynn, Sancho, and Dulcie retreated back into the master suite as bullets tore into the manor house, shattering the French doors. A Stinger missile took out the balcony. It exploded in a fireball and flaming pieces rained down on the terrace. The billionaires scattered, scrambling for cover.

Flynn, Dulcie, and Sancho hurried down the spiral staircase to the first floor just as a dozen commandos came bursting through the front doors. Flynn changed direction and immediately ran back up the staircase, taking the steps two at a time. Bullets ripped into the mahogany banister. Sancho and Dulcie scrambled to keep up. They reached the second floor and skedaddled down the corridor. The boots of the commandos echoed up the stairs as they charged after them.

Flynn found an open door at the end of the hall. He dashed inside and motioned for Sancho and Dulcie to hurry. He slammed the door shut and lodged a chair under the knob. They could hear the commandos stampeding closer, their boots clomping down the corridor.

Flynn quickly opened a small window, grabbed Dulcie, and pushed her through. He climbed out after her, but it was a tight fit. "Come on, Sancho!" Sancho was considerably wider than Flynn, especially in the ass department. He simply couldn't get his butt through the window frame. The commandos pounded on the door as Flynn pulled and Sancho pushed. The pounding grew louder and Sancho couldn't believe that his fat ass was going to be the cause of his demise. He wiggled, he grunted, but what finally propelled his posterior through the window was the sound of the door crashing open.

Flynn pulled him free and the momentum sent them both tumbling down the slanted roof. Dulcie slid after them, skidding and bumping over the bright red tiles, right off the edge.

Back on the dock, Mendoza mumbled some feeble explanation as Goolardo glared at him. "He drove right off the damn cliff. It was like two hundred feet down. There's no way anyone could survive that."

"Yet apparently, he did," Goolardo said.

"I don't know how."

"Well, that's rather obvious, isn't it?"

"I just thought—"

"The man is a menace."

"He's just a nutjob. A headcase."

"Yes," Goolardo said. "And that's exactly what makes him so very dangerous."

Chapter Twenty-Eight

Blood covered Randall Beckner's blue silk Guayabera shirt. He hid, on his hands and knees, beneath the long mahogany table on his veranda. Squatting beside him, looking wide eyed and terrified, was Bill Mumson of Mumson Microsystems. It was Mumson who pointed out the blood. Mumson didn't actually say anything. He just pointed wordlessly with tears brimming in his eyes. At first Beckner wasn't sure whose blood it was. He was too full of fear to feel any pain. And then he felt the shredded material and realized that the blood belonged to him. He was injured, but not too badly. At least he didn't think so.

"Is everyone all right?" he shouted.

"You bloody asshole," Rupert Breen yelled. He was on his belly on the far side of the terrace and he looked pissed.

"Let's not panic," Lakshmi Mandar said in a panicky voice. He was crouched by the wall with a pasty-faced Warren Davis.

"If I want to panic," Breen said. "I'll bloody well panic!"

"My arm's bleeding!" Sergei Belenki sounded like he was about to cry.

"I'm gonna sue your bloody ass off!" Breen shouted.

"Just stay calm," Beckner pleaded. "Everyone just keep calm. My security force will be here any second now."

"Your security force is who fucking shot at us," Quinton Blackstone barked. He hid under a portico with Richard Cook and Prince Adnan Bin Hassan.

Beckner started to crawl out from under the table when he heard rifle fire from inside the manor house. He ducked and crawled back under. Bill Mumson was trying to tell him something. His mouth was working, but no words came out. Beckner smelled something very unpleasant. What the hell was that? And then he realized that one the richest men in the world probably just pooped his pants.

"What I want to know," Prince Adnan said. "Is where the bloody hell is *my* private security detail?"

"They're being detained." Harper's voice was calm and firm as he marched out onto the veranda with a detail of ten men, all armed with assault weapons.

"Thank God," Beckner sighed as he crawled out from under the table on his hands and knees and pulled himself to his feet. "What the hell is going on here?"

"I'm sorry, sir, but we have ourselves a situation."

"Who's detaining my men?" the Prince demanded.

"That's not really germane to the subject at hand," Harper said.

"What the bloody hell is happening!" Breen was on his feet and in Harper's face.

"Sir, back off right now."

"I will not back off!"

"Back off or I will put a bullet in your face!"

"Do you know who the bloody hell I—"

Harper fired his weapon right over Breen's head. The rifle's report was staggeringly loud and Breen immediately shut his mouth and backed the hell off. He looked stunned. Confused. Terrified. "Thank you for shutting your fucking piehole, Mr. Breen!" Harper's voice was almost as loud as his weapon. No one said a word. More automatic weapon fire could be heard inside the manor house. "If you do exactly as I say, none of you will die."

"Are you working for them?" The question came from Beckner. He looked hurt and horrified.

"No, sir, I work for you. But time is running out and if we don't end this discussion right the fuck now, you are not gonna make it. So, let's go! Now!"

"I need to change my pants." It was Mumson. He was still under the table.

Harper ignored him and shouted orders to his men. "Grab your man and move! Now!"

The commandos swarmed across the terrace, each one grabbing a different billionaire. They all followed Harper into the manor house. Bill Mumson was the last one out. He shuffled forward slowly with his thighs squished together and said sotto voce, "I really need to change my pants.

Dulcie was done. This whole being rescued thing just wasn't working out. She hadn't exactly been happy with Mike. He was abusive and mean and selfish and stupid. He was a lousy lover; clumsy and rough and only concerned with his own pleasure. He never wanted go to a movie or out to dinner. He could be condescending and just plain cruel, but she knew that Mike loved her in his own fucked up way. He kept a roof over her head, food in the fridge, and all the chronic and crystal she could do. It wasn't perfect. It wasn't even good. But it was a whole hell of a lot better than being with this fucking nutjob. At least when she was with Mike she wasn't being kidnapped by drug lords and driven off cliffs. Her life with Mike consisted of lots of boredom punctuated with brief moments of pleasure and longer moments of pain and loneliness, but at least it was predictable.

Dulcie mulled this over as she sat in a smelly garbage dumpster with Sancho and James, hiding from Harper's security men. The smell was worse than any stink she'd ever encountered. She gagged. Finally, it was too much. Death would be a welcome relief. She abruptly stood, straining to lift the lid.

"Dulcie, sit down," Flynn ordered.

"Fuck you." The lid fell back with a loud clank and she clambered out, falling into the dirt. She stood up, still gagging, and brushed off the garbage and maggots clinging to her dress.

Flynn climbed out after her. "You're right. For all we know Goolardo could already be spiriting away his targets."

Sancho stayed in the dumpster and said, "I'm not going fucking anywhere."

"Stay put then, amigo. Dulcie, I appreciate your enthusiasm, but you're not a field agent either. You have neither the training nor the constitution for it. You'd be better off here with Sancho."

"I don't think so," Dulcie said.

"Fine," Flynn replied. "You can come with me, but only if you do exactly as I say."

"How 'bout I don't," Dulcie said. "How 'bout you go do whatever crazy fucking thing you want and I'll find my own way out of here."

"Good thinking. That way if one of us is caught, the other still has a chance to complete the mission."

"Whatever," Dulcie muttered. She started to walk away and then stopped. Tears filled her eyes and that only made her angrier.

Flynn saw how emotional she was and put his hand on her shoulder. "You're upset."

"No shit."

"I know it seems bad, but you know what Winston Churchill said about surrender?" When Dulcie expressed zero interest in Flynn's pop quiz, he continued, "Success is not final, failure is not fatal: it is the courage to continue that counts." Dulcie turned her back on Flynn and angrily walked away. "Good girl! That's the spirit. Never say die!"

Harper and his squad escorted the billionaires down to the docks where Goolardo waited with Mendoza. Goolardo smiled at the frightened billionaires. Beckner was out in front with Harper. Breen was still furious, but kept his mouth shut. Mumson shuffled the slowest as his tighty whities carried a full load.

"Welcome gentlemen, and thank you for interrupting your busy schedule," Goolardo's voice was crisp and cheerful.

"Who the bloody hell are you?" Breen asked.

"Your kidnapper."

The billionaires looked bewildered. Beckner turned to Harper, his eyes full of hurt and reproach. "You *sold* me out!"

Goolardo smiled at Harper. "You didn't tell them?"

"Didn't want to take the time," Harper said.

"I think we can spare two minutes to tell them why they're coming with me."

"Coming with you?" Sergei Belenki started at the mini-sub with trepidation. "On that?"

"Indeed gentlemen."

"No bloody fucking way," Breen announced.

"Then you'll have to do without the antidote, Mr. Breen."

"Antidote?" Three of the billionaires said the word simultaneously.

"To the bio-toxin in your system. I won't go into detail as to how it got there. Suffice it to say, if you don't come with me rather quickly, your chances of survival decrease exponentially."

Sancho felt nauseous and foolish sitting all alone in the dumpster. The tension of sitting there in the dark waiting for someone to find him became unbearable. He hadn't heard a single gunshot for quite some time. What if everyone was dead? He lifted the dumpster lid and looked around. He didn't hear a sound.

"Fuck it," he mumbled and climbed out. At first, he wasn't sure which way to go. Finally, he decided to head for the docks. Maybe there was a loose dinghy he could jack.

He hiked around the side of the Manor House, staying close to the landscaping so as not to be seen. Soon he could hear voices, actually one voice. A loud irritated elderly Aussie who sounded like he was about to pop a blood vessel.

Sancho hid behind a pineapple plant and watched the showdown between Goolardo and the billionaires fifty yards away. He couldn't actually hear what anyone was saying, just the occasional shouted curse from the angry Aussie. He looked around for guards or commandos and caught sight of James Flynn darting out from behind a banana tree. Flynn moved in a serpentine fashion, staying low to the ground, running quickly from one clump of shrubbery to the next. Like a ninja. Like a Comanche warrior. Like a mental patient. He was graceful and swift and he appeared to be making his way towards the helicopter.

"Oh shit. Oh no," Sancho mumbled. The chopper was parked on its helipad and there was one lone commando guarding it. The soldier wasn't paying much attention to anything but the heated discussion on the docks. Sancho almost shouted a warning as Flynn snuck up behind the commando and put him in a choke hold, rendering him unconscious. "Oh, shit. Oh, no..."

Sancho was already running as Flynn climbed into the Apache Attack Helicopter. What the hell was he doing? He wanted to shout to him, but he didn't want to draw any unnecessary attention. He could see Flynn pushing buttons and pulling levers.

"James!" It was a loud whisper; not loud enough for Harper and his men to hear. Unfortunately, it wasn't loud enough for Flynn to hear either. The chopper rumbled to life. The rotor blade spun and the sound caught the attention of Harper, Goolardo, and all ten billionaires.

Sancho finally reached the chopper to find Flynn still fiddling with the controls. "*What the hell are you doing?*" Sancho had to shout to be heard over the loud thwacking of the rotor blade.

"He's not getting away!" Flynn yelled.

"Who?"

"Goolardo!"

"Dude, he's in a submarine!"

Flynn thought about this for a moment. "That's a good point!"

"Plus, you don't know how to fly this thing!"

"That's where you're wrong, my friend! I may not have flow this particular model, but—"

"Dude!" Sancho was staring at six commandos charging up the hill for the helipad. "Let's talk about this somewhere else!"

"Hop in!" Flynn patted the seat next to him.

The commandos moved as one, their faces grim, their eyes cold. Sancho had to make a split-second decision. He could die in a hail of rifle fire or crash and burn in a helicopter. It wasn't much of a choice, and Sancho made his decision more from instinct than careful consideration. He clambered up into the copter. The commandos were less than twenty feet away. They raised their weapons.

Sancho screamed, "Get this fucking thing out of here!" Flynn pulled back on a lever and pushed a big red button. Sancho heard a loud hiss and rush of exhaust as two sidewinder missiles were suddenly launched.

"Oops," Flynn said.

The commandos hit the dirt as the missiles zoomed right at them, just missing them. Sidewinders are heat seekers and Goolardo's luxurious mini-submarine had twin 300 horsepower turbocharged marine diesel engines. The next largest source of heat near the docks was Mendoza. Luckily for him, the engines generated a much higher core temperature. As stunned as Mendoza was, he was still able to appreciate the look of dumbfounded shock on Goolardo's face when the two sidewinders plowed into his twenty-million-dollar submarine.

The explosion was intense, creating a massive fireball and shockwave that knocked everyone in the immediate vicinity off their feet.

Chapter Twenty-Nine

"Stop them!" Harper screamed. He was on his knees, on the burning dock, pointing at Flynn and Sancho, both still sitting in the Apache Attack Helicopter. Flynn frantically flicked switches, pulled levers and mashed buttons, but even though the rotor was turning, the chopper refused to leave the ground.

Four breathless commandos aimed their weapons at the grounded bird

"I almost have it!" Flynn pulled back two levers at the same time. Nothing.

"Goddammit! We gotta go!"

Sancho grabbed Flynn by the arm and dragged him off the chopper as assault rifles barked. They half-ran, half-fell down the other side of the helipad hill. Bullets whistled by.

"This way!" Flynn took off into an abandoned sugar cane field and Sancho followed. There was nowhere else to go. Bullets cut through the cane, shredding it all around them. They ran as hard and as fast as they could, plunging deeper into the dense vegetation.

Goolardo couldn't hear a thing. He was stunned and dizzy and as angry as he'd ever been. He always had an issue with anger management. It didn't take much to set him off and more than a dozen men had died at one time or another as a result of his inability to contain his fury, but this...*this* was beyond the pale. That madman would have to die, slowly and painfully. He looked at Mendoza. Was that chingado smiling? Was that pinche pendejo enjoying this?

When Mendoza saw Goolardo's angry glower, any hint of a smile immediately disappeared.

The billionaires were reeling. Ears were ringing. Some were on their knees. Others were staggering aimlessly or on the ground.

Sergei Belenki started to cry. "Are we gonna die?" Bill Munson clutched his stomach. "I'm a little nauseous.

A discombobulated Richard Cook agreed. "I feel rather punk as well."

"It's Anthrax, isn't it?" Belenki blurted. He staggered towards Goolardo. "You infected us with Anthrax!"

Goolardo saw Belenki, moving his mouth, but all he heard was a faint ringing. The sound gradually grew stronger and behind it he heard a mumbling crowd; a muffled jumble of voices. The voices grew more distinct as the ringing receded. Rupert Breen's voice was the first to cut through the indistinct blabber. "I am really starting to lose my bloody patience!"

"I've lived through a lot worse than this," Quinton Blackstone said. "I survived a hotel fire by hanging out a third-floor window by one hand…for fifteen minutes! So, I'll be damned if I'm gonna let this little son of bitch kill me!"

"What?" Breen asked.

"This little son of a bitch!" Blackstone pointed at Goolardo.

"We're all going to die here," Belenki whimpered.

"What?" Breen repeated. He was still suffering the effects of the explosion and hadn't yet regained his hearing.

"We're all going to die!" Belenki yelled into Breen's ear.

"Is it Ebola?" a pasty-faced Beckner asked Goolardo. "Is it botulism? What did you infect us with? Viral hemorrhagic fever?"

"What does it matter now?" Goolardo said. "That stupid asshole sunk my submarine!"

"What?" Breen shouted.

"I was going to take you to the antidote!"

"Take us to what?"

Warren Davis helped up a stunned and bleeding Ingvar Knudson and said. "Why don't we fly?"

"Yes!" Belenki was ecstatic. "We can take my custom 767! It'll easily hold everyone!" Goolardo nodded and smiled, "You gentlemen humble me. You're all professional problem solvers and just like that…problem solved." He turned to Belenki. "Is your pilot on the plane?"

Belenki nodded enthusiastically. "That's where he sleeps."

Harper stepped forward. His uniform was torn, but he didn't seem the slightest bit rattled. "If you gentlemen want to come with me, I'll take you to the runway." He stepped closer to Goolardo. "But first I have a question for your kidnapper."

"We're running out of time," Belenki cried

Harper ignored him. "Do you actually intend to get an antidote to me and my men or were you planning on letting us die here?"

"I'm a man of my word," Goolardo said. "As soon as we're airborne, I'll radio my compatriots and the antidote will be air dropped. Anything else?"

"So, you're telling me I'm just gonna have to trust you?"

"What other choice do you have?"

"I can call your bluff."

"Yes, you can, but what if you're wrong, Mr. Harper? What happens then?" He locked eyes with Harper and Harper held his gaze. They stood there staring each other down.

"Please," Belenki pleaded. "Can't we talk on the way!"

Harper nodded and glanced at the billionaires. "Follow me, gentlemen!"

They followed after Harper, a rag tag group of frightened and bewildered billionaires. Mumson, bringing up the rear, said to Breen marching in front of him, "I wish I could change my pants."

"What?" Breen shouted.

Sancho heard the commandos push their way through the sugar cane, their boots crunching on the fallen stalks. His heart pounded and his breathing grew ragged. He tried to stay with Flynn, but the fruitcake was as fast as hell and as graceful as a gazelle. Sancho didn't want to lose him.

"Flynn!" he shout-whispered to him. He was afraid to call any louder; afraid to give away his location. Suddenly, a hand grabbed him, pulling him down. He looked up to see the furtive face of Flynn, his finger in front of his lips in the universal symbol for silence. Flynn rolled him into a ditch and quickly pulled dried sugar cane stalks over both of them. The sound of the boots crunched closer. Sancho heard voices. Shouts. Curses. Soon the crunching moved past them, growing more muffled as the commandos hurried away.

Sancho realized he wasn't breathing and let out a lungful of air. "Oh, Jesus," he whispered.

"Shhh." Flynn froze.

They listened and waited, and when the closest commando sounded like he was fifty yards away, Flynn poked his head out from under the sugar cane.

"Are they gone?" Sancho whispered.

"What's your name?" Flynn replied.

"Excuse me?"

"Your name."

"You don't know my name?"

"I know it, but do you know it?"

"Well, yeah."

"Then say it. What is it?"

Had Flynn finally totally lost it? "Sancho."

"So, you know who you are?"

"What do you mean?"

Flynn said it again; quietly, but firmly. "Do you *know* who you are?"

"Yeah."

"Say it. Say your name again."

"Sancho."

"So, you have complete control of you mind and your faculties?"

"I guess so."

"Then he doesn't have control of your mind?"

"Who?"

Flynn was losing his patience. "Goolardo."

"No."

"I'm guessing Q made sure we were all immune to the effects of his technology. Perhaps our food contained chemicals which created an immunity."

Sancho had no idea how to answer Flynn. Finally, he decided to humor him. "I guess."

"Dulcie probably knows the details."

"Probably—" Sancho's voice was drowned out by a deafening roar and the crack of a rifle. An Apache attack helicopter hovered directly above them, flattening back the sugar cane, creating a clearing, exposing them to the sniper half-hanging out of the chopper.

Crack! He fired again and if not for the sway of the chopper, he would have taken off the top of Sancho's head.

"Shit!" But the chopper was so loud Sancho couldn't hear his own voice. He did, however, hear the sniper's bullet whistle past his ear. They both scrambled to their feet as the sniper squeezed the trigger again. They took off running and the helicopter floated right above them. Sancho raised his hands in surrender. He glanced at Flynn to see him pulling out his laser pointer. "Forget it!" Sancho screamed. But Flynn was determined. He aimed the laser pointer at the chopper as the sniper squeezed off another shot, this one ripping through the top of the shoulder pad of Flynn's suit.

"Dude!" Sancho screamed, but Flynn was a man on a mission and wasn't about to be deterred.

The red dot bounced around the cockpit and the sniper saw the dot dancing on the side of the pilot's head. His eyes widened with panic and he leaned in close, screaming in the pilot's ear, "He has a laser sight! It's right on your head!"

The pilot freaked and pulled out of there so sharply, the sniper fell right out of the chopper. He plunged thirty feet down, landing silently and probably painfully, somewhere in the sugar cane.

Flynn was already running. Sancho hurried after. His lungs burned. His head swam. I keep this up, Sancho thought, I'm going to have a fucking heart attack. Flynn located the unconscious sniper. He couldn't find the man's rifle, but his sidearm was still in its holster. He unsnapped the leather cover, drew the man's weapon, spun around and started running again. Sancho lurched after him.

Flynn ran flat out through the sugar cane field and out the other side. He was on a runway that crisscrossed Randall Beckner's private airport. Sancho came bursting through the sugar cane a second later, sucking air something fierce. His face was bright red and he looked like he was about to blow a ventricle. Across the tarmac, he saw a-half-a-dozen commandos moving in formation

Flynn continued on, keeping low, running across the tarmac in a zig zag fashion. Sancho was too tired to zig or zag, so he just ran straight through. If someone shot him at least he'd have an excuse to lay the fuck down.

Sancho saw another contingent of commandos. If just one turned around, they'd be sitting ducks. They had no cover whatsoever. Flynn quickly changed direction and Sancho huffed and puffed to keep up with him.

"Pendejo…" wheezed Sancho as Flynn headed towards a corporate jet sitting next to a fuel truck. They heard the helicopter before they spotted it and Flynn ran faster. Sancho's thighs were on fire. His lungs felt close to exploding. James ducked behind the massive landing gear of the corporate jet. Sancho was just grateful to stop running.

Flynn heard indistinct whispering. Slowly, he turned around to see the open door of a cargo hold. Dulcie's face emerged from the shadows. "Come on." she whispered. Flynn grinned and clambered up into the hold. It was five feet off the ground and Sancho was too damn tired to pull himself up.

Flynn grabbed one arm and Dulcie grabbed the other. They grunted and pulled and Sancho wiggled like a dog trying to get out of a swimming pool, kicking his legs to get his belly over the edge. Finally, he was in the cargo hold, hiding in the darkness. It was as hot as hell, but he didn't care. The Baja sun had turned the space into an oven, but at least he was alive. At least he was lying down. At least his heart continued to beat, even if it was pounding like a cheap bongo drum.

"Is everyone all right?" Flynn whispered.

Sancho nodded. Dulcie frowned and said, "I won't be all right until we get the hell out of Mexico." She was about to say something else when they heard the voice of Francisco Goolardo.

"Is this the aircraft?"

"Yes, sir," Sergei Belenki said, his voice tight with anxiety.

"Very nice," Goolardo replied. "It's quite large. If we were having a cock measuring contest, your dick would definitely be the winner. All right, gentlemen, please follow Mr. Belenki."

They heard approaching footsteps and retreated deeper into the shadows of the cargo hold, hiding behind whatever they could find. Hunkering down, they stayed silent and motionless. A loud electric hum signaled the door to the cargo hold closing. Dulcie and Sancho exchanged an "oh, shit" look as the door shut tight with a loud metallic clank, plunging them into darkness.

Chapter Thirty

At one hundred and sixty feet from nose to tail, Sergei Belenki's custom Boeing 767 was one of the largest corporate jets in the world. It had a galley the size of a restaurant kitchen and a full-time chef. There was a large lounge with leather recliners, an entertainment center with a seventy-five-inch HD-TV, two wet bars, two full bathrooms with shower stalls, two half baths, a master suite with a California King, a Jacuzzi, and sleeping quarters for fifteen.

Goolardo marveled at Balenki's portable party crib, but noticed that on this particular flight none of the billionaires were having much fun. They sat in the large lounge, strapped into their seats, under the supervision of Mendoza and two thugs. All three carried Mac-10 machine guns. Goolardo occupied the co-pilot's seat. The man who usually sat in that chair had run off and was probably hiding somewhere in the sugar cane. Goolardo had a holstered 9mm Glock, and the pilot couldn't keep his eyes off it.

"Captain," Goolardo instructed. "Follow my coordinates to a T and this will all soon be over. If you try to be a hero, you will be responsible for the death of not only your employer, but his fellow multi-billionaires. And oh, yes, you will be quite dead as well. Are we communicating?"

The ex-air force pilot nodded grimly. He wasn't at all happy, but Goolardo didn't expect him to be. They taxied the 767 to the end of the runway. It was long enough to accommodate Jumbo jets and stretched from one side of Angel Island to the other. They fired up the massive engines and quickly accelerated down the tarmac. Goolardo allowed himself a tiny smile as they took to the sky over the Sea of Cortez.

Dulcie flicked her Bic and the lighter illuminated their tiny corner of the cargo hold. The flame trembled as they lifted off. The hold was fairly empty as Belenki and the other billionaires were in too big of a hurry to bring any baggage. The air temperature was in sauna territory and sweat trickled down her forehead, burning her eyes.

Flynn smiled at her. "How did you know?

"Know?"

"That they would take this aircraft?"

"It was the only goddamn plane on the runway."

"Then maybe it was fate," Flynn said.

"Or just bad fucking luck."

"For Goolardo, most assuredly," Flynn replied.

Randall Beckner wrinkled his nose. He glanced at Mendoza and the two thugs guarding them. Then he turned to the other billionaires. "What the hell is that smell?" Prince Adnan Bin Hassan of Saudi Arabia pointed to Bill Mumson with his thumb. Mumson sat alone. There was an empty chair between him and every other billionaire.

Rupert Breen glared at him. "You crapped your bloody pants? Jesus fucking Christ!"

Tears filled Mumson's eyes. His shoulders shook as he started to cry. "It's all right, mate," Richard Cook tried to console him. "He doesn't mean anything by it."

"Fuck if I don't," Breen said.

"Rupert, give the bloke a break," Cook urged.

"Bad enough we've been bloody kidnapped! But then this dill drops a load in his bloody daks!"

"We need to stay calm," Warren Davis said. "We need to stick together."

"Who died and made you fucking C.E.O," Breen replied.

"He's right," Randall Beckner said as he pinched his nose closed. "It does us no good to argue."

Breen glared at Beckner. "How could you let this happen? We're all fucking infected or poisoned or who the hell knows what and it's all your fault!"

"Actually, it's more *my* fault," said Goolardo, as he stepped from the cockpit and carefully closed the door.

"My legs feel numb," Ingvar Knudson mumbled.

"I feel sick," Sergei Belenki said. "Sick and dizzy. Very dizzy..."

"What did you do to us?" Li Chu Young demanded.

"I told you what I did," Goolardo said. "Your lives hang by a slender thread and I alone hold the knife."

"My people will pay you whatever you require," Prince Adnan said.

Goolardo grinned. "Of course, they will. All your people will."

"But if I die," Prince Adnan promised, "You will never live to spend a penny. My family will hunt you to the ends of the Earth."

"Are you threatening me?"

"There won't be a place on this planet where you can hide," Breen said. "Even if you get a billion-dollar ransom for each of us, how do you propose to spend it? Do you actually believe you can get away with this? We didn't get to where we are by being poofters, mate. Whether we live or die, you're not getting out of this alive."

"Rupert's only speaking for himself," Beckner said. "He doesn't speak for the rest of us."

"You can feed him whatever line of bullcrap you want," Breen said. "But the truth is, he's a dead man." Breen unbuckled himself and stood up, his eyes never leaving Goolardo's face. "You do *know* that, don't you? There's only one way for you to get out of this in one piece. Give us the antidote and let us go. If you do that, if you let me go, I have little reason to spend my resources hunting you down. But if you don't—"

"He's right." Quinton Blackstone unbuckled his seatbelt as well. "I'll be damned if I give you a dime. So I die? So what? I'm eighty-five years old."

"But I'm only thirty-five," Sergei Belenki cried.

Goolardo laughed, much to the amazement of every billionaire there.

"You think this is funny?" Quinton Blackstone asked.

"What's funny is how predictable you all are. I assumed that some of you would try to threaten me. That was to be expected. You're all rich and powerful men. But I've been threatened by men far more frightening than you. The Cali Cartel in Columbia put a price on my head years ago. Every government in the world has, at one time or another, wanted me dead. You see, I already have more money than I could ever hope to spend. I made it by peddling a product that generates its own demand. A product that requires no marketing. No advertising."

"Drugs," Warren Davis muttered.

"Very good, sir, yes. Your country's archaic drug laws have made me a billionaire."

"Then why kidnap us?" The question came from Sergei Belenki. "If you're already a billionaire, why—"

"Because he's a greedy fuck," Breen said.

"Actually, Mr. Breen, that's not really true. As you know all too well, there's only so much money a man can spend."

"Then what do you want?" Beckner asked.

"How about a little respect."

"Respect?" Breen spat. "Are you kidding me?!"

"I'm a business man. I manipulate markets. I obliterate my competition. And I make billions. But do you see me on the Forbes Four Hundred list? Am I celebrated for my accomplishments? No. I'm considered a pariah. An outcast. A criminal. You gentlemen control governments, pay for legislation, have politicians at your beck and call. Are you telling me you don't break any laws? You're no different than I am, yet Mr. Beckner has *never* invited me to his annual gathering. Am I not good enough? Am I not worthy to be in your presence?"

"No," Breen replied. "You're not."

"Rupert don't—" Beckner said.

"Don't what? He's a bloody—"

"What?" Goolardo shouted. He had Breen by the throat and suddenly the media baron didn't seem so defiant. "*I'm a what?*" He pushed him backwards and Breen stumbled and fell. "What am I Mr. Breen?!"

"Just tell us what you want," Cook kept his voice calm and measured. "We'll give you whatever you want."

"What do I want? I want it all!" Goolardo shouted. "*All or nothing!*"

"Nothing it is then," James Flynn replied.

Flynn stepped from behind the small curtain that led to the stewardess station. Sancho was at his side. He tried to look as confident and masterful as his mentor, but the sight of Mendoza filled his stomach with ice.

Goolardo was dumbfounded. He moved his mouth, but nothing came out. He glared at Mendoza and then back at Flynn and finally a single shrill word erupted from his mouth like steam from a tea kettle.

"You!"

Flynn smirked and held the gun loosely, the muzzle hovering between Mendoza and his boss. "You don't seem very happy to see me."

"You're like a goddamn bad penny!"

"Who the hell is he?" Breen demanded.

"The name is Flynn. James Flynn." Flynn heard the rousing theme music that always followed the announcement of his name. It was mysterious and exciting and no one heard it but him.

"You can't save these men with a gun," Goolardo said. "Put it down or they will all die."

"I don't make deals with mad men," Flynn replied.

Mendoza sighed and rolled his eyes.

"Please put the gun down," Beckner pleaded. He pointed to Goolardo. "This man's the only one who can save us."

"It's true," Warren Davis said. A few of the other billionaires nodded in agreement.

"Listen to me very carefully. You are under the sway of a new kind of mind control technology," Flynn explained. "Your thoughts are not your own."

"Whose are they?" Belenki asked.

"His," Flynn said, pointing to Goolardo with his weapon.

"I don't think so," Cook said.

"You're not supposed to," Flynn replied. "If you thought so, the technology wouldn't be working very well, now would it?"

"What technology?" Lakshmi Mandar asked.

"The mind control technology," Flynn repeated. "You see? He's already trying to make you forget what I just told you."

"Who?" Mumson asked.

"Him!" Flynn pointed at Goolardo. "Concentrate. Fight for control!"

"Of what?" Li Chu Young looked confused.

"Of whatever it is you think you should be doing and then do the opposite," Flynn replied. The billionaires looked mystified. Even Goolardo seemed bewildered as Flynn elaborated on his explanation. "Of course, now that he knows you know, he'll make you think that you're thinking about something you're not actually thinking about. So, don't think about *that*. Instead, concentrate on what you thought you should think about, but didn't."

"Mr. Mendoza," Goolardo shouted. "Kill that crazy chingado!" Mendoza and the two thugs squeezed the triggers on their MAC-10 machine guns and Flynn didn't fire back. Instead he tackled Sancho, saving him from certain death. Bullets ripped into the hull of the plane. One blew out a window. Flynn grabbed onto the bottom of a leather recliner and waited for Goolardo to be sucked through the broken window. Much to his dismay and disappointment, however, no one was sucked through anything. Instead, oxygen masks dropped from the ceiling, obscuring Mendoza's view of Flynn.

Flynn fired his weapon and hit one of the thugs in the knee. The man jerked back the trigger of the Mac-10 as he fell, taking out his fellow thug, before hitting the floor. Mendoza charged Flynn and Sancho stuck out his foot. The big man tripped and tackled Flynn as he fell.

Goolardo and the billionaires all grabbed oxygen masks as Mendoza wrestled Flynn into the stewardess station. Sancho jumped on the big man's back, his hands covering Mendoza's eyes. Mendoza tried to shrug him off, but Sancho held on like a cowboy riding a Brahma bull. Flynn hit Mendoza in the chin with an elbow and the big man growled and rolled over onto his back, squishing Sancho beneath his bulk.

Flynn rolled onto his knees and searched for his weapon as Mendoza aimed his Mac-10 and pulled the trigger. Flynn skedaddled under the stewardess curtain and crawled quickly up the aisle between the billionaires.

"Keep your heads!" Flynn shouted. He lay flat as the bullets flew through the cabin and peppered the cockpit door.

"Stop shooting you stupid baboso!" Goolardo screamed.

Mendoza rolled to his knees and then his feet. He burst through the little curtain and lumbered up the aisle for Flynn, grabbing him, taking him down. The billionaires, still breathing through their oxygen masks, watched as Mendoza sat on Flynn and brutally pummeled him. Goolardo stepped past the vicious one-sided battle and angrily made his way to the cockpit. He pushed open the door and went inside, closing it tightly behind himself.

Flynn futilely tried to fight back, but Mendoza was twice his size and seriously pissed off. As Mendoza throttled him, Flynn glanced at Beckner and the other billionaires, all watching wide-eyed. Flynn's voice was constricted as he called to them. "I could use a little help."

"You bloody idiot," Breen's voice echoed in the oxygen mask. "You're going to get us all killed!"

A magnum of champagne exploded against Mendoza's skull. The big man slumped forward, his hair covered with glass and champagne bubbles. Flynn used whatever strength he had left to push the big man to one side. He saw Sancho standing over him, his nose bloody, and the broken neck of the champagne bottle still in his hand. Flynn glanced at the label decorating Mendoza's head. "A 1990 Dom Perignon? Are you out of your mind?"

Sancho couldn't help but smile.

The cockpit door opened and Goolardo walked out with a pistol in his hand and a parachute on his back.

"Going somewhere?" Flynn queried.

"I'm afraid you've given me no choice." Goolardo abruptly opened an emergency door. An alarm sounded and a red light above the door blinked. Goolardo had to shout to be heard over the rushing wind. "As you can see, we're a little short on pilots!"

Flynn looked past Goolardo into the open cockpit. The pilot was slumped forward in his seat with a bullet hole in his back. The billionaires looked absolutely terrified. Actually, only their eyes were visible as the oxygen masks still covered their faces.

Breen removed his mask to shout, "What about us?"

"It's always about you, isn't it Mr. Breen!" Goolardo said.

"We're all going to die," Sergei Belenki sobbed.

"Yes, you are, Mr. Belenki, but not from any bio-toxin. That was simply a ploy to get you gentlemen to come with me." The billionaires all looked flummoxed and then furious. Goolardo chuckled.

"We're not infected?" Beckner said.

"No, and in that respect, Mr. Flynn was quite correct. I used mind control on you gentlemen."

"You son of a bitch," Warren Davis sputtered.

"I never intended for any of you to die. For that, you can thank Mr. Flynn."

Everyone turned and glared at Flynn as Goolardo positioned himself to jump. A hand grabbed Goolardo by the ankle. Mendoza.

The big man growled something obscene in Spanish and Goolardo shot him in the shoulder. All that did was irritate his large lackey. Mendoza slapped the gun out of Goolardo's hand and the drug lord slammed his knee into Mendoza's nose. Goolardo pulled his leg free and Flynn launched himself across the cabin. He grabbed for Goolardo as the drug lord ran for the open door and managed to get a hand on his rip cord.

The chute shot out and hit Flynn in the face before it landed on Mendoza like a net. The big man struggled to get out from under it and tangled himself up in the suspension lines, bumping his boss right out the door. Goolardo's body weight wrenched Mendoza forward and he stumbled towards the opening, grabbing at anything and everything to slow down his unplanned exit.

Two feet from oblivion, Mendoza grabbed the door frame and gripped tight, one hand on either side, his massive muscles straining to keep himself in the plane. Goolardo dangled in the air from the emergency door, screaming, yelling, and spinning in the wind like a fishing lure.

From the safety of the cargo hold Dulcie heard the gunfire, the shouting, the falling bodies, the terrified screams. The longer she waited down below, the angrier she became. Flynn was like every man she had ever met. Condescending, pushy, a total control freak. He figured he knew what was better for her than she did. Well, fuck him, thought Dulcie. If she was going to die in a fiery plane crash, goddammit, she wanted to know it. She called the little elevator down to the cargo hold and rode it up to where all the action was. As soon as she saw the situation, however, cold fear quickly replaced her righteous indignation.

"Are there any more parachutes?" It was Bill Mumson. He hadn't spoken since his embarrassing crying jag.

"I don't know," Belenki mumbled.

"You don't know!" Breen shouted.

"*I don't know*! Belenki shouted back, his voice ragged and frightened.

"We're all going to bloody die!" Breen concluded.

Li Chu Young exhibited an eerie sense of calm. His voice was measured and firm and, other than Flynn, he was only one present who wasn't pissing his pants. He had accepted his fate and was fine with it. "We all have to die sometime," he said.

"Eventually," Flynn replied. "Inevitably. But not today."

Chapter Thirty-One

The center instrument panel on a Boeing 767 has thirty-six dials measuring everything from airspeed to altitude. There are also fifty-two buttons, switches, levers, and other assorted doohickeys. There are even more buttons, switches, and thingamabobs located on the instrument panel overhead and on the massive control console on the pedestal between the pilot and co-pilot. None of them meant anything to Sancho and he was pretty sure that they all were equally inscrutable to Flynn. Yet, there he was, strapped in the pilot's seat, wearing a headset, and smiling confidently.

Sancho sat in the co-pilot seat and the view out the cockpit window made the hair stand up on the back of his neck. Dulcie was strapped into a third seat that flipped down from the wall. Her jaw was clenched tight and her hands were balled into fists. They had dragged the pilot into the main cabin. He was still breathing, but out cold and Flynn had instructed one of billionaires to keep pressure on the wound to staunch the bleeding. Sancho wished that he was just as unconscious.

"You know how to fly this thing?" Sancho didn't sound hopeful.

"Certainly."

"Are you kidding me?" Dulcie said.

"Aircraft today are so advanced they virtually fly themselves." Flynn grabbed the wheel and the aircraft lurched off kilter.

"Oh, my God," Dulcie cried.

"Chingao!" Sancho shouted. His hands dug into the sides of his chair as the billionaires in the main cabin all began to yell obscenities in various languages.

"Cao!"

"Kukjävel!"

"Chodu!"

"El Khara Dah!"

"Fuck!"

Mendoza strained to hang on to the emergency door as Goolardo dangled dangerously in the wind, his body occasionally bumping up against the fuselage.

Flynn released the wheel and the 767's autopilot took control. Soon the aircraft was once again level. "Touchy, isn't she." Flynn smiled.

"Dude, what the fuck?"

"Don't worry, my friend. I may not have flown this particular aircraft, but I'm instrument rated and have over two hundred hours on jumbo jets."

"Are you talking about that video game?"

"Flight Simulator, version 10. It's extremely realistic and very advanced."

"It's a fucking video game!"

"The Navy trains their pilots using an almost identical program."

"But they also fly the real thing, ese!"

Richard Cook poked his head into the cockpit. "How's it going?"

"It's all under control," Flynn said.

"If you need any help—"

"We do," Sancho replied. He shot from his co-pilot seat as if on a spring and pointed for Cook to sit.

"I've piloted smaller aircraft and hot air balloons," Cook said. "But nothing like this monster."

"A jumbo jet *is* a bit more involved," Flynn agreed.

"Where were you planning on laying it down?"

Sancho grabbed Cook by the shoulders and pushed him towards the co-pilot seat.

"I don't want to be in the way," Cook said.

"Sit!" Sancho pleaded. "Please!" As Cook settled into the seat, Sancho whispered frantically into his ear. "He doesn't know what the fuck he's doing."

Cook looked back at Dulcie and she nodded in agreement, eyes wide with terror. Cook glanced at Flynn who was staring quizzically at the control panel.

"Are you a licensed pilot?" Cook asked.

"I have a license to kill," Flynn said cheerfully. Cook was no longer smiling. "I'm thinking we should put down in Loreto. I believe they have a runway long enough to accommodate an aircraft of this size."

It was then that Sancho noticed the mountain range directly in front of them. Below them, the Sea of Cortez crashed upon white sand beaches that stretched all the way to San Filipe.

"We probably should begin the automatic landing control sequence," Flynn said.

"Automatic landing what?" Cook said.

Flynn started turning knobs and pushing buttons and the 767 violently pitched forward towards the ground.

"Bloody hell!" Cook yelled.

"Sorry," Flynn said. "I may have overcompensated for the altitude and wind speed." He was calm and unflappable as he pulled back a lever. The aircraft pitched further forward as the engines screamed and everything vibrated.

"Jesus Christ!" Cook shouted. "Do you even know what the bloody fuck you're doing?!"

"We'll soon know," Flynn mumbled. He turned the wheel and the plane banked sharply towards the 5000-foot-tall wall of mountains. Sancho's hand trembled as he pointed at the craggy peaks. He tried to say something, but nothing audible emerged from his mouth. Dulcie's face was as white as an albino's ass. She looked like she was about to spew. Flynn just looked perplexed. He pulled back on the wheel and adjusted the flaps and the plane barely cleared a rocky outcropping. Sir Richard Cook, the famous billionaire daredevil, shrieked like a ten-year-old-girl.

The airport at Loreto was just ahead, and now Sancho could hear someone yelling in Spanish over the radio. It was the air traffic controller for the tiny airport. He was telling Flynn to immediately pull up and abort his landing. If Flynn understood him, he gave no indication. Sancho, unfortunately, understood every word. He tried to tell Flynn, but nothing came out of his mouth.

Dulcie vomited on the back of Richard Cook's head. The billionaire didn't notice as he was too busy screaming in terror at the plane lifting off the very runway they were attempting to land on.

"Come now, Sir Richard," Flynn said. "Things are never so bad they can't get worse."

As Flynn reached for the white throttle lever, Cook leaped out of his co-pilot seat. On his way out the door, he bumped into someone pushing to get in. It was the pilot. Bleeding, woozy and off-balance, the injured pilot staggered past Sancho and sat his ass in the co-pilot's seat. Seeing the aircraft looming towards them, he immediately grabbed the stick and pulled up as hard as he could. The Cessna lifting off the runway was now so close that Sancho could see the frightened face of the pilot in the other plane.

He heard Richard Cook running down the aisle, yelling, "We're all going to die!" This did nothing to alleviate the concerns of the other billionaires, who all began to yell and scream in their own native language.

Sancho looked over at Mendoza. The big man's grip was slipping. His knuckles were white and every muscle in his neck was taut as he desperately tried to hold on to the edges of the open door. He assumed Goolardo continued to spin in the wind as the 767 barely cleared the top of the Cessna. Even though they avoided a mid-air collision, Sancho wasn't exactly relieved. The jet was approaching the runway far too steeply and much too quickly.

"Pull!" shouted the pilot, and he and Flynn pulled back on their sticks. The plane was shaking from the strain, the sheet metal close to buckling, the ground rising up much too fast. Sancho closed his eyes and prepared for a very sad end.

They hit the runway hard. The plane bounced and bounced again. The landing gear skidded and burned rubber. Smoke rose from the tires, but the pilot held on and kept the plane level all the way down the tarmac. He didn't lose control, even when they bounced beyond the runway, through a wire mesh fence into the desert.

The 767 eventually came to a stop. The pilot killed the engines and what astonished Sancho the most was the silence—the only noise the sound of his heart pounding. Flynn grinned and patted the exhausted pilot on the knee. Blood and sweat covered the wounded man's face. Tears filled his eyes. Dulcie let out a sob and Sancho couldn't believe he was still alive.

Some of the billionaires were cheering and screaming with joy. Others were smiling and laughing. Richard Cook and Sergei Belenki were crying. Randall Beckner gave Bill Mumson a high five. Mumson grinned. Not only was he still alive, he was no longer the only billionaire with a doody in his drawers.

Mendoza fell to his knees and collapsed on the floor of the plane, his muscles burning with lactic acid. Goolardo continued to dangle, his feet just above the ground, slowly turning like a marionette tangled in its own strings.

Flynn unbuckled his seat belt and stood, his pale face shiny with perspiration. He took a step and staggered and clutched his stomach. Sancho caught him and lowered him to the floor of the cockpit.

Dulcie saw the blood first. It oozed through Flynn fingers and saturated his shirt. "Oh, my God," she whispered.

Now Sancho saw it. "What the hell…"

"Did you get shot?" Dulcie asked.

"Apparently so," Flynn said. His complexion was chalky white. A yellow film covered his eyes.

Tears blurred Sancho's vision as he cradled his compadre's head. Flynn cocked an eye brow and smirked. A tiny bit of blood leaked from the corner of his mouth. "You know, Sancho, my hiding in your car was no accident. I knew I could depend on you. I knew you could do whatever you set your mind to…"

Sancho's voice was a sob as he picked up Flynn's hand. "Don't you die on me, ese."

"I wouldn't think of it," Flynn said. And then his eyes rolled back in their sockets.

Dulcie laid her head on his chest and cried as Sancho held his friend's cold, motionless hand.

Chapter Thirty-Two

The boy was in that awkward stage between childhood and early adolescence. He was ungainly and overweight and his face was blotchy with acne. His clothes never fit him correctly as they were all hand-me-downs. His foster father would cut his hair at home, in the bathroom, with an electric clipper made by Ronco. The boy always ended up with a crew cut and the short hair only served to accentuate his chubby face.

He had crushes on four different girls at school and not one of them even knew he existed. There was red-haired Jessica Babcock in his math class. She sat in front of him and smelled like lemonade. She had narrow shoulders, a tiny butt, and the largest chest in the seventh grade. When the bell would ring, signaling the end of the period, he'd have to hold his books in front of his groin as he walked to his next class.

There was blonde Mindy Taylor in social studies. She was a cheerleader and on Fridays wore that short orange and black cheerleader's outfit. She had a high-pitched laugh and would stick her tongue out between her teeth when she giggled.

April Zelinski sat next to him in science. A tall, skinny girl with short dark hair, she was a forward on the girls' basketball team. She always wore jeans and t-shirts and she never wore a bra. She was also his lab partner and together they dissected a frog. He couldn't help but notice that her nipples poked out from her t-shirt like pencil erasers and he tried not to stare, but it was like trying not to look at the sun during a solar eclipse.

His English teacher was his biggest crush. Mrs. Jensen wore very short skirts and would often read to the class from a stool in the front of the room. She read Hiawatha and Beowulf and he never heard a word as he was too distracted by her flashing panties. She would smile at him and compliment him and actually acknowledge his existence. The longing he felt for her was physically painful.

She'd reminded him of his mother.

His mom had always made him a snack after school. They talked and she loved hearing what he had to say. He, in turn, loved making her laugh. Her abrupt absence left a cold, dark hole in the middle of his soul.

He missed her laughter more than anything.

His dad would get home from work and, after dinner, he would help him with his homework. Sometimes they'd stay up late, after his mom went to bed, and watch movies on TV. His dad loved action movies with Steve McQueen and Clint Eastwood. They watched westerns and war movies and spy movies. They bonded over James Bond and his dad insisted that the best Bond, in fact, the only Bond that mattered, was Sean Connery. His father thought Roger Moore looked like an old woman. Put a wig on him, some lipstick and a dress and he would make a passable Queen Mother. His dad had a complete collection of the Bond novels in paperback and the boy read them all, multiple times, cover to cover.

His life had been perfect, but now his parents were dead and nothing would ever be perfect again. No one cared whether he lived or died. His foster mother hardly ever talked to him. When she did, it was only to criticize. His foster father always seemed to be irritated. He told the boy he was stupid. He told him he was fat. Whenever his foster father looked at him, the boy could feel the hate. But then everyone hated him. All the girls at school thought he was a dork. Bullies regularly kicked his ass. He was bad at academics, bad at sports, he was bad at everything. He was a failure. A loser. A fat, stupid, ugly, worthless dweeb.

At age thirteen he tried to hang himself, but all he did was dislocate his neck. His foster parents decided he wasn't worth the trouble and gave him back to the state. He ended up in a group home where he made another unsuccessful attempt to end his life with a box cutter.

He couldn't even do *that* right.

At age fourteen he was institutionalized for clinical depression. He withdrew completely and didn't talk to anyone except for the people on TV; Mr. T and Clint Eastwood and Johnny Carson and Sean Connery and Bruce Lee. They taught him things. They told him how to live. How to be. He mimicked Bruce Lee's every movement until he could do a perfect back spin kick. He mirrored all the exercise shows and slowly lost weight and sculpted his body until he was solid muscle. He became exactly who he wanted to be; someone confident, masterful, fearless, charming, intelligent, and accomplished. A ladies' man. A man of action. Someone who could handle any situation. Do anything. Save anyone. Even himself.

A telenovela played on the waiting room TV, but Dulcie paid no attention to it. She was watching Sancho; his eyes closed, his hands clasped in prayer. Dulcie hadn't prayed since she was fourteen. She was a lapsed Catholic who hadn't been to confession in ten years. She'd decided back then that it was all just a bunch of bullshit, but maybe she should pray. Just in case. What if he died? What would she do? What would she do if he lived? She was in love with a mental patient, a fucking nutcase, someone who didn't know who the hell he was.

But then who the fuck does?

She heard sniffling. Sancho was crying again. She crossed to the other side of the waiting room, sat next to him and held his hand. Sancho's hands were warm. Her hands were never warm. She was always so cold.

"He better not fucking die," she said.

"That fucking asshole," Sancho muttered.

"He's a total fucking psycho."

"What the hell was he thinking?"

"It's a miracle he didn't kill us all." Dulcie's eyes burned with tears.

"And that stupid fucking laser pen."

"What a fucking lunatic."

"When he tried to burn a hole in that fucking door…" Sancho left the thought unfinished, but the memory made him smile. Dulcie giggled. Which made Sancho laugh. Now they both were laughing. Laughing and crying at the same time. Sancho felt like he was going crazy, which just made him laugh that much harder.

When the doctor walked into the waiting room, they both were laughing their asses off. One look at the doctor's unsmiling face, however, and the laughter instantly ended. The doctor wore scrubs and his surgical mask hung from his neck. "Your friend's in recovery. We removed a bullet and from what we can tell, there's no damage to any major organs."

Relief flooded through Dulcie like a hit of Crystal Meth. Sancho started to cry again.

"We need to keep him here under observation for a few days. He suffered a very serious trauma and lost a lot of blood, but otherwise he's fine."

"So, he's gonna be okay?" Sancho asked. He couldn't quite believe what he was hearing.

"Yes, sir," the doctor said. "The prognosis is very positive."

"That fucking asshole," Dulcie said. She had tears in her eyes, but she was smiling.

Sancho watched as James slept. He was in a semi-private room on the fifth floor at Providence Saint Joseph Medical Center in Burbank, right across the street from Walt Disney studios. Sancho sat by his side on a chair by the bed. From the window, he could see the Seven Dwarfs holding up the roof of the Team Disney Building. Each dwarf was sculpted out of stone and stood nineteen feet tall. Dopey stood above the rest, holding up the highest part of the building.

Flynn slowly opened his eyes. His arm rested in a sling and his chest and shoulder were swathed in bandages. Sancho saw the initial confusion on his face. But once their eyes met, he could tell Flynn knew exactly where he was.

"Sancho? You're still here?"

"Dude, I'm not letting you out of my sight."

Dulcie laughed. She was sitting on the other side of the bed and Flynn's face lit up when he saw her. "Dulcinea."

"Hey," Dulcie said.

"Darling, you look absolutely ravishing."

"Well, you don't. You look like shit." She stood up and leaned in to kiss him on the forehead. He tilted his head at the last second so that her lips connected with his. She didn't resist and melted into the kiss. When he put his hand on her ass, however, she carefully removed it. "Let's not go crazy."

"You don't think a dying man deserves a last request?"

"Dude, you're not dying." Sancho patted him on the arm. "According to the doc, you're doing fine."

Flynn took Dulcie's hand in his. "Perhaps Dulcie and I should try a test run? Make sure all the naughty bits are in working order."

Sancho grinned. Dulcie shook her head. "I don't know about you, James."

"What don't you know?"

"I don't know anything. I don't even know who you are."

"Of course you do," Flynn said.

"Do I?"

"I'm not the man everyone thinks I am."

"No?"

"No," Flynn replied. "But I do know that person. That little boy who lost his family. That fat little boy who had no friends. I knew him very well. He was like a brother to me." Sancho looked at Dulcie as she held Flynn's hand. "But he's gone now. And he's never coming back and it's up to the rest of us to go on with our lives. It's all we can do. Which is why…" Flynn tried to sit up, but the effort made him wince. "Which is why I have to finish this mission."

"But the feds already arrested everyone involved."

"Goolardo?"

Sancho nodded. "Mendoza too." In his mind's eye, Sancho could see the Federales cutting through the nylon parachute lines. A frazzled Francisco Goolardo hitting the tarmac with a thud. His hair was wild and his face was splattered with bugs. They loaded him on a stretcher as Mendoza was led from the plane in handcuffs.

"Kursky?" Flynn asked.

"Dead."

Flynn nodded.

"They picked up Mike too," Dulcie said. "When he finds out I ratted him out…" Her voice almost broke.

"You have nothing to fear from him anymore, Dulcinea. I'm sure he's going to go away for a very long time. He's a bastard and a coward and you deserve much better." Flynn glanced at Sancho. "What about Grossfarber?"

"They gave him the boot," Sancho smiled at the memory of a humiliated Grossfarber carrying his box of belongings past a gauntlet of mental patients all laughing and hooting and waving good-bye.

"It won't be the same without N," Flynn said sadly.

Sancho smiled. "Nickelson's back, dude."

"Who?"

"N."

"How is that possible?"

"Got me," Sancho said. "But he's already back at work."

"Well, then, I have to return to headquarters."

"You're going back?" Dulcie was surprised.

"Well, of course."

"But why? Now that you're out…"

"Out?" Flynn chuckled. "Once you're in, you're *never* out."

Dulcie looked like she was about to cry. "Why can't you—"

"Stay with you?"

"What?" Dulcie immediately straightened up. "No, that's not what I—"

"Dulcie, it's all right."

"But I'm not inviting you to—"

"Shh." Flynn put his finger against her lips. "You need a different sort of man than I am. I'm not right for you at all. You need someone who can be there for you, day in and day out. My life is too dangerous and I can't afford to love too deeply. It's just…it's too risky." Flynn cradled her face in his hands. "But I'll always be your friend and if you ever need my help, you'll know where to find me." Flynn gently kissed her on the mouth and she just about swooned. He glanced at Sancho. "What day is today?"

"Saturday."

"Saturday? Shouldn't you be somewhere?"

"Somewhere where?"

"Didn't you have a previous engagement?"

"Saturday, right…today's…Shit! My date! Dammit! What time is it?"

Sancho pulled up in front of a tiny house on Ranchito Avenue in Van Nuys. He stared at the house for a while and checked the address. This was definitely it. So why wasn't he getting out of the car? He felt light-headed. Queasy. He knew if he didn't go through with this he could never face Flynn again. All he had to do was open the door. So he did. His legs wobbled, but he forced himself to stroll up the front walk and knocked on the door. He heard someone inside moving around and then the front door opened and Sancho saw someone he didn't immediately recognize. She was beautiful and petite, maybe five feet tall, with long dark hair and a luminous smile.

"Alyssa?"

The girl nodded. "Sancho?"

She looked so different away from the drive-through window. She wasn't wearing the El Pollo Loco uniform and her hair was down. She was more even beautiful then he remembered. He stood there awkwardly in the new suit Flynn had picked out for him. He had a new hair cut as well, but the brain below the hair was totally blank. He didn't know what to say and felt himself blush. A sweat broke out under his arms. And then Flynn's voice echoed in his head. "Women want to give it up, Sancho. The trick is to allow them to."

Sancho smiled suavely. "You look lovely," he said.

Now it was Alyssa's turn to blush. "Thank you."

Sancho offered her his arm. She smiled and took it and together they headed down the driveway. Flynn's gleaming Aston Martin DB 7 Advantage Volante was parked at the curb. Cardboard covered the broken driver's side window and there were a few stray bullet holes, but otherwise the car was flawless. Alyssa couldn't hide the surprise in her voice. "Nice car."

"I agree," Sancho said as he opened the passenger door. She climbed in and sat in the soft leather seat. He carefully closed the door and walked around the rear of the car, pumping his fist in the air, mouthing a silent, "Yeaaaaah!"

Chapter Thirty-Three

James Flynn breezed into the activity room wearing a casually elegant Armani suit. The social area was busy with people playing games, watching TV, talking and laughing and breaking balls. Flynn was pleased to see the place back to how it used to be, back before the arrival of the sinister Grossfarber.

Ty, the rotund nineteen-year-old black kid, came running up to him. "James! Hey! How ya doing, motherfucker?"

"Couldn't be better, Ty."

Flynn bumped fists with him and Ty plopped himself down on a couch facing the TV. The fact that there was no room for him didn't even enter his mind. The two people sitting on the sofa squished themselves to either edge as Ty jammed himself between them.

Flynn found Q sitting at a table, playing Uno with three other elderly patients. "Q! You're alive!" Q glanced up at him and then back at his cards. "Where in God's name were you?"

"Oxnard," Q said, without looking up.

"Why Oxnard?"

"Why not?"

"Why not indeed," Flynn replied as he continued his promenade.

"Hey," Q said, looking up from his cards. "Have you seen my laser pen?"

But Flynn didn't hear him as he was already greeting, "Sancho!"

Sancho grinned and shook his hand. "Hey, dude!"

"It's good to be back."

"Nickelson was looking for you. I think he wants to talk to you about something."

Flynn nodded as they walked side by side down the corridor. "So, how'd your date go?"

"Good."

"Of course it did. How could she possibly resist you?"

Sancho grinned as they walked into the anteroom just outside Dr. Nickelson's office. Miss Honeywell, Nickelson's large, no nonsense African-American secretary was back behind her desk, working on some paperwork.

"Honeywell!"

Honeywell looked at Flynn without emotion. "What?"

"You look more delicious than ever." She rolled her eyes and continued typing and Flynn sat on the edge of her desk. "Did you miss me?"

"You're sitting on my Ho Ho."

Flynn looked to see that he had, in fact, nearly flattened her snack cake. "Believe me, darling, when I sit on your Ho Ho you will most definitely know."

Before Honeywell could make a crack, the door opened and Nickelson walked out with a pretty, young nurse. "If you have any other questions, please don't hesitate to—James!"

"N! It's so good to see you're safe and sound."

The pretty nurse looked at Flynn with obvious interest. "James," said N. "This is Nurse Winston. Today's her first day."

Flynn took her hand in his and softly kissed it. "It's a pleasure." Nurse Winston was too flustered to speak as Flynn offered her a devilish smile. "I do hope we have a chance to get to know each other better."

Dr. Nickelson shot Honeywell an "oh, shit," look and Sancho smirked.

"James, do you have a moment?" Nickelson motioned to his office. "There's someone here who wants to speak with you. You too, Sancho."

Flynn and Sancho followed him into his office, where billionaire Randall Beckner waited with a large, unsmiling bodyguard and a female assistant. The assistant was attractive in a serious Harvard MBA "I wear glasses" kind of way. Her entire demeanor changed when Flynn entered the room. She suddenly looked less severe. Color rose to her cheeks as she moistened her lips with the tip of her tongue.

"Mr. Beckner," Flynn said. "It's good to see you again, sir."

"It's good to see you too, Flynn. How are you feeling?"

"Excellent, thank you. Very fit."

"First of all, I just wanted to thank you for what you did for me and my guests."

"No thanks are necessary, sir. It's what I do."

"Well, Mr. Flynn, you do it very well, which is why I'm here. I'd like to offer you a job."

That startled Flynn and he was rarely, if ever, startled. He glanced at N. Then back at Beckner. "What sort of job?"

"I'd like you to head up security on Angel Island. Mr. Harper severely disappointed me. You, on the other hand, knew just what to do. I can offer you a very generous compensation package. You *and* your partner." He motioned to Sancho.

"You wanna hire me too?" Sancho was nonplussed.

"You seem to work together quite well."

"Yes, we do," Flynn said. He smirked at Sancho and then addressed N. "How do you feel about this, sir?"

"It's an unusual offer. But your last adventure proved to be highly therapeutic. If Mr. Beckner thinks you're adequately qualified, I wouldn't want to stand in your way."

"Of course, you wouldn't. As long as I've known you, you've always looked after my best interests, sir."

"I think you're ready for the world," Nickelson said. "The question *is*...is the world ready for you?"

"Well, Mr. Flynn?" Beckner said. "What do you think?"

"I think I belong here, sir. I'm sorry, but I believe my country needs me more than you do. The offer is very flattering, but I'm going to have to turn you down. Sancho's a free agent. He can do whatever he wants."

"You think I'd go without you?" Sancho said. "No way in hell, ese."

Flynn slapped Sancho on the shoulder. "Good. Because I do think we make an excellent team."

"I can't say I'm not disappointed." Beckner reached out. "But I understand."

"Thank you," Flynn said as he shook the billionaire's hand. "If you ever need me, you know where to find me."

Flynn then shook the huge bodyguard's hand and finally the hot female assistant's. She held on a little longer than necessary, holding his gaze with her big brown eyes. When she let go she left a scrap of paper in Flynn's hand. Flynn waited for Beckner and his people to leave before he glanced at the paper to see a name and a phone number. Sancho laughed.

Flynn smirked, carefully folded the paper, and dropped it in his pocket.

Nurse Winston was still in Nickelson's anteroom, filling out paperwork, as Beckner and his team left. The assistant caught Honeywell's eye and casually asked, "So this Flynn...is he a doctor?"

Honeywell laughed. "No, but girl, you better watch your ass, 'cause he sure does love to operate."

~ * ~

If you enjoyed this book, please consider writing a short review and posting it on your favorite review site. Reviews are very helpful to other readers and are greatly appreciated by authors, especially me. When you post a review, drop me an email and let me know and I may feature part of it on my blog/site. Thank you.

~Haris

Message from the Author

Dear Reader,

I was a shy, skinny, bookish, bespectacled, and insecure twelve old living in the suburbs of Chicago when I first realized what I wanted to be when I grew up. I wanted to be Alexander Mundy in *It Takes a Thief*. I wanted to be Illya Kuryakin in *The Man from Uncle*. I wanted to be part of the Mission Impossible team. I wanted to be Jim West, Derek Flint, and Matt Helm. I wanted to be James Bond.

Those men had no fear. They knew karate and could scuba dive and rock climb and sky dive and ski and shoot the eye out of a flea at fifty yards. They were confident in any situation and were comfortable in their own skin. I think that was the biggest wish fulfillment fantasy of all for an awkward pre-teen struggling through puberty, and that's what inspired *You Only Live Once*.

At twelve I was terrified of girls. I was always picked last in gym class. I lived a life of perpetual embarrassment. In hindsight, that's probably how most twelve year olds feel, but at the time, I didn't know that. So I started lifting weights. I became a gymnast. I boxed. I studied karate. I became a rock climber and learned to ski and scuba dive. I even studied in London for a year and traveled the world. But I never did become an international super spy.

Instead I became a screenwriter and game writer, creating wish fulfillment fantasies for other nerdy twelve year olds. Thank you for indulging in my fantasies. I hope you enjoyed the journey. I do believe Mr. Flynn is just getting started.

Please connect with me on Twitter and Facebook and feel free to ask me anything. This is a two way conversation.

~Haris Orkin

About the Author

Haris Orkin is a playwright, screenwriter, game writer, and novelist. His play, *Dada* was produced at The American Stage and the La Jolla Playhouse. *Sex, Impotence, and International Terrorism* was chosen as a critic's choice by the L.A. Weekly and sold as a film script to MGM/UA. *Save the Dog* was produced as a Disney Sunday Night movie. His original screenplay, *A Saintly Switch*, was directed by Peter Bogdanovich and starred David Alan Grier and Viveca Fox.

He is a WGA Award and BAFTA Award nominated game writer and narrative designer known for *Command and Conquer: Red Alert 3*, *Call of Juarez: Gunslinger*, *Tom Clancy's The Division*, *Mafia 3*, and *Dying Light*, which to date has sold over 7.5 million copies.

Haris has contributed chapters to two books put out by the International Game Developers Association; *Writing for Video Game Genres* and *Professional Techniques for Video Game Writing*.

www.harisorkin.com
https://twitter.com/HarisOrkin